# THE LEPER AND OTHER STORIES

## BY MILOVAN DJILAS

# The Leper
# and Other Stories

MILOVAN DJILAS

*Translated by Lovett F. Edwards*

HARCOURT, BRACE & WORLD, INC., NEW YORK

"War" was first published, as "La Guerra," in *Tempo Presente*.

# CONTENTS

THE LEPER AND OTHER STORIES

# War

RUNNING FROM EAST to west, the great river flowed into a still-greater river. It always has been and always will be that a lesser river flows into a greater. Around these rivers, as around all rivers, there have always been battles and wars and frontiers, for life follows rivers, and they divide or link together men as chance may have it, according to time and circumstance.

For three months the battle had been raging about this great river. But because the opponents had equal forces, neither was able to drive back the other, especially in winter, which had now set in, for winter demands more men and

3

material for an offensive. Along the banks and between the rivers, the armies dug in, mustering their forces, so that in spring, when it thawed and the green leaves began to appear, they could destroy one another. The front intersected the great river—but to all rivers, and to this one, too, it matters not a jot if a front intersects them. Thence the front ran to the south and the southeast, where it joined the other, still-larger, river and flowed with it—it is all one to any river whether there are battles along its banks. The front was torn with trenches, dugouts, and every sort of excavation, a belt of land scarcely thirty miles wide, which embraced the two rivers, the great and the greater. To the land, too, it was all one if the front crossed it or did not cross it. It was all one to the meadows and the vineyards, to the villages and the towns.

But it was not all one to the people who lived along the riverbanks, though they were not to blame for the war. The soil and the sun were good for man, and men lived there. War means oppression or lordship over men and their lives and cannot but disorganize human life wherever it may be; it would disorganize the lives of these men even if they did not live there, as soon as it reached them.

Because in war there must always be two opposing armies —for without them there would be no war—each will do its best to destroy everything that might be of value to the other. In war there is nothing human or created by human intelligence or craftsmanship that would not strengthen an opponent, so the most certain way to weaken the opponent is to destroy everything that might be of benefit to him. War has no understanding, nor can it choose what could be or could not be at any given moment of advantage to the opposing side. Therefore in war the most sensible thing is to destroy everything—houses and fields, cattle and roads, bridges and

museums, and, naturally, first and most important of all,
human beings and the manner of their lives.

In its withdrawal westward the enemy had broken down
all the bridges over the rivers and destroyed all the boats,
even those so small and insignificant that lovers could hardly
find space in them—and because they are in love, they want
to hold one another close and save one another. Nowhere
near the front or even very far away from the front—for the
front may be here today and there tomorrow—was there a
bridge, a ferry, or a raft. Worse still, even those boats and
wherries the fishermen had hidden from the advancing army
had been requisitioned by the retreating army, not so much
that they might be of use to it, as that they might be of value
to the enemy for transporting spies and agitators, or if, by
any chance, they might advance again.

But men must go on living even in war and despite war,
and so, behind the front, they renewed the river crossings.
They had no materials and, because they were sensible men,
they knew that every new boat or ferry would be requisitioned. Therefore all their comings and goings were by the
military motor ferries, for an army must have, and did have,
means of crossing the river. An army exists in order to have
everything that its adversary has and has not and even what
it might have.

The soldiers on the ferry were good fellows—all soldiers
are good fellows when they are not being soldiers, and even
when they are soldiers but are not at war—and they trans-
ported the people, their beasts, and everything else free on
their ferry. They were the more considerate because they,
too, belonged to the people of the country over which the
war was being waged. They did so only at the times when
the ferry was not working for the army, or for the war—
which was quite natural, for they were there and did what

they did and were what they were only because of the war.

The enemy planes preferred to fly by day, so the ferry worked for the army at night and for the people usually by day. But the people, even though they were not in the army, soon became aware of this and avoided the hours of daylight. For the most part they crowded to the crossing points in the evening, when the enemy planes no longer flew and the home army had not begun its transport, or in the early morning, when the enemy had not yet begun his flights and the home army was no longer crossing.

All that morning, as dull and chilly and damp as many a winter morning, especially in wartime, a lament could be heard from the left bank of the river where the front was. The soldiers and the three officers on the bank—a major of the counterespionage service, his assistant, a captain, and a lieutenant who controlled the ferry and the crossings—knew that it was one of the peasants. Only the peasants wailed so incessantly, loudly, and senselessly when they brought back from the front a corpse of a brother or a father, and even more were it a son or a husband. The officers had been willing to come and help the unfortunates to cross even before twilight, but they had to hide the ferry in the willows because the enemy reconnaissance planes emerged out of the clouds all day, and at all times of the day, as if they took pleasure in watching the river, which was neither blue nor silvery, but muddy-colored, and the willow clumps, drowned in gloomy, rotting marsh, merged into a gloomy leaden sky.

The grunting ferry had been dragged from the marsh earlier. The dark lowering clouds came right down to the water's edge, and the twilight had begun to gather, so the officers decided that there was no further danger from the planes.

The keening, which had ceased, suddenly began again, as

if waiting for the motor to fall silent and the ferry to nuzzle
the bank. A crowd of peasants, men and women, with their
beasts, crowded onto the ferry, and among them an elderly
bearded peasant who urged his mettlesome horses with mut-
terings to get on the ferry. He used the sort of phrases he
used at home, but more tenderly and more sadly, for there
was an unpainted pine coffin on the cart, upon which a peasant woman, also elderly, and muffled to the mouth and eyes
in a kerchief, laid a bony hand, fearing lest she be separated
from it.

"Come, my grief, bear my sorrow to my lonely house,"
mumbled the peasant, twitching at the reins, while the peasant woman, with laments and even more grief-stricken words,
put her other hand on the coffin, embracing it.

The captain, fair, emaciated, and thickset—he could have
looked quite different, for he was only important because
he was a captain—shouted almost angrily at those who were
already on the ferry to make room for the cart, and even
jumped to the bank, seized the reins, and pulled the horses
forcefully onto the ferry. "Leave it to me, uncle. I grew up
with horses. You there! Make room!"

The horses recognized the strong and masterful hand and
followed the captain, champing and testing with their hoofs
the solidity of the planks and the depth below them. The
peasant thanked the captain, calling down blessings on him
and on the whole army. So, too, did the peasant woman, with
more subdued and even more sorrowful keenings. The captain seemed embarrassed by so much gratitude. Rubbing his
hands as if to brush dirt off them—the reins had in fact been
muddy and greasy—he unobtrusively and modestly rejected
it. "It's nothing! It's nothing, uncle. It is our duty to help
the people. That is why we are here. But who have you got
there, in that coffin?"

"Who?" the peasant wondered sorrowfully. "It's an ill day for me. It is my son, my only son. I have given two already, and now it is his turn. That is who."

The captain clearly wanted to say something consoling that at the same time showed understanding, something like "Yes, freedom costs very dear!" but he could not find the right words, or else it seemed to him they would be superficial in face of the peasants' grief. She was obviously the mother of the dead man. So he remained silent and only sighed. But in his place the lieutenant, at the tiller, spoke. He, too, was fair, but tall and with mustaches so sparse and blond that they only served to draw attention to his baldness; he, too, might have looked different, for he was important just because he was a lieutenant. "What will you? War is war. Men die every day. Sometimes we carry more dead than living."

A tall, thin, elderly, and wrinkled peasant turned to the father with the question: "Are you bringing your son back from the front?"

The peasant told him that he had gone to visit his son at the front and had brought him clean clothes and food—he, too, had fought in a war and knew very well what soldiers needed. At dawn the day before yesterday the enemy had attacked and, as ill luck would have it, his young, green son, who was not yet twenty, had been killed by a shell. "All his guts had been blown out, and neither his father nor his mother was in time to hear his last wishes," he added as if he were talking to himself and his wife, but all the more despairingly.

And the mother ended her death-wail with: "What can we tell you? It is our burial. Our line is over forever."

The thin peasant, playing with the Adam's apple in his scraggy throat, went on as if he had not heard the father and

mother. "Mine, too, was killed, a month ago, but I did not
bring him back. Let him lie with his comrades. But you,
how did you find a coffin at the front? There is no wood
there and no carpenters—nothing!"

The father turned aside, as if he had not heard the last
question. "And I don't even know where we shall take him.
It is just our peasant foolishness to find consolation only in
the grave."

The captain said that others, too, had brought back their
dear ones, though certainly without coffins. "The Command
of the People's Army respects our customs, though it would
indeed be right for a soldier to lie among soldiers."

The ferry nudged the bank, the horses shook themselves,
and the captain again seized the reins and led the horses,
who now went gladly, their hoofs eager for firm earth beneath them.

A path led along the river dike, and the army had made
and graveled a road from the landing place through the mud
and the stagnant puddles. Along that short, narrow road,
flanked on both sides by thin mud churned up by the wheels,
the travelers began to line up, one behind the other, ready
to show their papers to the major, who had not yet appeared
from the little hut alongside the road. The captain led the
horses onward without paying any heed to his place in the
queue. The people stepped aside into the mud unwillingly,
but without protest, for this was a dead man and, what was
more, was being escorted by an officer. But the thin peasant
—he whose son had been killed a month before—pushed his
way through, waving the stick in his right hand as if it were
helping him to move more quickly, and hurried toward the
hut, paying no attention to anyone. Furthermore, when the
lieutenant warned him to keep in line, he only turned and,
still hurrying onward, waved his arm impatiently and

pointed with his stick to the hut, shouting: "I've urgent business up there!"

After that—silence; only the cart creaked over the sand and feet sloshed in the mud. Everyone realized that the thin peasant had something important to tell the major in the hut.

For his part, he did not conceal the fact, and when the cart reached the dike, the major was waiting for it and gave a sign that it should move aside. The peasant stood behind him, watching him, grinning knowingly and cunningly and shifting from one leg to the other. "I heard, I got to know today," he bragged, "that there is something in that coffin. And you, Captain, you mustn't be offended that I said nothing to you. I was afraid lest they tip the coffin into the river. I waited till they got across, and there is a higher authority. And you mustn't be angry either," he said, turning to the parents. "It is our duty to speak up if we notice anything suspicious. War is war."

The father and mother had stopped, confused, dumfounded. The mother was the first to come to her senses and she began to curse the peasant's malice and lies, and to implore the major. "Have pity, leave us with our sorrow for a day."

Emboldened and aroused by her support, the father stood at ease in front of the major and also began to plead with him; his attitude was firm and soldierly as much as imploring. "Be understanding, Comrade Major. We are parents. This is our son. Our village is far away."

The major was dark, youthful in appearance, and very alert, with an expression more inquisitive than cold—and he, too, might have looked different had he not been a major. He replied to the peasant as though he were not speaking to the man standing there before him but to someone who was not there, to whom it was laid down in regulations that he must be amiable. "We must inspect everything, according to orders. You needn't worry."

Then he went over to the cart and, tapping with his finger on the coffin, ordered it to be opened.

The soldiers quickly obeyed, and without much difficulty took the coffin off the cart. The mother lay on it, moaning softly: "My empty home! My empty home!"

But the soldiers had nothing to raise the lid with, and that encouraged the father to implore the major once more. "Don't lay sin on your soul. Have understanding."

It seemed that the major was not listening, nor could he have been, for he was examining the travelers' papers. Nonetheless, he said to the father, and perhaps to the travelers, too: "All right, all right, everything will be all right."

A truck came, and the major stopped it with a wave of a hand full of someone's papers. The captain knew what he had to do, and asked the driver for a hammer and a pair of pliers. He gently removed the mother from the coffin, but she stayed nearby, crouched and withdrawn, with fists clenched to her face and moaning even more despairingly about her empty home and her black fate.

The soldiers at once pried open the lid, and the major, who had by now finished examining the papers, gave a sign for it to be raised. Inside, there was a clean-shaven, brown-haired youth in peasant dress. He rolled his eyes, made a movement to rise, then smiled shamefacedly and remained lying there.

"Is that your son?" asked the major.

"My son," the peasant answered. "Two of my sons have already been killed."

"A deserter?" the major asked next.

"No. I wanted to save him, to keep my line alive. What

do land and house and state mean to me if all my family is extinguished?" answered the peasant unemotionally.

The travelers had stopped in curiosity, but the major ordered the soldiers to move them on, and they all quickly and raggedly retreated before the rifles. The driver, too, went away as soon as he got his tools back; clearly all this did not interest him, or perhaps he had more important things to do, or troubles of his own. Only the thin peasant remained. No one drove him away, and he remained standing there as if he had some special right to do so. He spoke, almost to himself. "And I thought it was a spy or something of the sort. I didn't mean any harm, may God help me! May God help me!"

Crouching by the coffin, the mother began to smooth the youth's hair away from his brow, damp with sweat, consoling him. "Don't be afraid, my soul. He is a good man, a good man—he is one of ours, the people's."

Enheartened, the youth sat up in the coffin, but the major made a sign to him to lie down again. As at a command, he lay down tensely.

"Captain, do your duty!" ordered the major.

The captain quickly drew his pistol and, as if he had been waiting for the order, cocked it. Without waiting for any order, the lieutenant took the mother by the shoulders and firmly, though not roughly, took her from her son, lifted her to her feet, and moved her a few paces away. A soldier pushed the father aside with his rifle and placed him beside the mother.

Then the captain straddled the coffin and fired into the youth's heart so quickly and skillfully that, it seemed, the shooting was all over before the barrel touched the young man's chest and before either of the parents realized what was happening.

It seemed, too, that the young man realized it only when the bullet entered his heart. He cried out, his body arched, and his head and limbs beat strangely on the planks, and then he fell back like an empty sack.

The major said irritably: "Now take him away!" And at once added mildly: "We are doing, and will go on doing, our duty."

The parents did not hear him, but broke into wails and sobs, grieving for their son. The soldiers, by force, but not roughly, kept them away from the coffin, which they put carefully back on the cart, not forgetting to tie it down. They placed the lid on the coffin; they no longer had any tools, and the ferry had to leave again as soon as possible, for a line of military trucks was waiting on the road.

As soon as the soldiers had finished, the horses moved away of their own accord. The peasants followed the cart. And the thin peasant wondered to himself: How could I have known that?

Probably a knot had fallen out of the wood at the bottom of the coffin, for the blood flowed out, black and silent. The mother kept her hand on the coffin, wailing incomprehensible words, and the father, lamenting, walked beside the horses, forgetting to urge them on.

The lieutenant said: "Funny people, these peasants; they are wailing now just as they were before."

But no one listened to him, either. They were all far too busy looking after the traffic.

# Old and Young

THERE ARE SOME MOMENTS when armies cease fighting. These are usually at mealtimes, and sometimes when they pause for breath and prepare for fresh encounters. In the mountains these intervals may last for an entire night, or at least almost until dawn, for the fighters are worn out by the previous day's scrambling through the ravines, and it is difficult to move in the darkness over narrow, unseen, and precipitous tracks.

In the Lim Valley there had been fighting day and night on the Koma Mountains. Not only were the regular armies fighting, but the Albanian and Montenegrin herdsmen were

fighting to decide who was to hold the valley and who the
mountain slopes. They had been fighting for centuries;
either they joined one or another of the armies or they
formed themselves into guerrilla bands whenever war or
invasion threatened. States rose and fell, but the mountains
and the plain remained, as well as the unsettled feuds between clans of two differing languages and two differing
faiths. For the past hundred years the Albanians had taken
up arms whenever the authority of the state was weakened,
and the Montenegrins every time it was re-established. In
the current foreign invasion, complicated by civil war, states
and armies changed more rapidly than ever. The Montenegrins and the Albanians around the Koma Mountains went
on with their unfinished centuries-old feud, allying themselves sometimes with one army, sometimes with the other,
according to which offered the best prospects.

In the spring of 1944 the Germans, foreseeing that they
would soon be compelled to leave the Balkans, started an
offensive in the Lim area to prevent the movement of the
insurgent Yugoslavian army toward districts far more important to them. The Albanians around the sources of the
Lim also moved to the offensive, the more indefatigably and
inevitably because their mother country, Albania, had already been surrounded. The Albanian leaders, expecting a
German collapse and certain that this offensive was the final
death throe of a great state, began even more bitterly to
settle accounts with their old enemies, who had now been
transformed into opponents of their traditional way of life
and had found support among the malcontents in their own
clans.

Though these peoples and tribes had waged war there
from time immemorial, they respected the unwritten primitive law: Do not fight with the weak; fight only with fighters.

The Germans, however, fight as war demands. Though normally they live according to rule, and each individual has his fixed place, in war they have no rules; everything is permitted if it helps to destroy the will and the power of the enemy. They strip war naked and reveal it as it is—senseless destruction for the survival of a senseless ideal. But here they could still keep the unwritten law; they did not have to burn and kill without reason. In this case they did not have to scramble about the mountains. The Albanians were there for that, and because of their traditional hatred for the Montenegrins, the Germans could use them against the revolution. They themselves could keep mainly to the roads and to their motorized columns.

In this battle to the death in the Koma Mountains, modern armies and contemporary ideas tangled with half-outlaw peasant bands; the influence of the great powers sharpened the blood feuds of the clans, and revolution clashed with reaction.

The old men understood what was taking place and interpreted it according to what had been in the past.

The old man was wise, but even he did not understand what was happening; nothing of this sort had ever happened before.

But this did not greatly concern him, for he had no one to lead or to teach, and his granddaughter was too small to understand.

Nonetheless, he knew what he must do. He retreated after the revolutionary army, not because he loved it or considered it to be his, but because it alone did not kill children and old people, no matter to what clan or faith they belonged.

So he, too, found his way to the Koma Mountains—too far for his legs and too high for his lungs. The paths were muddy, and it was cold and damp, and there was not a single flower to give old age a flavor of youth, or youth a flavor of forgetfulness.

The soldiers had already finished their evening meal when he, with his grandchild on his back, found his way to the burned-out mountain hamlet looking for warmth, food, and shelter.

The hamlet had been burned in some earlier offensive, but some of the cottage walls were still standing. The soldiers had made use of them to lean against and to keep off the wind. They had put up shelters for the wounded made from tent covers and a few boards they happened to find there.

They scarcely greeted the old man when he came closer to the campfire, but at once offered him soup and a place among the wounded.

The little girl woke up as soon as he took her from his back and looked wonderingly at the strange faces about her. She began to rub her eyes, but, warmed by the fire, soon went to sleep again in the old man's lap.

She was so dirty that her features and complexion could hardly be seen. She might have been about three years old. Her clothes were ragged and too big for her, and from the tangled pigtails, which her mother or some kindhearted woman had plaited for her, God knows when, dangled a red silk ribbon.

As soon as he took the plate, the old man woke the little girl, but with such tender words and ticklings behind the ears that the soldiers looked at him with inquisitive interest. Such gentleness was rare amid such evil. The nurse, a tall girl with a severe, swarthy face, took the little one from the old man and began to ask her questions, skillfully and cleverly, as if she were her own child.

The little girl recovered after a few mouthfuls and gently took the spoon from the nurse, lisping: "I know how to eat by myself."

The nurse laughed and hugged her. "Eat, then, little heart. In the morning we will give you some milk. We have a cow, and you and I will go to milk her."

Out of the darkness appeared a small, young courier.

It was obvious to all that the commander looked gloomier than before when he had read the message. He twisted his mustache and began to chew it. Everyone noticed this. The old man, too, noticed it, and stopped halfway through his meal.

Everyone was curious, but no one asked anything. In any case, they would soon know what the situation was from the orders the commander would give.

The old man wanted to ask, but feared that a question might be taken amiss or that the soldiers might become suspicious of him, so he kept silent.

The commander took a notebook out of a leather bag and began to write orders by the firelight. The nurse leaned over his shoulder, reading word after word with lips moving.

"Don't be afraid," whispered the nurse to the old man when the order was finished. "Just you stay with us. They won't drive us out of here so easily."

The old man sighed gratefully and, since he had finished his food, asked where he could wash his plate. The nurse took the plate from him and shouted some foreign name, which the old man at once forgot. A freckled, hook-nosed girl, red as if her hair were afire, rushed up out of the darkness and without a word took the plate the nurse handed to her and again disappeared into the darkness.

The little girl, too, had lapped up her soup. She was not yet satisfied, and licked the spoon, but did not ask for more. She was already used to not getting more than was given to her. The commander noticed her, though he was still writing.

He said curtly: "The little girl is hungry."

The nurse took this to be a command and, from the goatskin bag that was hanging on the packsaddle where the commander was sitting, took bread, wrapped in a clean white cloth, and a blue enameled vessel like those the peasants use to store yoghurt. She carefully cut a slice of bread and then even more carefully spread on it some clotted cream from the vessel and offered it to the little girl.

The child gulped it down greedily and smiled. "My mother used to spread it this way, but they killed Mama; yes, they did, they did. I saw the blood running from her throat."

The freckled girl ran up, picked up a blanket on the way and laid it beside the fire. Then she disappeared again into the darkness.

The nurse folded the blanket across and put the little girl between the folds. "Go to sleep. Tomorrow I will comb your hair for you."

But the little girl sat up, crossed herself, and said: "I pray to God for you: bless Mama—no, Mama and Papa are not here any longer—bless Grandad and this auntie and that uncle and all these good people and deliver them from evil."

The commander and the nurse looked on, smiling. The commander asked: "Who taught you to pray to God?"

The little girl replied innocently: "Grandad, Grandad taught me."

The old man was obviously embarrassed; this was a god-less army. But he only muttered to the little girl: "Sleep, my berry; sleep, Grandad's darling."

Wrapped in the blanket, the little girl smiled, closed her eyes, and said drowsily: "You must sleep, too, Grandad."

The old man silently took out a short pipe, stuffed it with home-grown tobacco from an oxskin pouch, and slowly inhaled the smoke, gazing into the fire.

"This is like being at home. But I have neither hearth nor home," he concluded, and looked away from the fire into the night, into emptiness.

The nurse lay down by the little girl, putting a knapsack under her head. Then, as if at a command, an older soldier, certainly the orderly on duty, got up and threw fresh wood on the fire.

The commander, too, made ready for sleep. He lay down on his military greatcoat, turned his back to the fire, and put the case containing his binoculars under his head for a pillow.

"Where are you from, uncle?" the commander drowsily asked the old man.

The old man began without hesitation. "From the Plav Lake; a Serb. What else could I be? My people have lived there from ancient times, and from ancient times we have been at feud with the Albanians. They killed and were killed, but we survived without law through Turkish and German times, right up to a few days ago, when the Al-banians, dressed in German uniforms, attacked us. They burned everything. They razed our houses, killed and burned my daughters-in-law, four sons, and thirteen grandchildren. Only I survived, for it was my misfortune not to be there. A neighbor, an Albanian woman, saved this child, as if it had been her own. So, night and day, with her on my back, through armies and through dead and wounded, over hills and ravines . . ."

The old man stopped, turned once again to the fire, and then went on: "So, out of so many of us—the house was smashed like a ripe pomegranate—there is now only this little one, and it is her alone that I live for."

But the commander and the nurse seemed only to be waiting for the old man to finish his tale to go to sleep. The older soldier, too, lay down and drowsed off.

The old man was not offended; it was as though it were all one to him if he were talking to someone or to no one. He calmly knocked out his pipe, leaned over the little girl and tucked the blanket about her neck. Then he bent over the nurse and adjusted the greatcoat over her and looked at the commander; but there he had nothing to do, for a soldier by habit sleeps uncovered. So he began to rake the embers and stir up the fire. Somewhere down in the valley a machine gun broke the silence of the night, and the wind began to whistle around the bare heights. The old man gazed at the fire, again filled his pipe, and said aloud, as if everyone were listening: "God has said that this army will win."

# The Execution

ALMOST EVERY EVENING I used to inspect the section staff buried in the mountain snowdrifts about five and a half miles from the little town. It was cut off from everything except the war that was raging through the land and that imposed a bloody settling of accounts and paid no heed to the ruggedness of the countryside and the harshness of the weather, and still less to the centuries-old stubborn silence and isolation of the hamlets and those who lived in them.

Withdrawing before the German offensive, the revolutionary army broke into the Italian occupation zone and drove the occupying unit, few in number and not over-combative, out of the little town to remain throughout the winter cut off from its main body in a wild district and amid an insurgent people. The revolutionaries purposed to spend the winter there to recuperate, so that in spring they could return to the districts from which they had been driven. But if for the German command its task was finished as soon as it had completed mopping-up operations, the counterrevolutionaries, who enjoyed German support, did not think in this way; for them, as for the revolutionaries, the struggle was not yet over. It was a fight to the death—their own or their adversaries'.

News had reached the section staff over the past two or three weeks of a muster of counterrevolutionary forces on the right bank of the river. After forcing its way through the mountain ravines, the river now divided men of the same blood, language, and tradition into two opposing worlds. There had also been news about a regrouping of the Italians in the neighboring town. The inhabitants, both those in the villages and those in the town, had suddenly and as if by agreement been seized by a morose taciturnity and a bewildered apprehension. No one knew anything for certain, but everyone instinctively sensed an offensive, the invasion of another army and the establishment of a different authority.

The first clashes had already taken place along the riverbanks, and the section staff daily sent into the little town wounded men and that lumber of VIP's and material which clusters around every command during a lull in the fighting but which during a withdrawal becomes a nuisance and an encumbrance.

The staff also rapidly concluded all those tasks that during a battle, or especially during a retreat, it might not be able to carry out properly. It buried its records and the arms for which it had no ammunition. It gave instructions to political and intelligence agents for their work behind the enemy lines, and it made decisions about prisoners and suspects.

It could be felt in the staff that haste and tension were growing greater from day to day and from hour to hour. Part of that was owing, or so it seemed to me, to the fact that the staff was situated, so to speak, right at the center of the stage, at the point where the stream broke through the mountain defiles into the meadowland near the river and in the large white house of the local teacher, shot a few days before, whose mother, wife, and three children were huddled in the wooden cookhouse in the courtyard, whence they more and more openly hissed bitterness and lust for revenge.

That evening the usual heightened tension awaited me there: the intermittent machine-gun fire, in the open, sud-denly seemed nearer and more vicious; the teacher's mother quickly, as if afraid that I had the evil eye, pulled an in-quisitive grandchild back into the dark hut and slammed the door on her; and the duty officer told me that the mem-bers of the staff had not yet returned and that Strahinja, the courier, was carrying out his duties by the brook be-hind the house—he was shooting one of those condemned to death.

Of two minds about what to do until the members of the staff returned, I went out into the courtyard, told my orderly to put the sweating horses in shelter in the stable, and made my way into the undergrowth behind the hut where Stra-hinja, as I had been told, was carrying out the shooting. I had already seen plenty of people killing or being killed, and I would say that it was less curiosity than a sense of duty that took me in that direction. I had nothing else to do, and the thought occurred to me that the method of killing and of burying the corpses might be such that the enemy could later make use of it in its propaganda; it was, therefore, necessary to find out and to see that things were done correctly.

Already, some way away from me, through the sparse and leafless alders and willows, I could catch a glimpse of two men. They were Strahinja and a peasant, not much more than fifty yards away from the house.

They were standing beside the brook as if my arrival had interrupted them in some unaccustomed task. At first glance there was nothing to bring to mind a man condemned to death and his executioner. The nearness of the grave to the house surprised me. But when I looked around, I noticed that the watercourse was narrow and that there were steep and stony hills around it. In fact, there was no more suitable and out-of-the-way spot for a grave.

I could not help, however, commenting on the shallowness of the grave, which was scarcely more than knee-deep. Strahinja, with ill-concealed annoyance, replied: "You surely don't want me to dig him a deeper grave. He makes out he is tired and doesn't want to dig any more. Let him lie in a shallow grave if that is what he really wants. In any case, I have more work to do; there are three others waiting for me to put an end to their troubles before nightfall."

I had known Strahinja for a long time past, and the case of the peasant was known to me.

Strahinja had just turned eighteen, but his face looked even younger, almost childlike. He had been born in a village, but as a fourteen-year-old boy had gone to the mines. Since there were few workmen in the revolutionary army, he had soon distinguished himself. Fair, rather chubby, and thickset, he would certainly have attracted all the girls in the village or the workers' settlement in the kolo on a

Sunday, even as in the platoon he had become a general
favorite because of his simple good nature and considerate
openheartedness. Because of his courage and quick-witted-
ness he had soon been withdrawn from his unit and placed
in the courier service, and now he carried out such tasks, as
well as shooting those condemned to death by the staff. He
had himself offered to carry out this duty. And, not only
because of the increasing number of death sentences, but
also because of his invaluable skill, in this as in all else, it
soon became his main occupation.

He said that he had undertaken this task willingly, in
order to avenge himself on the counterrevolutionaries, who
had beaten him up at the beginning of the uprising. Perhaps
that was true. But it was evidently not the whole truth. In
contrast to all the other couriers, Strahinja did not show
any special interest in books and lectures—that is to say, for
so-called ideological self-improvement. He found the killing
of counterrevolutionaries a good way of distinguishing himself among his comrades and of underlining his lifelong
attachment to the revolution. It was a confirmation, not
only to himself, but also to others, of something within him
that Strahinja especially loved and that he wanted to stress.
It was undeniable that he was in no way one of those who
enjoy killing men, though he brought to his task a cold
accuracy and a terrible hatred.

Be that as it may, someone must carry out such tasks, and
Strahinja accepted them without demur.

However inescapable, it was nonetheless an unusual task,
as everyone on the staff and connected with it well knew.
Shooting at an unseen or faceless enemy, or even showering
bombs on a hamlet, is quite different from striking down a
particular man, with whom some sort of human contact is
inevitable and whose ways and looks, appearance and bear-

ing, force one to think about one's own fate. Therefore, men looked on Strahinja with a sort of wonderment, but also with a feeling of uneasiness. He, apparently indifferent, enjoyed both one and the other with a childish naïveté, mocking those who shuddered at his task.

As far as the peasant was concerned, he had been captured by a patrol behind the lines a fortnight before. The men in the patrol, who came from a village near his, witnessed that he was the brother-in-law of one of the counterrevolutionary commanders and had earlier been known as a canvasser for the counterrevolutionary party. Nothing else could be proved, and he had admitted nothing, saying that he had come into the revolutionary territory to buy tobacco, of which there was less there than in the district from which he had come. It was beyond question that he would tell the counterrevolutionaries all that he had seen and learned, and how much he had seen and learned was known to him alone. No one could assume the right of risking the lives entrusted to him without good reason, and the peasant would have to be killed.

He was a large and powerful man of about fifty, with a rugged head, already overgrown with curly beard and plastered with dirt.

It was strange how obediently, slavishly, he did all that Strahinja ordered him to do for his own death. I was at first afraid that the huge peasant, the more so because he was not bound, might throw himself on Strahinja. I wondered that he did not at least try to run away. It was still quite light; cloudy but moonlit. The whole countryside quivered in the bluish twilight. The snow was deep, but Strahinja would have found it more difficult to run through it because he was small and was wearing military boots. Then, too, the river was near, and on the farther side life awaited the peasant. But he seemed in a trance, as if doomed to death. Only a few ran; there are few who stand up against authority and organized force. And even those who ran did so as much because of the unendurable expectation of death as from the longing for life.

But something else, something perhaps stronger than anything else, paralyzed the peasant. That something was the certainty with which Strahinja was filled, his calm movements, measured speech, powerfully built body, and, even more, his simple ease of manner and familiarity with the peasant. In that familiarity there was something that bound Strahinja to his victim inevitably and unbreakably in the task they had to carry out together.

I could not see any stirrings of hope in the peasant because of my arrival, and it certainly never crossed Strahinja's mind that I could stop the execution of the sentence.

After his rather peevish reply to my comment about the shallowness of the grave, Strahinja turned to the peasant in a businesslike way. "You know, my friend, we ought to hurry up a bit. Neither you nor I can put off what has to be. You just undress nicely. You have a good jacket and trousers, and your sandals are quite new and of good leather. It is a pity that they should rot in the earth while our men go barefoot."

The peasant agreed submissively, as if that had been just what he had expected. "I will, Strahinja, I will, brother. It would really be a shame for them to rot."

He began to undress. First of all, he took off his jacket and laid it carefully on a heap of snow dirtied by the freshly turned earth. He had a powerful chest, covered with graying hair, and broad prominent ribs. His muscles were dark and knotted, and his forearms black with hair. He made no complaint, nor did he shiver in the chill air, though the trees were splitting in the cold. Equally carefully he took off his shirt and laid it on the jacket, then sat down at the edge of the grave and began to take off his sandals. When he had taken them off, he picked them up together in his right hand and placed them beside his jacket. He stopped for a moment, but since Strahinja said nothing, he took off his stockings and placed them in the sandals—the right stocking in the right one and the left in the left. Then he stood up, stepped out of the grave, took off his trousers, placed leg upon leg, folded them, and put them down on the sandals.

He did not take off his woolen pants, but, standing in a sticky mass of snow and earth, remarked: "Strahinja, brother, don't make me take off my pants. I am ashamed before you, and it is not well that I should be buried naked."

Strahinja agreed, but he was a little angry that the peasant had called him brother in my presence. "Don't call me brother. We are not kin, nor are we comrades. You may keep your pants. We do not take off a man's pants. It is not correct."

What Strahinja meant by "correct" at that moment it is hard to say. It was a word frequently used, perhaps the most frequently used word in the whole revolutionary vocabulary; in fact, it represented what was politically advantageous. But it conveyed also the sense that something—in this case the taking off of pants—was not in accord with regulations, written or established by custom, that were valid in the army and the staff, and thus in his work, too. There was also in that word, at that moment, the remnant of inherited popular custom, according to which it is neither nice nor lawful to bury a naked man.

Taking his revolver from his hip pocket, Strahinja put

his left hand on the peasant's shoulder and began to put him in position, still continuing to talk in the same tone. "Stand here, not there, but here, here! That's it!"

Without taking his hand from the peasant's shoulder, Strahinja stopped him at the edge, so that the whole length of the grave was immediately behind him. He explained: "You know, if you stand like this, you will be stretched out in the grave and I won't have to put you into position."

The peasant, as if only then fully conscious of what was to happen, began to wail from his dark mouth covered with dense mustaches. "Woe is me and my house! Woe, my wife and children! Woe to me, my land! To whom shall I leave you? Woe is me!"

His wailing recalled to me the bitter life of the peasants, an eternal struggle over land and kindred, and I was sorry for him. I could have ordered Strahinja to postpone the shooting and demand that the staff reconsider the peasant's case. But even had such a thought occurred to me, I would have had to reject it. Any sort of consideration for an opponent, as the peasant undoubtedly was, might, in certain circumstances, weaken the combat spirit and unity of the soldiers of the revolution.

And what would Strahinja think of such a thing? It was obvious that anything of the sort did not enter into his wildest imaginings.

Still holding the peasant gently by the shoulder, he raised the revolver to his forehead and, unexpectedly for me and seemingly also for the peasant, he fired. The peasant fell full length in the grave, where his body twitched and a death rattle came from his throat. Strahinja put back the revolver, picked up a shovel, spat on his hands, and began to pile back the earth.

"But he's still alive!" I could not stop myself from saying.

Strahinja explained, breaking off his work for an instant: "Yes, alive, alive. Of course he's alive! I have learned just where to hit him—straight between the eyes, but a little lower down, so that the bullet passes below the brain and does not kill him but stuns him. He must feel his death, the son of a bitch! What would death be if we did not feel it? And so," he said as he went on shoveling the earth, "I am burying him while he is still alive. Let him feel what it is like to die, how he ought to die!"

What was I to do?

I pulled out my pistol angrily and almost at random began to shoot at the peasant. I do not remember how many bullets I fired before the twitching and the rattling in the grave ceased.

Strahinja remarked: "We should save ammunition. That bandit"—till then he had not called the peasant names, but only friend or kinsman—"must feel death. What is death to a bandit if he does not feel it? Yes, feel it!"

I changed the magazine of my pistol, returned it to its holster, and went back to the staff without another word.

I was already well acquainted with the feeling that oppresses one in the presence of death and extermination—as if everything disappears and there is no sound but death and all that is connected with it. That evening I felt nothing of the sort until I emerged from the watercourse onto the open ground before the house. Then I noticed that the machine gun was no longer yelping and that the river, choked with ice, groaned softly and a blue brilliance outlined the house and the haystack and the bare saplings along the path.

# Woods and Waters

I HAD TO BE on Bjelasica Mountain by evening. I had to find my way in the darkness to a particular hut in one of the mountain hamlets and there, through the herdsman, get in touch with the outlaws. The wonderful August day passed slowly because of my impatience and the risk of discovery, but also quickly, for I was spending it in my native village after several years of town-dwelling and three years of languishing in prison.

I had left my birthplace when I was seventeen. Memory had refined and mellowed my recollections, leaving them vivid and colorful: fable and stone, snake and melody, man and cherry tree, all were unforgettably dear to me.

Therefore I returned to my home, at the age of twenty-seven, burdened by early experience and an overheavy knowledge of the world. Everything was different from what it had once been. It was no longer as it was in my memories. This was no longer my world, though its every detail at every moment came back to me, unique and intimate. Did that mean that there was nothing that could be experienced anew, even more moving in that it was nearer and dearer? I had been greeted with frightened or covertly welcoming glances from those I knew and those I did not know, for the police would not regard my arrival there as without motive.

The outlawed revolutionaries and the broken remnants of the revolutionary organization were waiting for answers and decisions from me, and only me, while I, in man and tree, in pool and stone, in the sky and in the grass, was searching for the childhood and youth preserved in my memory. Yet I was aware that I could, that I must, live among things as they were and must accept events as they took place. I must wander carefree through the village, visit frightened or indifferent relatives, and hold secret meetings at which it was up to me to find the answer to every misfortune and the key to every dream, while men and things and the place as a whole recalled to me a life without hatred and without torments, a life encased in memory or dreamed of for a distant future that would never be mine.

Letting it be known that I was going to visit relatives in a distant village, I went, just as the first shades of night were beginning to fall, to the thickets near the mouth of Jezerštica brook, where Ilija, a peasant of about my own age and from my own village, was to wait for me. He was to escort me to the mountain hamlet and act as my link with the herdsman and the outlaws.

Only three steps from the river one plunged into the impenetrable greenness of young willows and alders, creepers and burdocks, and at the same time into sultry, heavy silence. How rapidly and inevitably does nature renew itself! Nine years ago a cloudburst had ravaged the narrow valley of the Jezerštica, and already the young waves of the plants had covered its stony and pebbly banks. Very soon everything would again be forest and travelers'-joy, dense greenery, full of life and sound, like a river.

But I could no longer be, I was no longer, the boy who with fear and joy cleansed and revived in that brook my body and my dreams.

This was the spot where I had arranged to meet Ilija, by the little pool above the rickety bridge of saplings made by the local peasant after every flood so that he would not have to take off his shoes. I knew the pool so well that I could find my way there in the twilight or even at night. How many days, how many hours, had I lain in wait there for the trout and sat dreaming of adventure on that mossy stone up there on the left bank? This time, too, I found it without much trouble, forcing my way through a tangle of twigs and creepers and over fresh moist stones.

Nothing had changed at the pool, on the stones or around. The dark green of the forest had crawled down from the hillside, and a fine transparent flood of green foamed and waved in the valley. There on the mossy stone it was soft, softer than ever before, and the fresh burbling of the stream was sweet and familiar in the ripe green silence.

Ilija was not yet there, and I dangled my legs over the stone, feeling a cold shudder through my sweaty calves. In the depths of the pool dark shadows darted cautiously, trout surprised and frightened by the new apparition on the stone, and I shook myself lest I should fall into youthful fisherman's reveries. I whistled the agreed signal, and almost at once Ilija replied from the undergrowth about a dozen yards upstream.

I went on sitting, resting and dreaming on the stone over the pool; it was the stone of my shepherd and fisherman childhood. To the left, about a hundred yards away, flowed the Tara, a river of changing color and force, and beneath my feet the kindly, insignificant, and unknown Jezerštica, a brook singing its songs amid brakes and stones. On those stones, by common consent, the shepherd boys used to gather to cool off and amuse themselves with games, since from there the surroundings and the movements of the flocks to meadow and pasture could be seen. The shepherd girls, still unawakened to maidenhood, with modest budding breasts and downcast fiery eyes, wove there and sang and played knucklebones with the beardless but already muscular and openly unashamed boys. There, too, I used to read books truer and more exciting than fact, dream dreams lovelier and more real than any book, and day by day outwitted the daring and wary trout. There began and there ended the fishing. There was also a lookout beside the path lest a chance traveler, so rare in such a place, should pass by unseen.

Noticing that the world outside was once more what it had been before, a trout cautiously slipped down through the rapids to the depths of the pool. Now it was quivering gently, ready to dart away but also ready to lie at ease and jump lazily and cautiously at the flies.

What did it think? What did it think of the world outside its pool, out of the water? It lived unconscious of time, in a world that constantly offered it the necessities of its life. But I had to fight for ideals, for a world different from the one that existed. What would be my fate if I should leave my world of struggle and ideals?

But I was not a trout, nor could be, nor could I go back to my childhood, into a world and a self that no longer existed.

I had to acknowledge Ilija's reply. My desires were not his, nor could I share them with him. I slipped off the stone at his call and went back once more into the world in which I had to live, the world that did not permit me to be absent-minded.

Ilija's red, bony head, with its unruly quiff under his forage cap, emerged from the willow thicket as soon as I began to make my way along the bank toward him. We shook hands, whispering, and then quickly made our way upstream to get out of range of the road and away from unwelcome eyes.

It had been our intention to reach the mountain heights in a day, and not be caught by night in the forest areas. There Ilija could not act as guide, because he had never herded stock in those parts. But all this area was well known to me, as was the pale leafless sycamore moist with river spray and the glimmering shimmer of the beech. Along the green valley and by the river I delved still more deeply into my youth and childhood.

I explained to Ilija that the shortest way to Lake Biograd was upstream. I said that it was a very precipitous track and that we should certainly not meet anyone on it.

Ilija was one of those peasants who need a lot of convincing. Nonetheless, he agreed: good! But it would not be good, he said, to go as far as the lake itself; there might be campers on it, even though it was a working day, and probably there were also some of those "vulture" policemen around its shores.

Ilija often used the expression "vulture," which I had heard only in his district, but which on his lips had an even

wider significance than among the people. With him it
stood for everything spiteful and tyrannical. Taken in just
that way, that expression could signify for me all that I, too,
had known and experienced under the name of "police."

But how could I give up having a look at the lake when
I was only a few paces away from it?

From my earliest youth my longing for the lake had been
fostered by fearful tales in which it was so wonderful to lose
oneself. It was scarcely an hour from my house, but it was
deep in the forest on the far side of the Tara, and I saw it
for the first time from the mountainside. With my elder
brother, I had suddenly emerged from behind a knoll, and
there below us, in the dizzy depths, stretched the dark,
shadowy forest with the oblong lake, bluer and clearer than
a piece of the sky itself. It was like a morning when one
awakes from a dream. Everything seemed in vertiginous
movement amid the mystery of the impassable, boundless
forest.

I had dreamed of that first sight of the lake countless times,
so that dream and reality perhaps were confused in memory.

However that may be, every time I burst out of the forest
upon it, I still felt something of my first impression—of
morning and of dream. Through long years, for all my life,
that morning, that eye of the forest, glowed and shone in
dream and in waking, in prison and in conflict with the
realities of the everyday world.

Lake Biograd and the forests around it, huge trunks of
every kind of tree close-packed against one another, were
identified with my youth, with my first songs and my first
disenchantments, and, forcing my way toward it through the
freshness and dense greenery of the Jezerštica, I knew that
I would not be able to resist my yearning to see its dark-blue
eye shine once more upon me.

The Spanish Civil War had just begun. Ilija was not without a sense of humor, and remarked casually, jetting a particularly large gob from his thick lips, which gave an even more comic expression to his tales, that at the beginning of the Spanish revolt he had been of two minds on which side to be until he read the illegal press. It seemed a topsy-turvy sort of world, he said. Here, we are against the government, and out there we must be for the government. There had been quarrels and curses, and some men had withdrawn from us when we decided on which side we had to be.

So we went on talking about politics, sometimes with and sometimes without laughter.

Though we were not hurrying, we were perspiring, for we were leaping from rock to rock and were hampered by the denseness of the undergrowth. Our breasts ran with the blood of Spain. And here the police were firing on the unarmed people at the Belvedere, the main police stations groaned with rebels beaten up by the police, and men fled into the forests to escape from shameful tortures. Sweat burst out of every pore, and the icy breath of the brook chilled me. My memories crowded in upon me and boiled up anew. So immersed was I in my thoughts that I completely forgot the beauty and charm of the Jezerštica and my intimate association with it. I was enveloped by its greenness. I felt numb and dizzy with the heavy scents of roots and flowers and berries whose names I did not know and did not need to know. I would have died for the sake of some good news from Spain and I would have died for a crumb of hope for the hard-tried outlaws. I was overcome by the colors and the sweet exhilaration I had felt there on the stone. My heart was ready to burst under the first chill, wonderful beech on the Jezerštica. I was a man among men and a comrade among comrades, but I was also a trout and no longer worried if someone should catch me on the morrow. I was a branch which leaned over the stream and blossomed and grew green till broken by some passer-by.

"We will take care, but we will have a look at the lake!" I told Ilija firmly.

For a wonder, he agreed. "Well, it's worth seeing, and who knows where this road may lead us."

Ilija, too, had his own dreams and his own feeling for beauty.

But that journey did not, as I had hoped, lead me back to my childhood.

This was the same world, the forms and colors and smells I had already experienced and that I knew so well, but that seemed as if they had acquired, as for me they had, some different quality, different only because they had entered and taken root in the limitless cellars of my memory and thus acquired their own incontestable material existence. This was reality, known and irrefutable, but yet at the same time it was my consciousness—myself. The river would certainly continue to run without me, even as Spain bled whether I existed or not. Although the river did not flow for me alone, it flowed with me and I with it, which was for me one and the same thing. As for Spain, Spain was different; it was in my consciousness and yet far away from me, though I knew that I would live and die for Spain, either that Spain of the Iberian Peninsula or some other, any other.

That reality, that link between me and the world, was one facet of my being, my thoughts of Spain the other. I could not and did not want to deny this. This was a fresh life for me; far-off reveries gushed out from all sides and on all sides, wavering and merging not only with my present words and thoughts but also with the heavy scents of the juices from the broken burdocks and the murmuring sound of the Jezerštica. I knew that there is no other world but this, but my world and my dream of it and my memories were real to me and equally necessary to my life. I would do my duty; I would not forget Spain or the men fighting in the forest. But would I be able to do this if I had not dreamed, if there had not been that stone and the bitter, pale gold of the primroses in its cracks?

A little longer, another quarter of an hour, and we would be under the height of Prlo, below which are the sources of the Jezerštica, and I would feel it not only as a fresh wound on the dark-blue oak slopes, but also like a wound in my own body. Prlo would be forested and covered once more with grasses, for little by little, a thousand, perhaps a million, years from now it would reach as far as the lake and would swallow it up, even as the police would kill the outlaws. My lake and my comrades would disappear. But I would, I must, protect them, for how could I go on living if there should die within me what once there was, even though what ought to be may never return, even though it will never be?

For the first time I noticed, skirting the rounded shallow upper part of the lake, the intimate bond of plants and water. Gigantic limes and maples stretched out their roots into the water, reeds had grown out of it, and the lake, with unseen spores and capillaries, yearned toward the plants. The thickets were soft from the damp, and the trampled broken grasses breathed out their juices, white and scented. Our feet sank to the ankles in a mush of damp rottenness, and all about us milk-white juices spurted and foamed and hissed with moisture and growth.

This bond of water and life had no demonstrable link with the interweaving of my memories and the perceptible world around me, with my everyday life. Above all, they could not reveal the link between this wedding feast of water and plants and my longing to revisit the lake—that is to say, my childhood—despite the ambushes that always, behind every tree trunk in the forests, lie in wait for who-ever hides from them. The water and the plants were not, and could not, have been symbols of my memories and my immediate feelings. How could trees and water have any link with my fears of a meeting with the police, who would certainly hamper me in my intentions and my duty to find and meet the outlaws?

Nonetheless all this had some sort of mutual link, which I did not know, and did not even dream of being able to unravel. Or was this only so in those moments when I was intoxicated by my lake childhood and my ideal Spain? These were moments of living to the full, as real as I myself in the world around me.

As in a dream, or as in a moment of waking, I noticed how everything around the lake was huge and young. Leaves and trees and grasses were three times, ten times, larger than anywhere else, and even what had rotted—there were some old trunks which had fallen with their crowns in the lake, and those, it seemed to me, were exceptionally fortunate— had rotted with strong saps and scents and was burgeoning with fresh and vigorous life. The stumps were covered with fungi like sombreros, and around Biograd River, which hastened onward to fill the lake, we were met by the green flood of the burdocks, wider than umbrellas. I remembered that the frogs and snakes were bigger here than elsewhere and crawled vigorously, satiated and freely. I would not have wondered or been afraid if from these moist warm forests, which had never heard the sound of an ax, had crawled some mammoth, or if out of the swollen grasses one of the long-extinct saurians should raise its head. For everything was as if it were the first day of creation—mine and that of everything living. I, too, moved and had my being in the life of everything living, perhaps of everything which was to live, a life indestructible and outside time, in the perception and consciousness of my own human existence, inseparable from and undifferentiated from other living things.

The lake itself seemed like a piece of sky, peaceful and clear and translucent, and, so I felt, like a first kiss. It heaved gently with a measured even breathing. Yet there was some accord between its expressiveness and the rich, profligate burgeoning around it, as, so I again felt, between thought purified and harmonized and the apparently confused and opaque outer world. At every step and at every moment the forest received me, plundered me, with its outstretched fingers, and through the leaves and branches the lake lay awaiting me with its sunny, heavenly smile.

My sole intention was to do my duty toward the outlaws, and my sole desire was to rejoice in the lake. At any moment I could have moved away up the mountainside toward my duty, but I did not want to leave the woods and waters before I must.

I said to Ilija: "We needn't hurry; in any case we should not venture onto the mountainside before dark."

He agreed in a roundabout sort of way. "Night and the forest are for *hajduks;* by day in the forest, by night on the naked heights."

But soon Ilija smelled out in the forest the equally wary poachers. There were three of them. Those who could not yet make up their minds, about ten in all, would come only with the darkness.

All three had been my fellow villagers, and I remembered them well and knew all there was to know about them. They had, so I guessed, come to poach trout and were waiting for the twilight, when the first fish begin to bite and it is not very likely that the police would be trampling through the woods. Despite Ilija's overcautiousness, there was no sort of danger in meeting them, for even if they told the authorities that they had seen me, they could only do so on the following day, when I would already have had my meeting with the outlaws, and, furthermore, they would draw on themselves the suspicion that they had gone to the lake either to poach fish or to steal wood. Nor was it to be expected that they would jeopardize themselves for a secret that was not theirs. Moreover, the youngest of them, Bogdan, three or four years older than we were, was regarded by Ilija as being on our side.

Bogdan was one of those men whose innate ferocity would never have come to the fore, and perhaps would not even have existed, had he not been very short. But he was no strutter or blabbermouth; only his rapid movements and dexterity in everything he touched revealed the banked-up fires and bridled force. The peasants were aware of this characteristic, which could be very unpleasant if anyone questioned his honor or dared him to do something. Then this peaceable, unquarrelsome man would lose his temper and reveal an incomparable strength and cunning. For that reason they soon began to esteem him, though he was a newcomer, and they never took him to their hearts.

He had married into the village, and that in itself was enough to create in him a mistrust that they might underrate him. From his first day in the village and his first meeting with the villagers, he had felt bound to show that he was the master in his family. The tiny scrap of land that was his wife's dowry—a steep rocky pocket near the top of the hill—was so miserable that any mockery of Bogdan for feathering his nest might have been regarded as silly. But because there were few men in the village who had more, they regarded it as real wealth, and he was as easily insulted as if he were indeed dependent on his wife's patch of stones and one-roomed hovel, in which he could scarcely stretch his legs properly. At first this had its comic side. On several occasions he beat his wife, one might say for nothing at all, till the whole village echoed with her wails. After the first quarrel, when someone in jest had taunted him with having married into the village and with being unmanly and dependent on his wife, he revealed a fury that impressed the villagers. But it took years and continual effort on his part, ever ready to take offense at any hint of disparagement, before the village realized, or at least came to terms with the idea, that he was as much a husband and the head of a family as anyone else.

It was perhaps for this reason that he would do day labor for the richer peasants unwillingly and only when he got very favorable terms. In his deep-set greenish eyes and bristly mustaches could be seen a bitter spite and an entire absence of fear; this was even clearer in his words, which were as rare as if they had been coined in gold and always harsh as a jagged saw cut. As other men display their jewelry, so he paraded his determination to fight, and even to die, to defend his honor and display his equality with other husbands and men.

Even when the attitude of the villagers changed toward him, he remained the same: reserved and a prisoner of his stubborn pride and defiant integrity, fighting at every step with one or another, even when no one said him nay.

Something of that feeling he brought to his trout fishing. That was beyond doubt his passion, and not merely a poor man's need for food. He needed it to live at peace with himself and with nature, since he could not be intimate with his fellow men. His fishing was like a battle, if by fishing be understood entertainment and enjoyment, and by battle conquest and annihilation.

He brought to his fishing fury and even hatred, as if he enjoyed them, and he did not spare himself. This did not mean that he hated fish as a whole, or even individual fish. Quite the opposite! After he had caught them, he killed them swiftly and skillfully, spoke of them with understanding, and even referred to them with tenderness: "My sweet little troutlets!" But he loved to catch them to the last trout, and was not particular about how he did it. He wanted to prove to the fish that he could and would destroy them all. There were many others who were also not particular. But he was always thinking up fresh ways of destruction. He daubed mullein in quicklime and used it to dam their pools, changed the course of the brooks, and with long poles drove the fish from their hiding places into fish traps. He was the first to bring poison from the town and put it into floating lures, so that the fish were stupefied when they swallowed them.

In all that, he paid no heed to profit, nor did he grudge time. To fish without regard and without limits was his very being.

The second poacher, Tomo, was an older man, with ideas of honor similar to Bogdan's, inasmuch as he, too, would never stand aside for anyone. But in the manner in which Tomo fulfilled his ideas there was an enormous difference between them. Tomo did not try to demonstrate his manhood, even when it was contested. It seemed that he never even thought about it. He felt no need to order his actions by any sort of rule or by the demands of those about him. They had grown with his personality, his way of life and his way of looking at things. If I had not known that men may become anything, even moral beings, I would have concluded that Tomo had been born honest, so frank and spontaneously honest were all his thoughts and actions.

It was the living truth that during the war he had let his small son die of hunger and had not stolen so much as a chicken in the village.

I was unable to forget that little boy, my contemporary, and that famine during the summer drought, and whenever I chanced to meet Tomo or thought about him, I would remember his little son with the huge shadowy eyes, marvel at Tomo's inner force, and be filled with awe at the sacrifice he had made. There were others who felt the same about him, and many who declared that they would not have acted thus, but there was no one who did not wonder at what he had done. He had noticed this attitude toward him, but he remained indifferent, neither proud of nor humiliated by his unprecedented and harsh action.

It could be seen that in his own thoughts he had been incurably wounded by the child's fate. Else why had his smile and his witty tales, of which he knew countless, come to an end? Did he hold himself in leash lest they should burst forth again? Why was it that he never mentioned the dead child, or even that terrible hungry year?

He, too, was rather small, but without any concealed or bridled force. He was bony, thin, and lined by work and privations. And he, too, was sparing of his words. He selected them carefully and uttered them slowly, with great consideration, as if he feared that they might give offense or do harm. His words would be long in dragging out from between his few teeth and from beneath his bristly, still-chestnut mustaches. He would swear "by God's name." He did not do this so much from religious feeling, for he was not notable for that, but as if it confirmed and fortified that whatever he had said was exactly as he had expressed it.

He was perhaps even poorer than Bogdan. It was hard to imagine greater misery than that in which he had passed his whole youth and almost all his life, though he was neither work shy nor unskillful. His poverty was all the more striking in that he never tried to conceal it from anyone, as if he considered it an integral and inevitable part of his life. Later, though, after his children had grown up, he managed to acquire a modest holding; he moved from his reed cabin to a little house, pastured a dozen goats, and at last irrigated and cleared a hill of stones from the watercourse which he had toiled at as a youth. He, too, did not work willingly for hire, since he was occupied with his little stretch of stony land. He grubbed and toiled at it for more than forty years, whenever he was not fishing.

He was the oldest and the most experienced, though not the most successful, fisherman, for he was a little slow and old-fashioned. He fished every eddy slowly and carefully and still made use of hooks that he himself prepared from old knitting needles and hafted with twisted skeins of hair from a horse's tail. As with everything in his life, it was not possible to judge whether it was the keenness of a fisherman or the need for food that drove him to go fishing. He never noticeably displayed either one reason or the other; he was not especially pleased with rich and exceptional catches, nor did he despair at lack of success and poor results. It was simply something he had to do, and he did it conscientiously and devotedly.

He was not overkeen to share his experience and knowledge of the rivers with others, but he never refused unconditionally. For example, it was with him that I began fishing and learned its secrets. He was our nearest neighbor, and he taught me the more gladly because his own children did not show any inclination for fishing. I was attracted as much by his passion for the chase as by the thoroughness this inflexible man showed in this as in everything else.

The third fisherman, Maxim, was a foreigner, a Russian, driven by the tempests of war and revolution to our isolated village. He was a strange mixture of the inherited spiritual feeling of his native Russian steppe and his adaptation to our Montenegrin mountain mentality. Even aften ten years, he had not managed to learn our language, but in habits and even appearance—bony and with the sharp mountain expression—he did not differ from one of our own peasants. The strangest thing about him was that, in his new surroundings, he did not display any sort of hatred toward Communists, as if he did not differentiate between them and others, though he had fled from his own country because of them and had fought against them at the time of the Revolution. He maintained no links with his countrymen in the nearby town, nor did he ever correspond with any of them. He drowned himself consciously in forgetfulness and in a foreign land. It was not clear to me why he, a simple man and a muzhik, should have supported the aristocratic-intellectual counterrevolution, from which he dissociated himself as soon as he had left the soil of Mother Russia. He used to say: "It is all the same—white or red."

He never mentioned his family or his native district, and spoke unwillingly even about Russia, as if he wanted a leaden pall of forgetfulness to fall over everything that had happened before his arrival in our village. He had been deeply disillusioned by all that he had seen and experienced, and furthermore was serious and taciturn by nature. He was not religious in that strikingly submissive manner of the majority of Russian *émigrés*. He certainly believed in

God, but in this, too, he associated himself with local custom
—not too much praying or churchgoing. He used to swear by
a Montenegrin saint, Basil of Ostrog, and to celebrate his
*slava*, his name day, with the Widow Vasilija, a very poor
and honest woman with whom he lived.

What was the bond between these two, two beings from
different parts of the world, from two worlds?

She had already passed her fortieth and he his fiftieth
year when they found one another. One evening he, a chance
traveler, knocked on her door, and there he stayed. Though
they long remained unwed, he proved himself a good husband and stepfather. All that he earned he handed over to
her, and the neighbors abounded in details of his tendernesses toward her—unusual tendernesses, which were almost
comic in a society that did not show any sort of outward
conjugal affection. Vasilija revived and raised herself out of
misery and filth, thanking heaven and earth for Maxim.

But they did not succeed in escaping from their poverty.
He was obviously satisfied with the style of life he had, and
she, although she could have imagined something better, was
unable to do anything to attain it. They lived, growing old,
in a little hut on the hill above the village as unobtrusively
as if they did not exist, and the village grew accustomed
to them and their union, and since men quickly recognize
good and evil, the village soon regarded Maxim as an honest
man.

Nobody knew whether Maxim had brought his passion
for fishing with him from Russia or whether he had become
obsessed with it by associating with the local fishermen. But
he was unable to resist it and devoted himself to it whole-
heartedly and without thought of gain. That was well known
to the whole district. He fished for the sake of fishing; for
him the obtaining of food was an inessential and unim-

portant by-product. What was important for him was the solitary chase, far from men, from talk, from everyday life. What did he dream of, what did he remember, what was in his mind at his early risings? He always returned from his fishing smiling and carefree, as though from some secret and holy rite.

At first the three fishermen, each in his own way, were embarrassed at this meeting with me, an almost forgotten neighbor and one who was now proclaimed a Communist and a convict, because it must have occurred to them that my sudden appearance there was not without a reason. But we smoked and chatted, and they forgot their fears and apprehensions; in any case, they were themselves hiding and breaking the law.

I stressed to them my longing to see the lake once more, and then, to make my story more convincing and also from a real though vague desire to round off the experience that had started for me so suddenly and turbulently at the Jezerštica, I asked them to provide me with fishing tackle. I intended to fish only during the early twilight hours and as soon as the moon was up to slip away into the forest. It was too late for us to be able to cross the pathless forest before darkness. Black shadows crept across the lake and forest and fled away into the gloomy depths. We must wait until the moon rose and then go on our way. Ilija agreed with me, though against his will, since my intentions were unexpected and new to him.

The fishermen willingly supplied me: Bogdan with a hook and gut, Maxim with a line and a bullhead for bait, while Tomo pulled out from under a log one of his beautifully constructed rods.

Soon fishermen began to appear on the banks, now here, now there. The twilit darkness fell on the smooth dark waters; a wild duck called its flock to shelter for the night; a squirrel chittered for its lost mate, and we five went down to the lake to choose a suitable spot and begin our fishing.

I remembered Zukva to be a good place, sheltered by an old crabapple whose branches stretched out over the water. It must be somewhere near, about the middle of the lower lake on the eastern side, but I could not find it at once. Bogdan, who had already taken up his place, realized what I was looking for and told me that the old crabapple had fallen into the water two or three years before, and, in fact, about thirty yards away I could see a half-rotted trunk with its crown in the water, so that now no one could use that spot for fishing lest his hooks become entangled in the branches. But because I had no intention of staying all night and my hook was borrowed, I decided to try my luck just there. I began to reason it out; if I could find an open space between the branches through which my line could fall freely to the bottom, I might hit on a fishes' meeting place, for it is well known that they like to settle and gather around logs, roots, and every kind of snag.

Fishing in Lake Biograd and hunting in the forests around it had been forbidden ever since these parts had been attached to Montenegro in 1878. After their liberation from Turkish rule, the Morača and Rovača clans, when taking possession of the lands that had till then belonged to the Moslems, had presented, partly by compulsion and partly by good will, the lake and the woods around it to Prince Nikola, and he had put a ban on them, whence they got the name of Branik. But the local peasants, accustomed to freedom of the chase, did not respect the ban, and skirmishes with the gamekeepers were frequent. After the expulsion of the Montenegrin dynasty, the ban was even less respected. In the chaotic years after World War I, the wild goats were completely exterminated, and deer became a rarity. The stony depths of the lower lake and the grassy shallows of the upper still had trout in them despite the fact that swarms of poachers killed them with flails at spawning time in Biograd River.

Trout are the only fish in the lake. They are similar to the river trout in the streams nearby but have an even better flavor. They always fetch a higher price in the market at Kolašin, and fish gourmets are especially fond of their sharp juiciness.

Because of the wooded valleys between Bjelasica and Goreč, which stretch for about ten miles down to the Tara River, the lake is rich in food, but the trout will still willingly rise to a bullhead, a little fish one or two inches long, of which there are plenty in the lake. These are distinguished by a powerful bony head on a very thin body. They are very wary and move at great speed. The bullhead does not swim on the surface, but lies on the bottom, usually concealed under a stone. It allows its enemy to approach within four or five inches before disappearing unexpectedly and with lightning rapidity, so that it is impossible to follow it. Because the forests come down to the water's edge and there are no glades, fly-fishing is almost impossible on the lake, and from time immemorial—until the appearance of modern lures and nylon lines—it had been the custom to fish by night, from the bank or from floating rafts, with worms or grasshoppers, but best of all with bullhead. The hook is inserted in the bony head of the bullhead, and since the trout does not swallow it at once, one must let the fish get a good bite and let it nibble at least three times before one jams the hook into its gills with a sharp strike.

All this I knew well from earlier times; a man does not forget how to fish, or any other necessity of life. But I had only one bullhead; with one it is possible to catch only two, or, exceptionally, three, fish, for the voracious trout soon pull it off with their sharp teeth. The other fishermen did not have many more, two or three at the most, for their early twilight fishing, because they could get bullhead only after dark. Then human skill would manage to get more of them by a sort of chase with miniature tridents. The fishermen would turn over stones in the shallows, lighting the bottom with pocket flashlights, and then transfix the blinded fish with the forks.

There was, therefore, no real need to worry about bait. It was not so much the catch itself that I wanted, as to see the twilight and the night fall on the lake while waiting for the sudden electrical strike of the trout, which makes the whole body thrill.

The lake trout bite most eagerly at twilight or at dawn on the eve of, or just after, rain, and by day or in the moonlight only at the time of the spring freshets. The day had been clear, with no threat of rain, and the moon was due to appear early, by about ten o'clock. All that I could hope for was to get in some fishing in the twilight hours, and as soon as the moon topped the mountain peaks I would have to begin my inescapable journey up the mountain.

I began badly. At the first cast I caught my hook on some sunken branch. But I managed to free it by tugging gently at it; the wood was already soft with decay. Then I caught it again and yet again. I lost count of how many times, and twice Bogdan had to free it by rowing his raft over and sliding a long pole down the length of my line to the place where the hook was caught. Fishermen do not like to be distracted, and despite the fact that Bogdan replied to my excuses and thanks with a mild "It's nothing; we've all night before us," his impatience was noticeable when he added:

"But it would be better if you chose some other place."

My shortcomings were a godsend to Ilija, the more so because none of the other fishermen had yet caught a fish. Like all nonfishermen, he kept nagging and grumbling that we were endangering an important mission for a mere trifle. "There are no fish here. Anything you catch you are welcome to fry on my stomach! Try putting salt on their tails. Perhaps you'll catch them better that way! Truly there is no madder way of wasting time than waiting for something to commit suicide by hanging itself on a hook. We would be up in the mountains by now if we hadn't stopped to mess about down here!"

In truth, my own conscience was beginning to gnaw at me. I kept telling myself: "If my hook gets caught just once more, I'll give it up."

But I didn't give up, reassuring myself after every snag: "In any case, neither the catch nor the hook matters very much to me. I will find some opening in the branches or finally break off the hook."

My obstinacy became more and more feverish. The lake turned the color of molten lead and then as dark as pitch. Twilight faded. I could hear the joyful slap of the trout on the water, leaping after unseen flies, and the crack of twigs underfoot from the bank opposite.

At last I found a suitable opening for my line where I could cast my hook. I practiced casting into that place, so that even in the darkness I would be able to find it.

Even before that, just as I had found the opening at my second or third cast, the first trout appeared. It was over to my left. Tomo had already caught one; we could hear its rapid flapping as he pulled it in, and then Tomo's calm voice could be heard from the dark greenery. "Got one!"

But that was not my fish.

"The first fish is the first to come my way," I replied to Ilija when he spitefully drew my attention to Tomo's triumph.

I wheedled my line through the branches and waited for the first nibble. When it came I felt as if it represented years upon years of unfulfilled, inextinguishable yearnings, as if that moment represented something as sweet and fateful as life itself. Nonetheless, I managed to prevent myself from responding to the first nibble and reminded myself that if I did not take care I would get my line entangled with some branch or snag as I tried to land the fish. The line transmitted its tense quivering to me from the depths, but I waited for the third tug of the fish before I struck. Somewhere far away, within myself and in the dark depths of the lake, began the terrible mortal struggle with which nothing can be compared, since man does not remember his conception or his birth and knows nothing of his death.

I had so clear a picture in my mind of the branches on the bank that I felt as if I could actually see them, and landed the fish carefully, forcing myself to be as calm and collected as possible. I stayed where I was and brought the tip of the rod around toward the bank. I was well aware that the line was strong enough to take the weight of the fish—there are few trout in the lake weighing more than a couple of pounds —and I put it down among the stones with a gentle swing. Ilija, noticing that something was happening in which he had almost ceased to believe, stopped smoking. His cigarette had been glimmering with a weak reddish glow, which scarcely lit up his long nose and stony face. I was just about to shout to him to take the fish off the hook when he leaped up as if stung. He put out his cigarette and rushed toward the fish.

I remarked to him as indifferently as I could, but still loud enough for my fellow fishermen to hear: "Ilija, I've got one!"

And Ilija, who was taking the fish off the hook more impatiently than unskillfully, cried out: "Mashallah, a fish!"

When Ilija at last freed the hook, I reeled in the line and felt the bullhead. It was a bit chewed, but I reckoned it would serve once more. I lifted the rod, the bait splashed into the water, and, as if in answer, a bright light shone on the farther bank. I thought that someone was about to hunt for bullheads. But the light went out and someone to my right shouted, splitting the smooth, dark silence: "The *police!*"

On the far side a light flashed in answer, followed by a stream of curses. Soon the sound of men crashing through the forest could be heard. That was the fishermen on the far side of the lake running away, to the accompaniment of cries. "Stop, or I'll shoot! Stop, you sons of bitches! Stop! Stop!"

Although I didn't see the red flash from the gun barrels, shooting broke out and crashed along the farther bank so loudly that it seemed as if it were just in front of me. I paid little heed to the shooting, since I was convinced that the police had fired only to frighten and scatter the fishermen, but I noticed that the rod quivered in my hands from inward shock. The impact of the shots woke me out of the mild cool darkness and the almost unconscious communion with the dark waters, the fish, and the world around. I thought: A bullet is so small a thing compared with this forest night. How could it manage to hit anyone? But it was intended for a man, and I kept wondering who long after the noise of the shots had died away in the softness of the forest and the night. Once more I found myself back in the world of man's relation to man, and was faced with duties and decisions. Should we make a run for it or stay where we were?

Both near me and somewhere far off men were running and panting. Every sound was magnified across the lake.

Ilija's voice called softly to me. "Let's run, let's run!"

And though he did not actually speak it, I could hear him saying: "Haven't we already taken too great a risk for no reason?"

But still I waited. I was certain that the fish would go on biting, for they did not have, nor could they have, any connection with what was going on around them. And why hurry? The light once again appeared on the far side, crawling along slowly, now and again blotted out by tree trunks. The police clearly could not make a rush through the dense forest and the darkness, and from them could be heard unintelligible words and the clear thud of military boots on stones and wood. Even in daylight it would take them at least half an hour to reach us, and they could not approach us in the stillness of the forest without our being aware of it.

Nonetheless, the fishermen fled, though they must have known that the danger was distant and powerless. They must have been seized by panic, which in the sightless darkness had passed from one to all. Night hides the guilty, and the peasants felt themselves to be in the wrong. Night makes everything a pursuer.

I, too, was frightened. Might not another patrol appear behind us while we were engrossed in our fishing and made deaf by our enthusiasm, so that we would not hear them? But when I thought over such a possibility, I was convinced that the police would not be able to catch us. I would jump into the water, swim to some spot where there were no policemen, and then set out up the mountainside to fulfill my duties. That, however, would be a risky and foolhardy adventure. Ilija was right. We must get out, get out as soon as possible.

I was just on the point of saying to Ilija, "We'll go at once, as soon as this scare dies down," when a fish, once more, angrily and as if to remind me of its presence, made the rod quiver. Perhaps in any case I would have said nothing to Ilija, but that tug by the trout served me as a justification, to myself and also to him, that in fact I had not said what I wanted to say, what I ought to have said. I landed that fish also, though rather too jerkily.

I suspected that Ilija would not want to take it off the hook or would do so against his will. But he threw himself at it, unable to hold back a cry. "Oho! Mashallah, mashallah!"

There were only scraps of the bullhead left, and they could no longer be used. Then I remembered one of Tomo's stories: in earlier times, when there were fewer fishermen, and tackle and hooks were more primitive, the fish bit more easily and were less wary, so that it was not necessary to worry so much about bait, and the lake trout let themselves be caught on pieces of liver taken from one of their fellows. I called softly to Ilija: "Bring me a fish, one fish!"

I watched the light on the farther shore. It had stopped, and hung like a sort of scarecrow. I heard Ilija crawling along, scraping bits of bark off the crabapple. The police must have heard us; if nothing else, they must have heard the flapping of the fish on the stones, and must have been irritated by our audacity and would be discussing how to get at us.

Ilija touched my hand with a cold wet fish and asked me cautiously: "What do you want the fish for?" He, too, looked at the light, and I could read on his face, despite the darkness, a sort of inquisitive fear. I seized the fish and jammed the point of a penknife into its belly and began to clean it.

"I've no more bait, so I will use its liver," I whispered to Ilija.

He was astonished. "Will that do the trick?"

The cut stopped just below the lower jawbone. I quickly drew out the liver, cut it free, and put it by touch on the hook. Ilija withdrew, again scraping against the bark, and I cast the line into the favored place and began to wait, curious to know if the fish would bite on that bait, too, yet at the same time sorry that this might mean the end of the fishing.

But the fish took the bait with a sort of considered madness. At times they threw themselves on their prey not from hunger, but as if from some unbridled joy at a feast or ritual unknown to us. They did so without a trace of fear, driven by a need greater than themselves, and yet at the same time according to all their rules of cunning and behavior. The strangest thing of all—or so it seemed to me in the darkness and in the excitement caused by the presence of the police— was that, once caught, they made no special effort to break free. Overcome by the fascination of the game, they did not seem to regret that they had been caught.

No, I really could not bear to leave them; my dear little fish would have been too unhappy.

I called out to them, inwardly: "Don't worry, little fools. I will catch every one of you. Not all there are in the lake; I could not carry so many, and some must be left to breed for fishermen who come after me. But I want to catch every one of you who is involved in this terrible, senseless game. For we are one, though we are different and are in conflict. We cannot rejoice if we differentiate between the joy by which we live and the game by which we die."

At long last the passion caught Ilija up also. "Go on, go on," he said. "Those dogs are still far away!"

The police, hearing what we were doing, began to shout at us, to curse us and threaten us. We could see and hear them as they crashed along the bank. As I watched them I caught one fish after another and handed them to Ilija, who took them off the hook with a skill and speed that had noticeably increased.

Soon the police reached a bend in the bank. Now we could only hear them. The peak of Goreč suddenly shone, one of its stony spearheads lit by the moonlight. We came to ourselves, and began to hurry along the bank. Ilija went ahead, and about fifty yards on nearly tripped over a man squatting on the bank. It was Maxim, who muttered shame-facedly: "I couldn't go away, even if the police catch me. They are biting tonight as they have never bitten before."

The lake began to shine with a dull light, and only then, feeling tired and overcome by sleep, did we hasten through the dense forest and the darkness as black as pitch, toward the moonlight that was beginning to fall over the mountain peaks.

# The Foreigner

BOTH OF US had wanted to become close friends, always. We tried three times; in childhood, in early youth, and as grown men.

But with Miliko that was difficult, almost impossible. He was so poor that no one could be poorer, and so proud—overproud—that no one could ever have even hinted that he made friends to better himself. The fear lest anyone be able to reproach him for begging or self-interest or giving way to his longings or desires had been rooted in him from his earliest youth by the force of superstition and unbending moral prohibitions. He lived his life in merciless loneliness,

61

satisfied with his own integrity, so that it developed, was in fact bound to develop, independent of all standards and comparisons, and often even in contradiction to them.

Miliko was scarcely able to remember his father, who had died, so they said, from hunger in one of the Austro-Hungarian prisoner-of-war camps. The old people said that he had been brave and upright, and although he had been a poor and undistinguished peasant with the rank of a reserve officer, he had behaved like a regular officer from a famous and well-to-do family.

I imagined and pictured Miliko's father through his mother, Pava, who, it seemed, really possessed just those qualities.

Tall and bony, with dark, mottled skin—though she might have been a bit cleaner—she doggedly and proudly endured her widowhood and poverty. For her, they evidently meant the same thing. All her efforts and all her hopes were centered on her four children—three sons and a daughter—in the shack on the fringes of the stony, only partially cleared patch of land where her husband had settled after the cultivatable land seized from the Turks had been apportioned. He had made his home outside the village on the very crest of the ridge known as Ravens' Height.

The widow regarded it as her irrevocable duty to sacrifice what remained of her youth and strength to her home and children—a woman's testament and inheritance in a land of continual war, devastating epidemics, and the harshness of nature. Pava was exceedingly poor, but the most widow-like of widows; no one knew, or even hinted, that she ever had any connection with men. She herself never made any show of her restraint; she probably regarded it as something natural by the very fact that she was without a husband. Nonetheless, being naturally talkative, she spoke much of her poverty, though perhaps not so much of her poverty as of her irreconcilability to and inflexibility in penury, a penury so harsh that it was beyond the comprehension of the other peasants how she and the children endured their hunger and nakedness. She was clearly conscious of her integrity and still more of the exceptional nature of her attitude, and she almost boasted of it as the one treasure she possessed.

A slight froth used to gather at the corners of her dry, bluish lips, but not, as might have been thought, because of her talkativeness, but because she could not hold back her saliva. Two of her sons, the eldest and Miliko, were by nature taciturn, but they, too, had a similar froth. The other two children, the youngest son and her daughter, Dunja, who was older than Miliko, also possessed her inexhaustible self-reliance in poverty, but showed it in a different way.

The eldest son was already of school age and, though in poor health, often worked as a day laborer. Too weak to get involved in open quarrels, but sufficiently straightforward not to make use of plots and stratagems, he was well able to preserve his pride and honor. The youngest son, an undernourished and embittered, but decent, child, was like the eldest, but more obtuse and more liable to pick a quarrel. Dunja, a plump brunette, who they said was very like her father, gave the impression of being rather silly, lazy, and fond of eating. She was in fact just that; she ate stolidly everything that was set before her, and worked little and not very intelligently. But whenever anyone in any way infringed her code of honor, she would react swiftly, infallibly, and with a fury not in keeping with her gay and simple nature. She left the service of my parents after some minor slight and fled back to the hunger and desolation of Ravens' Height.

Miliko, thin and bony like his mother, Pava, was the

strongest and healthiest of the sons. His boniness was not merely the effect of hunger and every kind of lack, but was more a result of his qualities, his vital, restless body and his keen, impulsive spiritual make-up. As a child he had not been strong, nor did he become so later, but he was the quickest to learn among those of his own age and one of the best pupils at school. This fact and her desire to preserve the reputation and prestige of her husband led his mother to send him to secondary school despite the still-greater penury to which it exposed both him and her. I do not remember him ever taking part in our childish squabbles, and though I was the stronger, I, like the others, avoided quarreling with him because of the ungovernable, unmeasured fury, especially in defense, that was evident in his dark fine-cut features and gray, almost undetermined color. What certainly contributed most of all to that avoidance and impression was that he, though always hungry and always without lunch, never consented to take even a crust from his companions. While we were eating, he would slip away unnoticed to avoid any possibility of being offered anything.

The name Ravens' Height attracted me, partly because it was right up there in the skies, but even more because I marveled at the thin, austere boy who was able, after gulping down a bowl of skimmed milk and a chunk of bread in the morning, to climb back in the evening to that height, the farther away because during the day he had not swallowed a single mouthful. Miliko's was a sad life for a boy; he was always alone, because he could make friends with no one lest it be thought that he was being friendly in the hope of getting some food. It seemed that the conviction grew in him that penury and loneliness went together.

Though we were not in the same class—he went to school two years after I did—we were often together for long peri-

ods, for all four classes learned in the same room, and often
at the same time, and we went home together for a good
part of the way. However, I cannot tell you anything more
of him and his family, and have only mentioned these details in order to illustrate what I have to say.

Later, during our secondary schooldays, nothing very noteworthy took place between us either. We still remained only
chance acquaintances, despite my desire that we should be
something more, which awoke in me after our every meeting.
The fact that we did not go to school in the same town kept
us apart, so that we only met in summer or on holidays.
Even then we saw one another only occasionally and by
chance, for our families, though not very far from one another, lived in entirely different conditions—his on the crest
of the mountains and mine down by the river. Ravens'
Height and its nest remained far off and unattainable.

But one summer I at last made acquaintance with Ravens'
Height.

I was by then a young man, and some job or other took me
to a neighbor's house on the crest a little below Miliko's.

Having finished my task and being already in the vicinity,
I set out through the sultry summer heat to visit Miliko. His
family had just put up a cabin of a single room with a fireplace and with a storeroom beneath. Seen from the village,
that little house below the wooded peaks was as lonely as a
bird which has forgotten to fly away with the flock or as a
patch of snow that has been too late in melting. From
nearby, it still seemed poverty-stricken. Owing to the steep-
ness of the slope, and to save expense, it was almost at ground
level, and the walls around the clumsy fireplace had not
been whitewashed. There was only the one little room, with
a fir-bark bed and a chest on which were laid some rough

woolen coverings. On the planks near the hearth there was a patch of tin and a wooden dish; a muslin cheese bag hung on a peg. There was neither stool nor tripod, and evidently they baked their bread on the tin slab and covered it with bare embers. But this was a great improvement, and a whole kingdom must have been destroyed to reach this stage from the shack and sleeping on the bare earth with the calves and kids.

Miliko was not at home.

Dunja had grown into a young woman whose blossoming masked her ugliness and whose modesty raised blushes from time to time on her dimpled cheeks.

When she had been a servant in my parents' house, we two had often squabbled and fought. Mother Pava reminded us of this, and those childish squabbles in a trice became charged with something dear and intimate. Dunja smiled timidly and amorously, and I was astonished to see that the weak clumsy wench, quick to quarrel and patient in enduring kicks, had become a strong and thickset young woman, charged with youth and vigor. It even seemed pleasant to me that Miliko was not at home, for he did not like to be reminded that his sister had been a servant, and I was a little afraid lest he should suspect my not quite uncarnal astonishment at Dunja's fresh and rounded figure.

This time, too, Mother Pava did not fail to stress, especially before a schoolboy from the big house, her integrity and poverty. She told me that her husband and my father had been great friends. That was, in fact, quite true, as was everything she said, though her home had been dogged by fate and had remained poor in everything save honor. But I noticed a change in her, and not only external; she behaved like a housewife who had at one time been well to do. Her lamentations and the froth at the corners of her mouth were still there, but she burst out with broad, expansive expressions and gestures, and had even grown a little fatter. The only heritage she had ever had was her children, and she had succeeded in bringing them up, fresh hands to help in the heaviest tasks.

I could not avoid being treated to the best they had—warm creamy milk, which Dunja, disappearing into the dairy made of rough planks, clearly drew from the tub poured out that morning. She put it into a blue cup, from which the enamel had already begun to chip. An improvement was also to be seen in the way in which Dunja served me; she placed the cup on the palm of her hand as if on a tray, and did not hold it in her fingers, as is usual with simple peasants.

I continued on my way to the crest of Ravens' Height through the cool shining green of the peaks, trembling with vague passion and my first thoughts about the destinies of human beings—Pava's and her husband's, Dunja's, Miliko's, and my own.

Miliko's father and his neighbor had cleared almost the whole shoulder of the mountain and had fired the land in order to obtain fertile soil. But the soil had been thin, almost barren, and below it the stone again appeared. They got only three or four small fields in the hollows and about as much meadowland on the slopes, while wild raspberries, blackberries, and other bushes sprang up on the fired patches. The land had proved suitable for pasture, but only in the spring, before the sun burned up every blade of grass on the bare, hard soil. Thinned out, the forest was no longer able to withstand the storms, which must have been fierce up there. Fallen trees blocked the paths, and broken beech stumps stood on guard. Up on the ridge, where the forest had not been thinned, it had held its own. Colossal beeches defied the heavens, but I knew that, sooner or later, their turn would come, either from ax or from storm. I sat down, perspiring, by one of them, nestling in its mossy roots as in a lap. So this, then, was Ravens' Height, just under the mountain peaks, bare and green, and above the village like a cloud, lonely and desolate but also suckled by some living, irresistible force. This was, this meant, life; destruction and renewal, death and birth. Pava had nourished life despite desolation and need, war and death, and soon she, too, would die. So would Dunja—be married, give birth, and die. Why should she not come up here with me, here between heaven and earth, so that, young and innocent, we should conceive a new life? Why should men behave as if they were different from all other living things?

Only later did I remember that I had not given a thought to Miliko, though he and my insatiable curiosity about Ravens' Height had been the reasons I had gone there. I had wanted to see where he had grown up and to solve the riddle of how men lived, of how they managed to exist. But I knew then that if I met Miliko, I would be secretly ashamed of my desire for his sister, set in train as much by the simplicity of life and death on Ravens' Height and the memory of my childish squabbles with Dunja as by a young man's desires. It may well be that the purity and indigence of Miliko's life and personality forced me to ask myself questions and to seek out my own faults; he had a similar effect, though quite unintentionally, on others also.

Only after my first year as a university student—Miliko was still at the secondary school—did this feeling of guilt that he provoked lessen. Dunja was already married, and Miliko and I went about more together, for he would come down to the river to bathe. He was now a youth, eager and alive to the joys of life, and he liked to listen to my tales of Belgrade and of a world that would no longer be evil and unjust.

It was then that I noticed a fresh facet of his character. He approached everything very cautiously and carefully, but when he had convinced himself, weighed the evidence and decided, he remained loyal and consistent.

He listened carefully and inquisitively to my exposition of the new society, but he elected for the revolutionary movement only much later, sometime toward the end of his studies, after he had confirmed everything and, I would say, weighed it all in his own mind. I remember that he explained to me as we were bathing in the cool pond under the sun's heat: "I have a duty to my mother to finish my education. She would have wasted so much toil if I were to be expelled from the university for political reasons."

He would only be able to join the revolutionary movement once he was convinced that this labor would not be in vain. That cautiousness was not due to fear—later, in prison and in battle, he showed himself to be very brave—and still less because he had become accustomed to, or desirous of, a comfortable way of life. No, he simply could not undertake anything of which he was not convinced and that could involve him in a useless waste of energy. Development, the conservation of life, not only human, was a moral duty to him. I would say that for him it was more important than the necessity of existence, though he could when he wanted see that duty in his own mind and detach it from his moral outlook.

Conscience forced him to join the revolutionary movement. On the other hand, that exaggerated conscience of his led him into the movement too late. Had the revolution not become a reality, he would never have become a revolutionary and probably would never have experienced such tragic and insoluble inner conflicts.

# 2.

WE DID NOT SEE one another again for years, not until the outbreak of the insurrection. Then, early in August 1941, we met in Montenegro, in our own homeland.

Miliko had been working only a year or two as an agricultural engineer somewhere in Slavonia or the Voivodina when he was caught up in the war and driven back to his homeland. I don't remember how he got there—probably the same way as had so many from certain units of the former Royal Yugoslav Army, which had disintegrated under the blows of the German and Italian invaders at the beginning of April 1941 and had dispersed without waiting for a clash with the enemy. His wife fled with him. I do not remember where she had been or where she came from, and at that time I was not interested. I can only say for certain that she had been born in some town of the Voivodina. She was an educated woman and, I think, had some university degree, but in what? No, I can no longer remember, if I ever knew. In the bloody maelstrom I would have completely forgotten her had Miliko's way and mine not crossed and if she had not met a fate unusual even in wars and revolutions.

In our village there was a long-standing and well-supported revolutionary organization. It was made up entirely of peasants, for the only intellectual, the teacher, was a supporter of the regime in power and was therefore bitterly at odds with the villagers. Miliko, who had recently become a member, had more moral than political influence among the peasant members of the revolutionary party. He had this influence on the other peasants also. But the peasants who had been members of the movement long before he had, and who had experienced its trials and dangers, looked more to themselves than to him. They welcomed him gladly enough, for he was a godsend to them in explaining and studying the revolutionary literature, some of which was written in the peasant manner and language, but some in terms foreign and incomprehensible to them. His wife was not a party member. But she, too, joined the movement there in the village, certainly after consultation with the higher committee; and she, too, was welcome to them, especially for work among the women and girls. She undertook such duties ably and willingly, though she did not introduce much politics into them. She mainly gave advice on hygiene and housekeeping problems, which aroused the interest of the peasant women. But little by little she drew them, too, into the revolutionary movement.

At the beginning the insurgents easily disarmed the Italian garrison in the town. But Italian reinforcements soon began to arrive, and it became clear that the insurgents would not be able to hold the town. So it was decided that the food plundered from the Italian stores should be taken by trust-worthy men to some isolated spot, where it could later be used for the insurgent units. This task fell to Miliko and the organization to which he belonged, both because of the suit-ability of the terrain, heavily wooded and far from roads, and because the military ability and long standing of the organization gave a guarantee that the stores would be con-scientiously protected. The food was brought by truck to the village, usually by night, where the members awaited it with horses and took it away to Ravens' Height.

It would have been impossible to keep this a secret from the peasants, even if a military organization had already existed. What happened, however, was expected by few, least of all by Miliko, who had been entrusted by the command and the higher party forum with the transport and safeguarding of the food. As soon as the Italian columns had thundered by on the roads, the peasants by night stole and apportioned almost all the food.

Seeing that the insurrection was coming to nothing and that the insurgent units, which at the time of the early victories had seemed all of one mind, were disintegrating into small groups, the peasants, as is always the case when authorities and states collapse, began to expand their properties. Suspecting that this was not the end of the struggle and that the insurgent cells would rapidly be reorganized, they plundered by night and in secret, and certainly by arrangement with the guards.

That was how Miliko and I met.

Miliko was embittered and despairing, the more so because it was obvious that some party members had taken their share in the plunder. He seemed to believe that any man by the mere fact that he had become a Communist also became morally pure and ceased to be what he had been before.

The question was posed: Without food what could be done for the units made up of those who wouldn't or couldn't come to terms with defeat? Without food one cannot live, still less fight, and to go on fighting was for the Communists and their sympathizers a question of life and death. It was to Miliko, who took on himself the lion's share of the blame, that we entrusted the task of restocking the stores and also, with the help of the most determined and loyal of the party members, of recovering the plundered food. That inevitably led to a clash between the insurgents and the peasants, and between Miliko personally and his own village. By plunder or by barter more than half the village had had a share of the insurgents' stores. The villagers justified their action by saying: "This was just as much our food as the Communists'. All of us helped to take the town."

It could be seen that Miliko was uneasy and embarrassed, both because of what had happened and because of the inevitable clash with the peasants. But less heed had to be taken of the last, since a reckoning with neighborly, parental, and other considerations was not only a duty but a condition of survival and struggle for every true Communist.

As I came to know later, Miliko half succeeded in his task. He found little food, but he somehow managed to convince the peasants that they should feed and help the few, and for that very reason firmer and more closely knit, groups which had been formed in the forests around the village—the nucleus of future military units.

Though trying to embitter the peasants as little as possible, Miliko was firmly on the side of those who had decided to fight. He tried stubbornly to reconcile one with the other. At first, he managed to do so quite successfully. Slowly the village came to life again, and those very men who had done the plundering rallied around the insurgent groups as if nothing had happened.

Nonetheless something *had* happened in the village. United in the first days of the insurrection, it was now split into those who unconditionally wanted to fight and those who were more or less willing to help, though they would have preferred to stand aside. This split took place even in the party organization itself; some members were expelled because they had taken part in the plundering of the stores and others fell away because they did not approve of direct action, fearing that it might lead to fierce reprisals.

During a discussion at Miliko's house of the plundering of the stores and the formation of a nucleus of future units, I came to know Miliko's wife, Gordana.

Miliko was then thirty, and she probably about twenty-five, though she looked much younger, like a girl of twenty. She was of average height and slender, but full-bosomed. Her large, firm breasts probably drew one's eye because of the slenderness of her waist and the delicacy of her long legs. She was proud of her breasts, and walked in a stately manner to emphasize their firmness and prominence. Her hair must have been shining chestnut, but here she could no longer take care of it, and it had become a sort of tawny, ashen color, as was her small and freckled face. Her hands, too, were small; the skin had soaked up soot from the hearths and that sullen, undetermined peasant grease, as if she had been milking and cooking, as perhaps indeed she had. Her dress was now in rags and had also turned an indeterminate color. She was obviously ashamed that she did not have better stockings, for in her haste she had put on her only silk ones, and they were now gone at the heels. She used to wear worn-out slippers, and it was noticeable that they did not fit her thin and delicate ankles. Her teeth were very striking, almost as striking as her breasts; they were close-set and slightly protruding, which made her look somewhat rabbity, mouselike, very humble and meek. That innocent animal charm was increased by her eyes, a little prominent, greenish in color, and very lively and penetrating in that freckled face.

Gordana was in no way a beauty. But in other circumstances, in her wealthy and civilized home town, especially in the atmosphere of comfort, settled family life, and apartments filled with modern furniture, she must have seemed a pretty and pleasing young woman. Here in the mountains, living in penury and backwardness, she had already lost her delicacy and refinement. Obviously she had done her best to blend with those around her, vainly trying to acquire the rough directness and unaffectedness of the village women.

She could not accustom herself to the way in which *rakija,* or plum brandy, is served among us, and hesitated whether to leave the bottle and glasses on a tray in front of us, as is done in the towns, or to fill the glasses and wait until someone drinks in order to pour out another. Mixing these two ways of serving, she was convinced that we, each in his own way, for there were both peasants and educated men among us, had noticed her confusion. So she became even more embarrassed and, blushing slightly and smiling wryly, left everything on the table and sat down on a chest.

It was an impossible situation, not because of her confusion—there were few who cared, even if they noticed—but because she was present at a meeting in which she had no part to play and at which her husband was bound to be exposed to harsh criticism for his slackness and lack of foresight in the matter of the stores and where he would be given fresh and even more difficult tasks. Miliko either did not realize that she should not be there or considered that she had a right to be present. So he kept silent, and all the others kept silent, as though there were an enemy among us. Gordana, unused to relations among Communists and the established rules of their work, in no way felt that she was out of place and even a hindrance. Someone had to break this embarrassment, and it was finally up to me to do so, not because I was in any way eager, but because I was the senior official and for that very reason called upon to do something. I said, with many excuses and assurances that it was not a sign of lack of trust, that she must leave us alone, for we had some work to do with which she had no direct concern. She burst into excuses, apparently embittered not at us but at herself for not having realized it.

There had been a certain improvement in Miliko's house,

though not much more than there had been ten years ago, during our childhood. The house had remained the same and was certainly full of bugs and fleas. But the stock were no longer shut in the cellar; a wooden stall had been built near the house. In the house itself there were a few glasses and some simple china. The old wooden bed had been replaced by a camp bed of some sort, and it had bedcovers and pillows. What was more, there were curtains of crude cloth at the windows, their lower edges fringed with thread.

But these changes confirmed rather than lessened Gordana's consciousness of poverty and backwardness. I felt that she was shocked not so much by the shortages and the dirt as by the calmness and indifference of these men toward them. She clearly could not understand how men could be so indifferent toward such inhuman, to her way of thinking, conditions of life. Disgusted astonishment showed in her face, though she quickly concealed it, when one of the peasants, a party member, spat copiously on the floor and then calmly rubbed it in with his sandal, which was made of an old tire. Brought up in different conditions, she was unable to see, and still less to understand, all that was in front of her. She could see the spitting on the floor, which she had scrubbed only the day before, but she could not see the significance of the sandal made from an old tire and not from plaited leather, such as for several years back had alone been made and worn. When they wore shoes, she probably thought, even these men would stop spitting on the floor.

Her inability to blend with her surroundings, which from an intellectual and political viewpoint could have been much greater, did not escape the notice of the local Communists. Already several of them had complained to me about her, saying that she was a lady who despised "us peasants," while others, half-educated schoolboys, insisted that

her attitude was due to "ideological immaturity" and "bourgeois upbringing." Both may well have been right. I myself
noticed that she did not find the poverty and primitiveness
so hard, but was horrified at the thought that she, too, might
become engulfed by them and grow accustomed to them. Perhaps it was that realization which made me repeat my excuses when she left the meeting at my request. If my memory
is correct, a sad and grateful smile lit her face, which seemed
to say: "Ah, I understand very well—though I might have
been warned before the meeting."

My way back led me over Ravens' Height.

Now it all looked different: huge masses of debris had
settled down and were rotting, while the young forest had
spread and sprung up unbridled. Uncut, uncleared growth
had conquered rock and desolation, glades and clearings. An
occasional stump remained, but rotten and fringed with
fungus, lost in the leaves and tangles of the blackberries and
creepers.

It was still summer, and the greenness had burst out everywhere, engulfing everything. Only up on the ridge had the
old beech trees survived, and I, I don't know why, was overjoyed by it.

Tired and perspiring, I sat down in the crotch of one of
them and remembered that somewhere nearby I had sat
down in this way ten years before, brimming over with the
first secrets of life and love.

But how everything had changed since then!

No, the forest had not changed, though it had won back
the areas filched from it and had become more luxuriant
and more beautiful; it was I who had changed, the life I had
lived and in which I had had so much hope. Then, sitting
there in my early youth, bursting with confused new thoughts
and fresh impulses, I had asked myself: Who am I, whence

do I come, and what do I want here on earth? With all my senses, not only my external senses but also those within me, I had noticed and understood as a whole not only everything material but also the sentient and thinking world. Then, there had been Dunja, with whom I had shared my experiences under the beech, in my hands and in my blood. Now, my body and my desires were empty of all women, and I would never have remembered Dunja or anyone else had I not sat there vainly trying to resurrect dead time and my own real existence.

Now, I noticed everything: the ant lost on a frond of fern, the humming of the centuries-old treetops, and the fresh crisp smell in the beech shade. But now I noticed it all in a different way, as something outside me. If I wanted to perceive some detail, it must be there before my eyes or I must force myself to plunge deeply in search of it. The world existed independently of me, and I was conscious of its, or my, isolation.

Human relations, especially, had been turned topsy-turvy, as if everything that belonged to them existed in a world not theirs, a world that someone with angry malevolence and icy abstraction had invented, so that in it men should be exterminated in the harshest and most unexpected manner. The stink of burnings and corpses which lasts for days and penetrates one's dreams, internments and shootings of even those dearest to us, and then that foreboding split; those who were opponents of our struggle incited men, with the excuse of preserving their homes and lives from the reprisals of the occupiers, to fire on those who still wanted to, who still must, fight. And there was that episode of the stores and our countermeasures. Did not all this throw human relations out of gear and make them inhuman and unreal? Then there was the civil war, which we revolutionaries preached inten-

tionally and rejoiced in fiendishly, and which was without
a crumb of joy, rending the living world and living men.
What was the good of that green age and youth on Ravens'
Height, the clatter of a disturbed jay and the scent of fern
and primrose? What good was that new song, that uncon-
summated passion? Everything lived for itself, outside me,
and I, too, lived as if outside myself, watching myself and
giving myself strict commands. I knew what I was doing and
what I would have to do; active war was my task and my
greatest, my only, hope.

Everything was so clear and definite, yet so strange and
distant—and, especially, not mine.

Below me were the terraces of my native village, with
white houses and bluish gardens and the river roaring fiercely
around its bends, and all about me the mountains breathing
heavily, heaving their wide shoulders and gently bending
their yellow heads. This no longer seemed a well-known
land, however, or my native village, perhaps not a village at
all, and if a village, then it mattered not whose. But it was
certain that today or tomorrow we must recover, if not
peaceably, then by force, the food the peasants had taken
from us and begin the disarming of those who would not
fight. For tomorrow—there had already been such cases in
other districts—they would guard the roads for the fascists
in order to avoid reprisals on their lands and supposedly to
preserve their homes.

I had to hurry, and I left Ravens' Height even more determined to carry out my duty and still more estranged from
the world, from men, from myself.

# 3.

IN THE SUMMER of the following year I again met Miliko, but far from our homeland and in greatly changed circumstances. In the spring of that year the revolutionary army had been driven out of Montenegro toward Bosnia, and later deep into it.

We marched for days along the mountain forest trails, through wild virgin country, ravished and terrible. The ruins of burned-out hamlets were our halts, and our camps at night were beside swift streams and bubbling springs, on meadows and mountain pastures. Grasses, ferns, and bushes had grown so vigorously in the desolate villages that it seemed that centuries must have passed since men had been driven from them or killed, though in fact it was not a year, not six months. Every moment there was something to remind us that men had been there only yesterday: the doorposts of the houses creaked, and doves cooed in the plum orchards, now gray and darkened and suddenly run wild. That was a land as wonderful and terrible as a madman's fancies and yet as real and insistent as a wound in one's own body. In that distant, imagined, and yet real world, creeds and classes and parties had been wiped out, yesterday and today, and each of them, faced with the inevitability of its own downfall, had done its best to reserve exclusively for itself all the necessities of life and to adapt them to its own ends. They slaughtered, burned, and exterminated neighbors and brothers along roads eager for the sound of horses' hoofs and in pastures where no sheep bells could be heard.

It was in one of these former Bosnian villages, while we

were camping in its luxuriance and desolation near a pleasant little river, that Miliko came to see me one afternoon. I had already heard what had taken place between him and Gordana and, suspecting that this was the very thing about which he wanted to talk to me, I went with him a little unwillingly. Confessions, when I must console the one who is talking even if he does not deserve it, always put me in a false position, but I decided to do all I could to help and advise him. Perhaps my mood was a personal and ambivalent attitude that others, too, had toward him—respect and avoidance, compassion and horror in his presence.

He spread a military greatcoat on the wall of a burned-out stable or kitchen, and we sat down among the ashes and the riotous greenery of the plants, facing the little river, which, darkened by patches of shade, smiled and chattered with thousands of sunlit ripples.

He was very thin—all of us had been starving—and froth appeared at the corners of his mouth, that same kind of froth that appeared on his mother's lips as soon as she began to speak. I also noticed something new in him: he often caught me by a button or a sleeve, by my belt or holster, not in order to hold my attention, but, rather, as if he wanted to attach himself to me. In his tone and manner, even though he stubbornly and skillfully tried to conceal it, I noticed a longing not so much for support and justification, as for consolation—yes, consolation. There was a certain stiffness in his speech and appearance, most unusual and striking in one who was usually so quick and sensitive. He would talk and then suddenly stop and look away. He had, too, a new turn of phrase: "Don't you think so?" By it he did not ask anything, but searched for confirmation of his words and, still more, of his unspoken mood and thought. But that abstraction had not lessened, had perhaps even strengthened, his decisiveness in the execution of his political and military duties. What is more, they alone had become absolute and important for him, gaining almost a mystical attraction and value independent of men and human relations.

Even before he had begun to speak it was clear that he had come to me not only, since I was a senior party official, to obtain ideological and political confirmation and explanation of his action, but because I was a childhood friend who, though we had never been intimate, understood him, so to speak, from the human angle. As a revolutionary I had always considered any differentiation between these two roles as incorrect and inconsistent. But in this case I felt a sort of embarrassment because it was impossible for me to be impartial. Partly because I felt it to be my duty, and partly out of respect for him and also because of our childhood together, I decided to listen to him carefully and patiently. As he spoke, even though I was scarcely aware of it at the time, I became more and more dumfounded and amazed at the unspoken, and at that time inexplicable, depth of his desolation and despair.

He was neither long nor monotonous in his tale. He left out what I already knew well, and if occasionally he laid stress on details, he did so only because they oppressed him and he could not pass over in silence what had become a nightmare to him.

His case was, as I have said, well known to me. But it is one thing to know and another to experience. Only through Miliko's narration could I conceive the incurable nature of his misfortune and the immensity of the desolation the war had caused him.

The Italian command posts had been for the most part slow in action and their intelligence was poor, and it was just for those reasons that the *carabinieri* were able to surprise Miliko and his comrades. In fact, having learned where the food store had been hidden and not knowing that it had already been plundered, the Italians, about twelve days after our meeting in Miliko's house, had surrounded the village at early dawn and begun a search of Ravens' Height. Miliko and his companions had managed to escape. The Italians found the food that had been recovered from the peasants and they had burned Miliko's house and those of the other insurgents. Miliko's wife, who had not been one of the fighters, was taken prisoner, together with the other women and the old men.

If I remember well, she was already suffering from some sort of stomach complaint, and in prison her condition rapidly grew worse. The Italian authorities had nothing definite against her, except that she was her husband's wife, so they transferred her from prison to hospital. Though they did not release her, there was no guard over her at the hospital, and later she was allowed to walk freely through the little town. But from that little two-street town, surrounded by barbed wire and alive with spies, she could not have escaped without help even had she been more experienced and in full health. Sometime in November or December the Italian garrison, fearing the onset of winter, when they would be cut off by snowdrifts in the midst of the wasp's nest of insurgents, withdrew to its main body. Gordana was among the prisoners whom the Italians did not take with them.

There was gossip that Gordana had been overfriendly with an Italian officer of the garrison who was at that time the only doctor in the little town. It was undoubtedly true that she had been seen with the doctor and that he had helped her with gifts of food and other trifles. That was enough, in a country torn by war and for an organization that drew its force from its uncompromising hostility, for a suspicion of shame and treason to fall on Gordana.

At that time the insurgents did not have courts, and military staffs and party committees meted out justice; naturally, the final word was usually with the latter. Well-known street women, who had given themselves to the enemy soldiers, were not punished by the insurgent authorities if they had not at the same time carried out any espionage activities; it was regarded as sufficient punishment that they be held up to public scorn. Miliko's wife was neither a street woman nor a woman of ill fame, but a member of the party and the wife of one of its local leaders. Her case could not be passed over and, still less, forgiven. That would demoralize the already unstable membership of the revolutionary movement. At that particular moment a widespread and sudden revival of anti-insurgent wavering and the consequent strengthening of the counterrevolutionary organization made her case more serious.

But because Gordana was the wife of a leading comrade, the insurgent authorities in the town did not arrest her, or even interrogate her—certainly at the request of the party committee—but referred the whole case back to the regional committee, of which Miliko was a member.

Miliko, so I had been told, had been aware of the relationship between the doctor and his wife before Gordana's case was brought to the notice of the committee.

"Gordana herself told me," he said. "She did not seem conscious of any crime against the party or the national struggle. For, she said, I gave nothing away, nor did I spy on anyone."

What is more, she continued to justify herself to Miliko; she was ill, alone, among prisoners who were for the most

part criminals. The Italian doctor had behaved kindly to
her, and but for him she might have died. She even said that
he was not a bad man; he was refined and cultured and was
not even a fascist, but had been mobilized and, like the
majority of Italians, plunged into a war he did not want in
a country he did not know. An intimacy had arisen between
them, she said, almost by chance, owing to the care he had
shown her as a conscientious doctor and from intellectual and
other affinities. The Italian, too, was lonely—so she told him
—in a conquering army in a hostile land. She became accustomed to his company and, though she felt uneasy among
the people who had begun to shun her and out of loyalty
toward Miliko, she no longer could, nor did she wish to, end
this friendship.

She never admitted that she had been the Italian's mistress, though Miliko had interrogated her about this all
night long. He felt the jealousy of the male, though perhaps
not very strongly, and this was not an essential feature of his
behavior toward her. But such a confession was in any case
unnecessary on her part; it was enough that she did not try
to conceal her friendship with an officer of the occupying
forces, or that she had received presents and attentions from
him.

From Miliko's account it could be concluded that Gordana
had till then always been faithful to him and that as a girl
she had always been among the unattainable ones, though
she had not been a virgin when he had first met her. He
had known every detail of her past; she had never tried to
conceal it.

But that had been the past! And it had not been an
enemy! And it had not happened in the midst of the insurrection, nor were the ideals of the movement to which he now
belonged involved, a movement that did not look on such a

friendship as a personal marital weakness, but as a shameful betrayal!

Her name, he said, had become a symbol of shame among the comrades, and that was especially hard for him. Gordana, whose name meant "the proud one," a friend, if nothing worse, of an enemy! Where was that pride? He had loved that name, both because of its meaning and because of its clear hard sound, and now, after she had fraternized with the occupiers, it seemed to embody all the suspicion and the humiliation, the insult and the hatred, that the war and the occupation had brought with them. His repulsion for her name was so strong that he not only avoided calling her by it, but it had sometimes seemed to him, and even now it seemed to him, that everything might have turned out differently had she been named differently. To what stupidity men come and what trifles beset them when they are anguished and embittered!

Another thing gnawed at Miliko even more: Gordana had assured him of her love, despite everything that might have taken place between her and the Italian. It was evident to me that his belief in Gordana's love, even were it well founded, was only the other side of his love for her. He loved her despite the pain she had caused him, perhaps even because of it, and he would have forgiven her everything. He even suspected that in the special circumstances her weakness for the Italian had not been a betrayal, even of the movement to which he belonged. But to forgive meant not merely to stifle the male in him and confirm his love, but also to separate himself from his comrades and the struggle that, because it was not his alone, he could not give up.

"And she, she understood nothing of all this!" he wailed. " 'Let them exclude me from the party if they won't understand,' she said, 'only you must forget and go on loving me.

Surely you, an intellectual and a man of the world, won't give any fateful or real significance to that, even if what they say of me really happened. He was an officer of the occupying forces, yes, but he saved me and many others, if by nothing else, then by his care as a doctor. Just think of prison, shootings, and burnings, and no human kindness or sympathy save from him!' It was as if she had come," Miliko concluded, "from some world in which war, death, and tears did not exist and in which men sinned only that they might be able to forgive one another. I was quite unable to recognize her. She was just the same, body and soul, just as tender, innocently devoted, and modestly submissive. Yet, it was not she. She spoke and thought in a way I could not comprehend. Or was it that we two, or I myself, had changed in those three months in which she had been a prisoner? And perhaps we were neither of us our real selves, but each in the given circumstances had gone his own way—and the ways had divided!"

Miliko, who had noticed that there had been whispering about Gordana and her behavior in prison, put her case to the committee before any information or orders had come from the town. He did not do so—and I was quite certain of this, even if he had not made a point of it—in order to appear blameless and sincere, but because he could not, did not wish to, conceal anything from the party and because he wanted help and a decision.

"It turned out differently from what I had expected," he said, "though I already knew what the decision would be. The more I expounded it at length and in great detail, the less I was convinced, to tell the truth, that Gordana must be shot. But there was no other solution, and it was I myself who had to carry out the sentence.

"While I was making my report it was clear to me what

the comrades on the committee thought, though none of them had as yet expressed an opinion and what, in the circumstances, Gordana's action meant. Each one of them had had someone dear to him either killed or interned; they were all homeless, their houses burned, their families dispersed. Each one of them had a burden upon him heavier than his own fate. They, the instigators and leaders of the insurrection, had urged the people to blood and fire and had transformed their own land into ashes and desolation. Treason had flourished in their own ranks, brother against brother, father raising his rifle against son. Only the day before, they had decided to shoot a party member, a relative of one of them, because he had handed over a rifle to the Italians, and I had agreed with them. A party member who had surrendered and then fled back again to our side had also been shot. The occupying forces and our local enemies had daily exchanges with us which left behind fresh corpses and burnings, pouring poison and hatred into overcharged hearts. Whenever I thought that human evil and loathsomeness had reached the bounds of imagination, a fresh incursion convinced me that I was wrong. Who could even have thought that to these men and in these circumstances Gordana's transgression could have been explained by psychological subtleties! For us that would have meant not only confusion and weakness, but also treason! The occupier's girl friend—a party member! What human weakness was this, while children were dying in burning homes?

"The conclusion, both for them and for me, was clear beforehand, logical, indisputable, determined by experience and example, imposed by the needs of further struggle.

"Though considerate and kindly to me as a comrade, not one of them volunteered to carry out the sentence. What is more, they did not even propose that soldiers from the local unit should do it. Not one of them wanted to be responsible for her death. All mutely held it to be my duty. Each one of them had settled accounts or was settling accounts with backsliding and treason in his own district and in his own village. The secretary said: 'I think, comrades, that it is best to leave the whole affair in Comrade Miliko's hands. We all have the utmost confidence in him.'

"So, by the very fact that I was a member of the committee and a fighter—and that I wanted to be and had to be—I automatically accepted the frightful task. To settle accounts with love that had treason in its heart—that was the task assigned to me. To show myself stronger than myself because of an ideal and because of social obligations! I behaved as I had to behave, as my social conscience commanded."

# 4.

THE SUN WENT DOWN behind the mountaintops, and dark shadows filled the valleys as Miliko went on with his tale.

"The committee meeting was held in the village school. The question of Gordana was only one of several matters on the agenda; we passed on to the others. I remember that I took part in the discussion as usual, but all the while I kept thinking of what I must do and considering how I would do it. Whatever I said or did, I couldn't help thinking about it. I said and did everything against my will, almost automatically, right up to the moment when I decided I must kill Gordana.

"And I acted, later on, automatically, surprisingly coldly, and very decisively.

"Since our house had been burned, my family had moved

down to the valley, to the house of one of my uncles, about
half a mile away from the school. You know where the
house is, at the crossroads, by the brook between the village
and the foothills of Ravens' Height. The path from the
school slopes downward and follows the brook through the
alder grove up to my uncle's house. So I thought that it would
be most suitable if I killed Gordana by the brook. The fact
that I must call her to the committee for her case to be heard
would serve as an excuse to get her out of the house. I had
already told her that I was putting everything before my
comrades.

"It was early evening—I had chosen that as the most suitable time—when I dropped in at the house and told Gordana
to get ready to go to the committee.

"The lamp had not yet been lit, and even now I cannot
explain how, in the half-light of the room, she could have
read in my face or from my actions what was going to happen. She said falteringly, though not sadly, for she was terribly exhausted: 'Miki'—she used to call me that, though no
one else ever did—'you are going to kill me.'

"Perhaps because I still loved her, I really wanted to spare
her any suffering I could. I had even decided not to tell her
of the sentence. So I said firmly: 'Don't talk rubbish, but
get ready.'

"She got ready meticulously, though she had little enough
to put on, and continued as if she had not heard me: 'Very
well, Miki, but don't let it be you who kills me. You will be
killing yourself. For I love you. Don't kill yourself, too.'

"She might have gone on in that way had my mother not
come into the room just then. We both stopped talking, as
if by agreement. I wondered that Gordana did not ask for
my mother's help and support, but she evidently had in one
way or another become reconciled to the idea of her death,

though till then we had not spoken of it. My mother tried to kiss me, but I moved aside. She said: 'Be merciful to her if she has done wrong. She is a foreigner.' I could see how much she had been tormenting herself all that week. Gordana's words had moved me, though they did not make me waver in my determination. But my mother's did not even do that. It was as if someone unknown to me had spoken to me from another world. I found an answer and explanation for them: Mother was old, a conservative old peasant woman who understood nothing. She went on talking in this way, and when the two of us set out, she saw us to the door and sent us on our way loudly and kindly, though we never said good-by to her. 'May you have a happy journey.'

"It was February, and the evening frost had already set in. Gordana was carrying her coat over her arm, and I told her that she would catch cold. The path was wide, and we could easily have walked side by side, but she kept ahead of me. She looked around. 'I'm cold,' she said. 'I would like to put it on, but it's still good, and the blood might spoil it.'

"I realized why she kept ahead of me: she was giving me the chance to kill her suddenly and unexpectedly, clearly not because she was afraid, but because she wanted to leave me the illusion that she did not know that I was going to kill her and to save me the unpleasantness of looking into her eyes while I did it.

"We went on thus, silently, for two or three minutes. The stream, swollen by melted snow, roared in the twilight. Suddenly I saw and heard everything so clearly. Gordana, without turning around, said: 'In any case, Miki, I should not be able to go on living. It is you I am sorry for.'

"She began to cry, but not in order to move me, still less to implore me. I did not feel sorry for either her tears or her grief, but I felt very bitter when I noticed that she was wiping away her tears with her fingers; we had grown so poor that she no longer had a handkerchief. 'It's nothing,' I said to myself. 'All this sentimentality and grief is inevitable in death, and what must be, must be.'

"In those moments I not only acted calmly and collectedly, but also there came unbidden into my mind a justification and explanation in which there was a suspicion of grief and reason; there were so many reasons, and none was refutable, why Gordana should not be killed.

"We had already covered the greater part of the path and had just begun to ascend the slope when I remembered that we would soon reach the school where my comrades were and that they would be hoping that it was already over.

"I took out my revolver so quietly that not even I myself heard its friction on the holster; I had earlier slipped the safety catch so that Gordana would not hear the click. I placed the barrel almost on the curls at the nape of her neck and fired. Her beret leaped onto the snow, and she fell to her knees, twitched, and buried her face in the snow at the edge of the path. I almost said aloud, astounded at my own cynicism: 'At least she won't be cold.'

"I did not look at her, but, almost at a run, skirted her body carefully, treading on the unstained snow, and hurried on to the school. The comrades there were awaiting me, solicitously, almost tenderly, but no one said a word about the shot they all must have heard.

"Gordana would have remained on the path overnight if my mother, with the help of some of the village women, had not brought her home. From thence, in the darkness, the keening could be heard. The secretary concluded: 'We will have to explain to the people what all this was about.'

"We gave the explanation next day at a meeting at the school.

"I, too, spoke. Not one of the peasants either approved or condemned my action. I felt, while I was speaking, as if I were in a place where there was nothing living. Even things became immaterial and transparent, and all those men and women, with deadened eyes and numbed faces, seemed to me like masks or puppets. Why was I talking to them? I could not get the idea out of my mind as I explained the reasons for Gordana's death and why I had had to be the one to kill her.

"My mother, shocked and grief-stricken, did not attend the meeting. I thought of her as soon as the meeting was over. 'To her at least,' I said to myself, 'I must explain everything. She is my mother; she will understand.'

"When I went out, the whiteness of the snow and the blueness of the moonlight intensified that feeling of unreality I had had at the meeting. Naturally, I knew the contours of my own district, but it was as if it were not mine and as if I were walking in some world of dreams. The peaks shimmered in the far-off blue; nothing was left of the fields but a stiff smooth whiteness, and the trees were black, as if someone had placed them there while playing a game. Every detail was familiar to me and yet, as if I were dreaming, everything was in contrast and quivering, deceiving my senses, and when I trod on the earth or caught hold of a branch, they seemed harder than usual and for that very reason more unreal.

"I remembered that in order to avoid the spot where I had killed Gordana I ought not to go along the bank. But that would mean making a wide detour. I was angry with myself, and exclaimed: 'Soon I'll be believing in ghosts!' and set out by that very path.

"Though I tried to think of something else, perhaps by that very effort I relived more and more intensely the moments of Gordana's murder and in such a way that at each step toward the spot I became more and more powerfully and directly aware of Gordana's physical presence, as if she were walking behind me. At every moment I expected to see her and to feel her take me by the arm, as she always did when we went for a walk together. Strangely enough her presence did not disturb me, but was almost a comfort to me. I know that people we have loved still go on living for a long time in us and beside us. But that spot! I was more and more horrified by it. I felt that I was losing my self-control, that my nerves were giving way, and that the familiar landscape seemed to be breaking into a thousand pieces, so that I was almost unaware of the white path which repelled me and yet brought me straight to the patch of blood. Certainly that patch existed and was still there. I wanted to keep away from it, but was ashamed to show myself a superstitious coward and so rushed onward, while Gordana held my arm and whispered to me humbly and lovingly, but indistinctly.

"I did in fact come to the stain. It was not large, but it seemed to envelop the whole countryside, probably because I could not stop gazing at it, so that I felt that I would never manage to either go around it or jump over it, but must tread right in it. With a final effort of will I leaped from the path. The snowy crust squeaked and broke, and I hurried on through the untrodden snow. I stopped for breath and looked around again; everything was familiar and more real, so I slowly returned to the path and, stamping the snow off my feet, went on my way to see my mother.

"But my mother did not understand.

"I had assumed that she, a peasant woman of patriarchal traditions, would approve my action as soon as I announced that Gordana had probably been unfaithful to me, since in almost all the national tales and epics, with which Mother had grown up and which she herself recited, unfaithful wives were most cruelly punished. But song and story are one thing and life is another. In song and story quartering an unfaithful wife or burning her in a tarred shift was fine and natural, but this—me, my action—this she simply could not comprehend or approve, despite the circumstances and despite the fact that it was a question of the destiny of her own son. She was not able to express her lack of understanding clearly, but I, knowing the nature of her reactions, felt it all the more. There was something of religion in her attitude, the belief in the existence of sin and the fear of punishment for it, but there was also something—I don't quite know how to put it—inherent, sucked in with her mother's milk, without which men would not be able to live. She said at last: 'You'—she was thinking of me and my comrades—'you know what you are doing; it is a matter of your lives. But for all that, it is a sin—it is a sin.'

"So I, misunderstood, broke also with my mother. What is more, I felt that many of the revolutionaries, even my closest comrades, did not really understand. Not that they criticized me or reproached me; none of them did that, and every one judged that, in the circumstances, there was nothing else I could have done. But the case was strange to them, unnatural, and they avoided me as though they were in awe of me.

"I don't know—perhaps the whole incident would have faded away, perhaps even the memory of Gordana herself would have died in me, had it not been for this attitude of men, this almost compassionate attitude, full of understanding, yet allied to this avoidance of me. That continually surrounded me and awoke in me the suspicion that I had not done the right thing, though I had only done what I had to do.

"It was for this reason that I wanted to hear your opinion also, the opinion of one who is more experienced and also a childhood friend."

He stopped speaking. It was already dark.

The chill mountain dew numbed our bodies and our thoughts. The young moon rose from behind the stony peaks. Only the smell of the ashes reminded us of war and destruction. Perhaps for that reason we moved away from the wall and set out downhill toward the camp. As soon as we crested the hillock, we could see the campfires in the valley, hear the clinking of the cauldrons and even the songs about the fighting around Madrid, which sounded the more beautiful there in devastated and Godforsaken Bosnia.

What could I say to Miliko? Probably nothing that he did not know already and that any other commissar could have said to him. Everything is conditioned objectively, and we do nothing but carry out the will of history and of the proletariat, whose executives we are. If some unpleasant duty should be allotted to us in the execution of its judgments, that should not break us, but temper us. Even as he had acted in the given circumstances, so should I or any other revolutionary have acted. The only thing he might have avoided was carrying out the sentence with his own hands. But the sentence had been given and had to be carried out, for even if that one case was without significance for the outcome of the revolution, it was nonetheless important, since revolution is nothing more than the settlement of a countless number of individual incidents, each one unimportant and insignificant; revolution is not only battles, but badly laden nags and the bruised soles of tired feet. Had he not carried out the sentence personally, it would have been easier for him today, but it would have shown both inconsistency and indecision.

That was the substance of what I could say to him, though certainly I did not say it so bluntly and tempered it with comradely warmth and friendly understanding.

I felt that I had convinced him, even reassured him.

We separated on the hillside; he went back and I went on to the camp. The river was roaring in the gorge like a tale of bygone times. The landscape, icily green, was stiff and glistening, and the mountain peaks reached upward into the pale blueness. I remembered Miliko's description of his parting with his mother, on the path where, the day before, he had killed Gordana. To hell with it, I thought angrily, his jitters have affected me, too!

We did not meet again. Or, rather, we met during the trek through Bosnia, but we did not say a word to one another except for the customary friendly greetings. I felt that he was ashamed of having spoken so openly to me, and I avoided approaching him so that he would not notice that I was aware of this, though it was not clear to me whether it was because he thought that I might regard his tale as a wavering of his revolutionary zeal or as his unextinguished love for a woman who had understood neither him nor his times.

But who knows if it were not something different both in me and in him? Hadn't I to avoid him lest he awaken in me something I had succeeded in concealing so that I might go on fighting? I had to fight if I wanted to preserve my ideals and my hopes through the storm of war.

Soon he, too, was killed. He disappeared in one of those hailstorms of steel to which the emaciated bodies of the revolutionary fighters were exposed for three whole nights in order to capture a little fortified city driven like a spear point into the body of the liberated country. I never learned on which night he fell, or how it happened. So how could I have known what he felt at the time?

As far as I was concerned, that part of him which had gone on living in me calmed down when I heard of his death.

This story is a true memorial.

# Šudikova

OURS IS ONLY ONE of the ways of life that have been and that will be, that they who came before us knew and those who come after us will know. To reopen that way anew each time is to live, to create one's own world. Thence comes the irresistible charm of digging up the past and dreaming of the future.

I was young, had only just begun to know the world, when I first discovered Šudikova. Today I rediscover it, as a grown man, in prison, about to leave the world. Šudikova has been with me all that time, perhaps from all time, and will always be within me.

The ruins of the little medieval Serbian church of Šudikova are on a shelf of the River Lim about an hour's walk
downstream from present-day Ivangrad (once, Berane), at the
very beginning of the Tifranska Gorge. No road leads to
it, as if there could be no path between us and the past
except that of the spirit. But the inquisitive traveler will
easily find it if he keeps to the right bank of the Lim as far
as the confluence of the little Budimka River and then
clambers for about a hundred, perhaps two hundred, yards
up the cliff above the Lim. He cannot make a mistake, for
there is no other access to the Tifranksa Gorge. Like everything built by man, the little church nestles in a spot accessible to men.

Nothing, or almost nothing, of Šudikova remains, even
in the inexhaustible peasant memory, except the fact that
the Turks, no one knows when or why, razed the altar
lamps of the Serbian faith, which in that remote niche must
at one time have threatened their overlordship. Nothing,
or almost nothing, remains to remind one of the life of the
priests and monks and the gatherings of the pious. There
remain only the foundations and the floor of the little
church, made of the gray and easily hewn stone that abounds
in the neighborhood and for whose working not much labor
is needed. No one knows when the church was built. As far
as one can judge, it must have been in the early years of the
Serbian state, in the twelfth or thirteenth century, if not
before, and the worn ornamentation on some of the stones
shows that on that spot, or thereabouts, there was some sort
of pre-Slav building. The shelf on which it is built is not
much more than three hundred yards long, and only about
half of that if one excepts the wide and gentle slope from
the Tifranska cliffs to the river. Overgrown with thickets
and brambles, it seems even smaller, powerless against the

plants whose invasion heralds the hour when even the last patch of grass as well as the ruins themselves will be swallowed up, so that the men of the distant future will never discover it unless someone comes to its aid in time. The mighty oaks and elms and lindens under which men gathered still stand there; the Turks did not cut them down, for they could not take them away, and they remain the sole living symbol of the little church's spiritual existence.

In Turkish times the builders of Balkan churches and monasteries sought out hidden and out-of-the-way sites, suitable for solitary meditation, yet accessible to believers and open to the skies and watercourses. Šudikova—it is not even known what the name means—faces a ravine honeycombed with countless caves for hermits; below, is the chill green river, and beyond, the parish valley, which stretches away as far as the Koma Mountains on the horizon. It was not so much the builders' aim that the little church should catch the eye, as to ensure peace and freshness for its servants and those who came to visit it.

Sheltered by a wooded ridge, it is a nest that men, profiting by the natural conditions and their own skill, adapted to their compelling need for a world different from that of every day, a yearning for the eternal and the unchanging. Its only wealth is rest for the eye and for the soul.

Djurdevi Stupovi, the monastery an hour's walk away upstream on the farther bank of the Lim, was built to dominate the plain, so that the eyes and ears of the faithful could easily find it. Its prominence and size confirm the faith and power that lay behind it, but Šudikova, on the contrary, is withdrawn into isolation and deafness, as if men were not necessary to it and still less to its faith. Out of the way, small, and of impermanent material, it is in no way especially striking; its beauty is not in itself, but in the link between man's work and nature, and in the skill by which men found and built a retreat for their thoughts of eternity.

Man never knows in advance why or how some place or object means so much to him. As man becomes wise only after the event, so only later does he fall in love with certain spots, finding in them affinities that at first sight he has not noticed and even discovering in them ideas that by their very nature cannot exist. Man subsequently confirms the presentiments that first attracted him by something that only later he grows fond of and that will only then become significant to him. It is the old story of the lover who falls in love at first sight as soon as he has heard the beloved's name.

So I, too, reading in a *Lovčen Echo* of 1925 an article on Šudikova by one of my teachers, felt a stirring of interest that here, near the little town where I was living, there was a ruined sanctuary where it was believed that the first ecclesiastical leaders of my people had their seat and that one of them was buried in it. Partly because of this article and partly out of curiosity, I set out to find the church. And today I would be willing to swear that, as soon as I had read that article, I had a presentiment that those ruins would have some special significance for me.

The truth is this: years passed, five, ten, twenty, thirty, when I never even thought of Šudikova. But I did not forget it. Every time I passed along the road on the far side of the river, and over those years this happened many times, I looked eagerly for it till I could discern, on the harsh enormous cliff, its little green nesting place, and from time to time pictures from my youth burst forth mingled with musings about the inevitability and power of men to find spots suitable for their spiritual, bodily, and every other form of life. Therefore, Šudikova appears to me today as an experience and a vision, a picture and a thought, with fresh and unexpended force—and that is what I want to express.

But why, why should it have remained thus concealed within me? Surely it was the hidden and lurking sense of my destiny, my dream and my awakening? Surely somewhere in the vast expanse that I have seen in the course of fifty years there must have been something that could replace it?

# 2.

THE CURIOSITY I FELT when forcing my way through the bushes, in the spring of 1926, in my search for the little church was transformed almost into panic as soon as I had found it.

There was no sound but the chirping of birds and the roaring of the river, as if in a dream or from some immense distance. All the tales of miracles and the belief in them became concentrated in my observation of all that was around me—the trees, the grass, the ruins themselves—quivering and poignant. Had anyone appeared at that moment, I would have been just as easily convinced that he was an apparition as an everyday being. Though I no longer believed firmly in wonders and visions, the place itself, isolated under the cliffs and the sky, which were, so to speak, one with it, the ancient ruined church, with its unknown graves, and especially the manner in which I had come upon it, seemed no more real than the legends and tales of the lives that had been passed there. All these things strengthened the feeling of unreality. This was not true reality, but as if reality itself were breaking up and dissolving. I felt that I could put my hand through all these things as if they were in a dream and did not exist. Though at first sight the outer world appeared unchanged, it seemed to me that I was witnessing visions that, although inexpressible, seemed even clearer than reality. I was myself a part of this; I felt oppressed in my innermost being by the church and the rocks, and within me I felt an intense joy in the chirping of the birds and in that suddenly comprehensible expanse.

I noticed this inner transformation even physically. It did not happen all at once, but I noticed it as soon as I had forced my way through the undergrowth to the clearing and saw on my right the gray stone ruin, a yard or so high. I was at first astonished that the coronation church of the Serbian archbishops was so small, no larger than the smallest village church. All at once I began to tread carefully, fearing to snap a twig or to make any sort of noise lest it break the silence within me. Every detail, every leaf and blade of grass and crevice in the rock, became clear to me, clearer than ever before, and I passed through this world, which was as real to me as I was myself, taking care not to awaken it, or myself. Beyond it there was nothing, not my past, not my hopes, not history, not other worlds.

Despite this panic and unreality, almost fright, I knew that I would not, could not, stop. I was not awaiting any miracle, and in the depths of my consciousness I knew that one would not and could not happen, though I would not have been surprised if it had. The miracle, I knew, had taken place within me as a special kind of experience, linked with a reality in which differences and frontiers between me and my surroundings, me and the outside world, had become lost. That sort of experience has happened to me in other places, too, before other buildings, at the Taj Mahal in India and at Sainte-Chapelle in Paris, just as it did at

Šudikova, but in a different way and never so intensely. I was quite unable either to foresee or to restrain what was taking place within me and against my will, with a sweetness much akin to love but instinct with mortal awe.

Graveyards and graves are, by inherited belief, the source of wonders and apparitions. But in that wilderness of Šudikova, where there was nothing and no one except myself, the feeling of awe and panic before the expected grave was stronger than in the blackest night in the most ill-reputed sabbath. I searched diligently for the priest's grave and was convinced, though I did not want to admit it to myself, that it was just for that reason that I had come there.

When I found it in a corner of the nave, I was disappointed because it was so unassumingly modest and commonplace. It was almost level with the floor and covered with cracked uneven slabs of that same soft and fragile stone from which the church had been mainly built. But I did not raise any of the slabs, not so much from fear as from reluctance to disturb dead bones. Slowly I began to return to reality, to a world that was not only mine but of which I was a part, and again began to look around me. I even sat on some hewn stone near the church. The birds sang in the vast expanse above me, and on the cliff the goatherds called to one another.

I did not feel this panic, and especially not this fear, on subsequent visits to Šudikova, but that feeling of identity with the world, that mortal emotion, broke out, though more mildly, whenever I set eyes on it from the road, even when I had not consciously remembered it. Was Šudikova, or that first impression of it, so intensely awe-inspiring that it became for me a reality that could not be restrained and could not be forgotten? Wasn't it, in the end, all the same what was in question, the place itself or the impression it evoked, seeing that they merged within me and expressed themselves as one?

The world and man, world-man.

# 3.

IT IS KNOWN that human life existed in the Lim Valley long before the coming of the Slavs, who began to arrive in the Balkans from about the sixth century A.D., and from the tenth century onward it was a cradle, though certainly not the only one, of the Serbian state and church. Tradition has it that the palaces of King Milutin were in the nearby village of Budimli—the King must have been glad to pass the summers there—and other villages in the neighborhood also have links with that famous ruler or with others of the Nemanja dynasty. Šudikova, small and out of the way as it is, must have been one of the oldest and certainly one of the more important centers of that early Serbian state. Since Turkish rule lasted from the end of the fourteenth century almost up to our own day, the church, razed but not forgotten, links and expresses the continuity of the Serbian people over almost a whole millennium. The similarity, indeed, is only apparent, and it is still vainer to expect its present aspect to reveal a picture of the downfall of the medieval Serbian state. It is notable and impressive for another reason: the men of this land found their way of life and expressed their spiritual existence in various and even contradictory ways. Armies and kingdoms came and went, but the people went on living by this river and amid these mountains, confirming the individuality of their spirit in this tiny sanctuary even after it had been razed and human life in it rooted out and exterminated.

But later, Šudikova had something more significant and universal to say—the way in which its people lived and also for what they lived.

Nothing of that could be concluded from the ruins themselves, but, rather, from the relation between them and their surroundings, from the church's narrow and unobtrusive isolation on the river shelf, as if a white bird had suddenly alighted on a green meadow. What was especially remarkable, even striking, was that men, amid so many suitable spots, had chosen just that spot to prepare for eternity. Could it be that their thought became embodied in the hardness and purity of the stone that it might the more completely remain within itself? Must man find in that tiny meadow amid the stony wilderness on which the little church was built a passionate enthusiasm for the supernatural, driven by the feeling that at least in ecstasy he could attain the sense of his existence and his fate? As if there were not the meadow or the little church on it, but that men were inspired by the thought that issued from it pure and white, unable to tell of and explain anything but one viewpoint, one moment of human existence and identification between man and the world. It cannot be put into words; it must be felt before it can be known.

Directly opposite Šudikova rises a harsh, black cliff on which is a fortress—Jerinin Grad—such as powerful men always build on the highways of human life, that in the name of their ultimate ideals they may maintain the lordship of their time and give a form to their society. Šudikova and Jerinin Grad are opposites, both in appearance and in position; on the one side asceticism and psalms, on the other armed men and force, both keeping watch over human existence.

There is no road near Šudikova. One must find one's own path to it, and there is no path from it through the impassable desolation of the rocky gorge. Near the fortress there is an unmistakable path down the valley of the Lim. No one now goes to the fortress, but it still waits.

Church and fortress, as is well known, served in different ways a common end. They are two forms, two aspects, of the same society. But how great are the differences between them! Šudikova stands amid the rocky precipices for what it is—small, simple, fragile, something outside and beyond its mission in time. It is the expression of inescapable and inextinguishable human longing to reveal the reasons for its own and man's existence, that by the linking of its transience with the unchanging and unattainable laws—with God as he was defined in medieval times—man should find consolation and tranquillity in this world of change and struggle. By its form and place Šudikova could only be an expression of its times. Just because it was that in all its heart and soul, it also expressed through its transience the inevitability of man's instinctive search for the eternal; it sums up in a single moment that linking of man's transience with the unchanging, that beauty which is outside time, as if it had not arisen among the storms of gloomy stone.

The fortress, too, is petrified human existence, the same as the little church, but differently expressed. It, too, is beautiful—a simple structure of stone and mortar on the crest of the sullen rock. Its beauty, too, is in the directness and obviousness of its intention; though its walls have now fallen, it seems as if it still lives to keep watch over men and their deeds. Faced with it, man feels his powerlessness, and it rises on the cliff displaying its onetime power over men.

Nonetheless, it is a part of the past that does not return.

But Šudikova has not passed away. All its living, direct, and material life has passed; but there still remains its meaning for man and his destiny, a meaning unbuilt and unhewn, in the very spot where man has found a way to take his place in it, paying heed only to its suitability for developing his thought and thereby the more perfectly to explore the innermost depths of his conscience.

Šudikova is spiritual life, as pure as it can ever be.

Every man must create for himself some way of life by the very fact that he is alive. And every man lives by it, trying to justify both it and himself and trying to link it with eternal law. Šudikova is an expression of that human inevitability, though certainly for a specific era. Its building was modest in every way, and the sound of its bells, lost in the tumult of the cataracts, was not often heard afar. But they summoned no one, only reminded those who lived there and the hermits in the caves around once again to examine their consciences, their actions toward men. Had they not indeed withdrawn from the laws to which men are subjected and which can only be attained by living and respecting the conditions of human life?

Every man must live in the spirit; no man can escape eternity—is not that the message of Šudikova?

4.

THOSE WHO BUILT Šudikova must have renounced, in fact wanted to renounce, much of what man lives by. They aimed at denying human existence itself in order the more fully to become merged with the pure and immutable laws—with

God, as they would have said. They withdrew from everyday direct contact with the fertile parish and its delights, living on the crust of bread given them by someone or other and on the clear water from the spring that still runs below the meadow. At least, so I imagine them, and thus, or something like this, they must in truth have been.

They certainly behaved in this way because in their times the belief was held that all bodily and material things were the cause and the source of sin and must be renounced to the limit of human survival and regeneration. But did they not somehow know, or, to be more accurate, did they not suspect, that man, changing his way of life according to circumstances, cannot approach, how much less assure, victory if he renounces not only the delights of life but also the very foundations of his own existence?

Men cannot exist without Jerina's fortress or without Šudikova. Individuals are attracted, and are bound to be attracted, to either one or the other, according to their inclinations and talents, but without devoting themselves wholly to either one or the other, for by so doing they would destroy that by which and for which they live—their own spiritual and bodily existence. A man turns to Šudikova, to eternity and his continuance, no matter how far it may be real or imagined, in order to exist, to justify himself in his own transience. Šudikova and the fortress confront one another and clash, but they are the two sides of the same coin.

Šudikova is that other side of human existence—that side which denies that very existence itself for an ideal and a vision. It would like man to be sinless, pure spirit, and obedient to law, as if he could exist outside sin and the body, as if there were a law beyond material things.

Šudikova wants sinlessness beyond space and time.

Just because it is, as an architectural conception, a very

consistent realization and expression of its times, Šudikova is imperishable beauty, the materialization, the shaping, of a thought, of a world that till then had never existed. It has created imperishable beauty just because it has seized a moment of life for certain men at a certain time and in a certain place.

Saying that it was just this renunciation that was the manner of existence for these men, or that it was the confirmation of their belief in the possibility of becoming linked to and identical with the eternal powers above us, Šudikova itself, by its position and its appearance, speaks of an eternal and ever-differing form of the unappeasable human longing to become one with the laws that govern man's life and by this very fact to become the master of his own fate. By the harmonious modesty of its form and by its isolation from human eyes, Šudikova is that unfulfilled yearning for the eternal.

The pious men of Šudikova had almost no idea of the laws that govern the world. God, they thought, was the prime mover of these laws, if not the laws themselves. The only thing man could do in this world of evil and transience was either to submit to the bodily and worldly or, by renouncing them, to assure for himself either eternal suffering or the salvation of his soul. By the very fact that it was material, the world for them was filled with demonic powers which at every step and at every moment lay in wait to storm the citadels of their sinful yet immortal souls. Just for that reason they wanted to renounce and destroy their dependence upon material things.

But in their building and the manner of their life they left behind them quite different messages.

Falling into ecstasy and prayer, they, too, came to know the eternal laws, certainly not by logic and understanding, but by flashes of emotion which blended with the eternal. Through their sanctuary they were linked with stone and water, with the breezes and the skies, the sun and the storm. Renouncing material thoughts, they became a part of it, one of the aspects of its existence. It could not be otherwise, in a reality that man can never control. Šudikova is the undying spark struck by the clash between the human spirit and the world of matter and everyday life. Therefore it is thought and beauty.

Its greatest, most final revelation is that it broke through the frontiers between man and the world, the world and law, law and material form; a pure shape of its times, it is the ultimate confirmation of the essence of man's life. There a man lived as a man, but he was also one with the cold rock and the flowing river, warning him of the transience of everything material, and with the skies, which, with the constant movement of the stars, warned him of the immutability of human destiny. There I could not stretch out my hand or open my eyes to link myself with final and irrevocable matter. Šudikova forced me unobtrusively to look into myself, into my conscience, and the world and all its laws became for me, even if not clear and comprehensible, at least accessible and friendly.

Wherever a man searches within his soul, there is his being, and wherever he strikes with his pick, he widens the horizons of his experience. Wisdom and beauty are only two of the inescapable and always different aspects of human experience.

Blended with soil and space, Šudikova is both wisdom and beauty.

What is there that is not encompassed by Šudikova?

The most complete inspiration and the most ultimate

truth, existence and transience, immediacy and the past—or should one say that this is one and the same?

The intoxication of eternity or the transience of the existence of the world and man.

# 5.

WE KNOW that the creators of Šudikova were as imperfect as other men. But we are speaking of their message, about Šudikova. And that says that its creators and holy men, believing that they were holding to the eternal laws, were in fact acting according to their conscience; through it and by it alone are the laws of human existence relative and accessible to man. By acting in this way they offered to their flock hope and consolation. It was as if they knew that an essential condition of the life of human communities is the sacrifice of prophets and leaders. Such a belief and manner of life they held, it seems, for several centuries, even to death in the fire and under Turkish swords. Certainly much changed even in their viewpoints and way of life, but the essential basis remained, as if they desired to remain true to the destiny, reputation, and standing of the church itself, unable and unwilling to break away from its significance, if one may so call its eremetical withdrawal and beauty.

From the very beginning, from the time when it was founded, the little church was an ideal, pure in every aspect. Its consistency, expressed in stone in a stony wilderness, was so strong and complete that it could not be annihilated by anyone. It is not by chance that no one built there or ever repaired it, and that not even destruction can affect its essence. It was possible to kill its priests and raze it, but what is essential remains and will remain undestroyed while there is still a stone left of Šudikova and while men still know where it is. And who knows but that they will remain eternal even after that, certainly not in any idea of continuance beyond the grave, but in some way inherited, as in a sacrifice to men, for a different life and in the name of different laws.

Men and buildings are not one, but they are dependent on one another and become identical even if they do not meet the same tragic end. The beauty of Šudikova is purely human. The same spirit, the same thought permeates the church as a symbol and its holy men as a way of life. But it wanted to express a truth, and it has succeeded—at that time it could only be a religious truth—and its people consistently adhered to that truth. Though it is unjustified to believe that one truth, one idea, even were it final, could exhaust and express the needs of all men, it is also true that human communities must inevitably have corresponding ideas, and that without them it would be hard for them to go on existing. The adherence of Šudikova to an ideal was an inevitable and established spiritual viewpoint and way of human life. The breath of a life, not so remote as it seems, still rises from its ruins, and its incense-laden prayers to a higher power are an admonishment to men of their duty to human existence, as if even now they arise unerringly from the shackles of that stony wilderness.

Šudikova is still a beloved and living survival of the people of this land. Unyielding and indestructible because true to itself, the small and disunited Serbian people stood fast against the invasion that flowed over three continents and reached the shores of two oceans, devastating lands and laying waste civilizations. And when everything had fallen, the Serbs still survived, isolated in their ideal, in the belief that the people and social groups, even individuals, were indestructible as long as they held fast to their spiritual heritage, which in the final analysis was identical with their choice of eternity and their sacrifice for the good of men. Šudikova passionately and consistently held that view even before the Turkish invasion. Was it not for just that reason that the Serbs have survived despite the fire and stake of an alien faith and rule?

Nothing is repeated, least of all history, and it is not true that civilization inherits from civilization. Every civilization must begin with the essential needs of a specific human community and must disappear when it is rotten-ripe for destruction. Šudikova is the purest form of the early Serbian spiritual feudal way of life, which cannot be repeated and cannot be renewed. Nonetheless there is in it—and this is what makes one catch one's breath and clouds one's reason— some undifferentiated human continuance, human existence as such.

But no, such a thing does not exist; no sort of all-embracing form exists, nor is there any form that could express all the others.

But why is this? Why does Šudikova remind one of the nonexistent, the universal and timeless?

It seems that just because its beauty logically expresses how the men of one certain time and place lived despite life and despite death, it at the same time reveals to all that the eternal and unattainable condition of existence—true to itself, to its conscience, its social conditions and ideals—is every time renewed and not by the various methods of comprehensible human laws.

Superhuman and eternal is the legend and the belief that the skeleton could raise this not overheavy slab and that the Tifrana caves would open their countless riches, if one may use the word of Mojsije, the last famous *iguman* of the monastery. But that, too, is truth and beauty, and to choose them is to decide for the good of men, for isolation in the wilderness, for Šudikova. What it shows to the greatest extent and which alone it believes to be true, to be the universal and revealed law, is in fact the purest and most cogent essence of its time and place and that the most consistent unselfish sacrifice is the guarantee of existence beyond its own times. Šudikova may also be the inspiration of an atheist who will find and build his own Šudikova.

Is not enthusiasm for its spontaneous beauty and the finality of its ideal a new and different partisanship? In truth, be it today or tomorrow, be it I or be it you, we cannot live without it. Can men be men without beauty, without creative thought, without sacrifice for an ideal, without renunciation of the conditions of their own existence?

The rivers will disappear. How much more Šudikova? The stars will move from their courses. How much more human ideals? But man will always have to confirm and conquer his own life by renunciation. How else could Šudikova be beautiful with the beauty of a star imprisoned in the rock, and how could it resist those who by its destruction wished to assure their temporal power and lordship?

To its beauty, as to all beauty, there is neither end nor beginning.

# 6.

I KNEW when I went there in the late spring of 1929 that that was my last meeting with Šudikova, for I was going out into the wide world and fresh experience, whereas it would remain unchanged where it had been built. But I had not imagined that this farewell would give me my final impression of it; every meeting with it had seemed final to me, since each was in some way new. How could I have known that once separated we would never be separated and that it would appear to me as an indecipherable unity of idea and reality, of beauty and of physical existence?

Everything, as if from time immemorial, was green and beautiful, and the sky, now indigo, now azure, was reflected in the river. Around Šudikova everything burst into new life, grasses and thickets, bird song and young snakes lured from their deep crevices by the scorching heat. Even the cliffs of the green-covered Tifrana swam to the south under white and fleecy clusters of cloud. In that frantic movement of life and color the little church, overgrown with fern and hellebore, was even smaller and more inconspicuous, more mortal, and what it wanted to say sadder and less imposing, but also less ambiguous. Everything was boiling, shimmering in the sun with life juices, threatening to cover even the last of its stones, destroying and obliterating the message of its ruins. But it did not heed that, and smiled from beneath the green hurricane confidently and unaffectedly, conscious that for it there was no death. There was no passion or resistance against the frenzy of the life about it and on it, and by just that indifference even to itself it seemed as if it called upon life to do its worst, even as it itself did not retreat from the truth it had stated for all time.

Two lives coursed independently, one of violent and uncontrolled forms and the other long ago incontrovertibly shaped and alive only in an ideal that it had taken for itself, though it was no longer necessary for anyone—the inevitable dissolution of forgotten ruins owing to unfettered, unbridled life.

But there was something that linked these two worlds. The universal spiritual life of Šudikova, its withdrawal into its own soul, into the human conscience, and finally its renunciation of reality, seemed to open the floodgates to life and give a warning that in just this way are opened the sluices against oppression, exploitation, and stupidity. The human yearning of Šudikova for eternity, for the reconciliation of human relationships with the immutable laws of human life and human nature, was a summons to freedom and to surrounding nature, to the flower to burst into purple and orange, to the earth to give it nourishment, to the river to seek new shores, and to the animals to increase and multiply without thought for the morrow.

That was the voiceless and timeless summons to a human being to regard life as a duty the more absolute and inescapable the more it was unreconciled with the law, with the freedom of the human individual and the community. The shining and transparent gates of nonexistent and unattainable freedom opened wide, for one more step toward it seemed possible from that riotous greenery and unspoken command.

All views of life, inseparable one from the other, were equally beautiful, and it seemed that the prayers of the hermits of Šudikova called to fecundity, as a holy duty to eternity, for the preservation of the human race. Two beetles crawled on a blade of grass, mingling in a love ecstasy, an eagle soared over the gorges, and in the deep shadow under the trees the mosses offered a shadowy couch soft as oblivion and sweet-smelling as unconsciousness.

Why, why did the girl not wish, not understand that she must come? Why did she not cease to be what she was—a relative and a conventional town-dweller—and be a young and uninhibited female, naked and eager for mating? For here everything vanished in the sultry noon, intoxicated with sap and silence—memory and prohibition, everything that must come to pass. Come, girl, the world is no longer remote. We can encircle it in our love and people it with our seed. The little church, too, has vanished in the close passionate trembling; the whisper of the grasses and the insects has fallen silent in expectation of the holy act. There is nothing under heaven between me and creation; there is no world outside desire and the longing for fecundity.

The speech of the grasses gradually became comprehensible; everything has it own speech, and this is the most beautiful of all. The cliff looked down in beauty; the sky wiped my eyes moist with longing; the Lim carried away thoughts and recollections into oblivion. The little church was no longer an ungarnished ruin, but was one with everything else—indestructible, undestroyed, eternal. It was no longer either beautiful or wise, was not able, even had it wished, to leave behind it any message; it merely existed as I existed, and, like me, was born, who knew when, and destined to immortality. Nothing will die, or can die, while this moment of intoxicating union lasts, with all that is, or was, or would like to be. Nothing will happen—all I know is that this love embrace will vanish with everything and with all material things. It will last as long as it wishes, and any endeavor will only break it and shorten it.

What can bring me back from that union in which the stone is as sweet and living as the ivy that embraces it, as yesterday, as today, as in an imagined tomorrow, even as the pine awaits carefree the stroke of the lightning on the cliff top? Can that tear me from this so evident, so irrefutable, so inspired identity with the world and time?

But this a shepherd boy did, a poor ragged goatherd who appeared cursing at his flock, which had moved from the shade and awakened him from his sleep on the stone. His goats were browsing near the cliffs, and he had slipped down to the little church so that he could see from the clearing where they had gone. He was for a moment embarrassed by meeting someone unknown, astonished that any human being should be there in his wilderness. He greeted me and sat down amiably on the ruined wall, dangling his legs in ragged stockings and worn-out sandals. He was already almost a youth and knew that this had been a church the Turks had destroyed, probably because they could not revenge themselves on the cliffs down which the insurgent serfs had hurled their army. That was all he knew. Nor did he need to know more; the church had no sort of meaning for him, at least no more than any other holy place. He had his pipes with him, and, though I did not ask him, he played on them like a child in the vision of a poet over some Greek or other ruin.

That was the symbol of victorious and omnipotent life.

Perhaps the youth was really right, like life, which pays no heed to messages and impossibilities. Perhaps I had imagined Šudikova, which was perhaps only a pretext for my thoughts.

Perhaps, perhaps.

The exaltation of union with the world was broken, before even the first gay notes of the pipes were heard. But the pipes and their song were nothing more to me than their perceived reality—subject and melody. And Šudikova was once more real, as it had been till then, with its beauty and its message. The shepherd and his pipes were more tangible but no more eloquent or more real than the church, as if I had vowed that what it had said, or what I had understood or fancied to be its message, I would experience and remember as the most complete and irreplaceable reality. That was painful; the living beauty of Šudikova forced itself upon me, despite the pipes, ever more unforgettably. One could not choose between it and the pipes, between it and anything else; it was as real as everything else and, though in vain, more beautiful, more inescapable.

It was not in vain, neither the suffering, nor the youthful love, nor the renunciation that was bound to come. That is life, even with the ruined church as an imagined reality. For it did not stand in anyone's way, and still less did it set up any barrier to life. Perhaps that is the one thing that should have been said, perhaps that alone is what I wanted to say—now, then, and forever.

# Fire and Knife

FOR ME, even the slightest memory of my childhood and youth is painful, almost unbearable.

But surely no man can fail to have such memories? How can a man live without his past?

Scourged and tormented by my memories in these long postwar years—they seem much longer to me than the years of war—I live in the past as much as in the years that now weigh upon me—that is to say, in the present. It is not only a matter of experience and memory; the happenings of the past have become an inexhaustible source of emotion, always flowing, in which I take refuge the more spontaneously and eagerly as my present conditions and prospects become more restricted and more uncertain.

Others, too, indubitably live in the past. But I see and feel its influence in everything that now is and everything that is to be.

The mutilated and unhealed past makes it impossible for me to adapt myself to the present or to console myself with the expectation of better times. I shall never be able to free myself from the past.

In everything that now is I recall what has been, and I cannot free myself from the horror that it might happen again.

Yet when it was happening to me, and happening to others about me, I was conscious neither of its significance nor of the depth of my misfortune. At that time a struggle was going on for bare existence and for a pure ideal, for the one does not exist without the other, so that what happened to me seemed inevitable and even logical. Today, on the other hand, those happenings seem to me even more absurd and inexplicable. The images have become blurred and softened by time, the details are no longer so clear, but my conception of them, that significance that man draws from events even when they have no real significance, has become with time painfully sharpened within me.

Had my home and my family been burned by chance, that would have been a misfortune I would always have remembered, but not, if I may put it that way, in an irreconcilable manner. I would have built a new home, life would have risen again from the ashes, and my memory of that earlier home would have gained a fresh and pleasant beauty.

But my home was destroyed by men, by my own fellow villagers, to revenge themselves upon me for being one of the prime movers of the insurrection.

With the burning of the house in which I grew up, all the ties and visions with which I had lived till then—my youth, my childhood, all my past—were also irrevocably consumed. Even harder to bear was that my very life was consumed in the flames. Only my great-grandchildren will be able to forget, if they are spared some similar fate.

The whole district has changed for me, without hope of renewal or consolation, by the very fact that the house has gone. All that remains are bare and smoke-blackened stone walls, and even these seem as if they had never belonged to my onetime home. It is as if I saw and understood that district and those people only through that house. Everything has been transformed and is as if it has ceased to exist.

It would have been better if I had not gone there. But I had to. Toward the end of the war my military duties took me once again to my native district. That was only the ostensible reason, however, a good justification for the irresistible urge to see once more the house in which I had grown up and, by reviving memories, to find healing for my wounded life.

I was the eldest child, and the only one who survived. During World War I three of the others died from Spanish flu. After the war three more were born, but war lay in wait for two, my seventeen-year-old sister and my eleven-year-old brother, and another sister had the good luck to die of some childish illness while still in the cradle.

My father, too, died without awaiting the new war. He had been a prosperous peasant, very adaptable and quick-witted. In his youth he had gone abroad to work, and, like many of our people, had brought back with him ideas for saving time and energy and for living a thrifty and comfortable life. Probably for this reason our house was bigger and finer than the others. I believe it was those ideas that led my father to sell the mountain land he had inherited and buy a property near the river in an isolated spot. It was almost as if they had played a part even in his death; he died when the property had been put in order and when I was sufficiently grown up—I had finished Teachers' Training College—to be able to take charge of the house and family.

Our property was in an unusual spot.

The left bank of the river was hilly, with small shelves of alluvial land, mostly settled and cultivated, while the right bank clung to the mountain slopes. The right, eastern, bank was almost entirely impassable; the cliffs and rocks rose more than three thousand feet from the riverbank. But on that side also, in the bends of the stream, the river had in a few places formed deposits, little sheltered shelves with very fertile meadows.

Our property was one of those little shelves, not more than about fourteen acres, but was the largest on the whole course of the river. It was a long oval, and immediately above it rose the cliffs and watercourses over which only one goat path led along the river to the highway. This path was scarcely passable for mountain ponies, but we had to use it when the river rose and we could no longer ford it, which happened even after the more severe summer downpours. Our property was thus enclosed, cut off by the river and the cliffs, open only toward the west, whence, from the shelf sheltered by the forest-covered hills, peeped out the thatched roofs of three houses, but behind which one suspected a broad valley and more frequent hamlets.

Our house, too, was unusual.

My father was afraid of landslides, and had therefore built the house farther away from the cliffs, on the moraines at their foot, so that from it almost the whole of the road that led along the left bank of the river could be seen above the alders and willows. My father had not built the house in the usual manner of our district, but like the two-storied buildings in the towns, with the floor raised above ground level, though without a cellar. My father had learned in the outside world that stock should not be kept in the house, and therefore he did not need a ground-floor storeroom. Instead, he had built stalls a little away from the house, under the cliffs, where there was always a spring of ice-cold mountain water. Our house had four rooms, two large ones facing outward and, behind them, the kitchen and my room, which had huge green-trimmed windows. I don't know why my father chose just that color, unless he had seen it somewhere or other, perhaps on the Dalmatian coast, and it had pleased him. But those lines of green, particularly in autumn and winter, when the hornbeams on the cliffs and the willows along the riverbank were bare, gave the whole of that restricted little spot a freshness and an especially inhabited look; they seemed to say that a man had made his home there.

Unlike the earlier owner, my father did not like keeping goats. They destroyed the young growth along the watercourses above the house, which he considered to be his property. This did not give rise to disputes with the village, for not even the goatherds came there, owing to the distance and the inaccessibility. Even though my father was not in the right regarding his property, time showed that he was right as far as the goats were concerned. After a few years the cliffs above the house were green with young growth. The land was unsuitable for sheep; there was no one who could climb up into the mountains with them in the summer. My father kept cattle, for which, in truth, there was not very good pasture, but it was easy to look after them. All that was needed was to turn them out into the scrub along the river or near the cliffs. Thus I was to a great extent spared the exhausting tasks of the village children of school age, for whom the herding of the stock during the summer made reading and games impossible.

All this meant that I grew up, so to speak, on the river—in its blue pools and silken fords, in its cool depths with the sun warming my shoulders, with its silvery, greedy, swift, and carefree fishes. I grew up with the sky as my cap, on the green meadows and amid the bluish-green maize and the young trees burdened with fruit.

In that dark-blue shady isolation it was inevitable that I should become overmuch attached to my family. And though I later went to school in the town, I remained bound up with those who lived in that house and with the property itself, certainly not because of its wealth, but because of its surroundings, associating them with my dear ones who lived on it and by it.

That tie remained unbroken, and for that reason I succeeded, two years before the invasion of the country, partly through my father's influence and partly because the district was isolated and no one was eager to serve in it, in getting the job of schoolmaster in my own village. That was a godsend to me because of my close bonds with my family and with the place—I am thinking of the property, and not of the village—and also because I was able to add my salary to the income from the land so that my younger brother, too, could be educated.

So, two years before the outbreak of war, I returned to my own village, to my birthplace.

I return there now, and I shall always return there, in fact or in dream, but never again will I find my home or myself.

# 2.

FOR A LONG TIME my district was scarcely affected by the war.
Only during the first offensive of the occupying forces, the
Germans and Italians, against the insurgents, sometime in
August 1941, did an enemy column visit it. The men from
my district took part in the fighting, but their duties took
them far afield until the summer of 1942, when, with the
help of the occupying forces, the opponents of the revolution
began to grow stronger and penetrate into even the most
isolated districts.

Up till then, or at least so it seemed to me, the men of
my district were all of one mind, though there was a group
that wanted to step up the fighting against the Moslems, and
it was not without considerable support because of the traditional hatred between the two faiths and also because some
of the nearby Moslems had taken part in the massacres of the
Orthodox population in the summer of 1941. But with the
outbreak of civil war, which flared up especially during the
occupiers' offensive in the spring of 1942, there was, even in
my own district, a sullen sense of division, which first was
expressed as indifference to and avoidance of military duties
and obligations and later by the running away of individuals
into the forest to join the opposing side.

All that was evident even in my own village, but, except
for concealed dissatisfaction, nothing happened. Only a certain Captain Manojlo, who till then had been an officer of
the insurgents, fled, with a few of his relatives. In the neighboring districts the insurgents had settled their accounts with
plotters and renegades in the most merciless manner, but in

my own village not a man had been shot, not even Captain Manojlo, for he was not caught, and right up to our withdrawal before the enemy, my village was regarded as a reliable revolutionary redoubt.

After our withdrawal I might have expected a change in the feelings of the peasants, some through fear and others because they had never liked the insurrection. Nonetheless I had hoped that this change would not be expressed in so revengeful and monstrous a form as in the districts nearby, for in my village the insurgents had given no cause. Therefore I, who was in charge of a battalion, concluded that it would be safe to hide a wounded political commissar with my people. The patrol of which I was one was exhausted and cut off and could no longer carry him.

All one rainy night we forced our way down watercourses and over rocks carrying our half-dead comrade, ourselves hungry and exhausted, with feet and hands torn and wounded. Though we were moving along the bank near my house, the way was unknown even to me, and it was only just before dawn that we knocked at my mother's window.

It would have been more comfortable for the commissar and less inconvenient for my mother and sister had we put him in the house, the more so since my father had built, under the kitchen, a secret and extensive storeroom. But I was afraid that the enemy might set fire to the house, though they had not yet done this in the villages they had captured. So we concealed our wounded comrade in a little cave hidden in the undergrowth above the house, the existence of which was known only to members of my own family. This was more inconvenient—my mother and sister could only visit him by night, lest they be noticed by some peasant from the far side of the river—but it was safer.

My people told me that the enemy had not yet entered our

village, though on the previous night they had captured the bridge, an hour's march away, and the former police station near it, and had thus made it impossible for us to retreat along the highway after the other units. We would have to hurry to get across the river before daylight so that we would not be seen by the peasants and in case the enemy entered the village and cut us off.

When I told my mother and sister about our wounded comrade, they accepted the task with the serious consideration they felt they owed to my comrade in arms, though with differing reactions: my mother, Marija, with fear, and my sister, Bojana, almost with enthusiasm. My mother said: "I am afraid, Stanko, my son, for the house and the child, though they will not do anything to us women."

But my sister cut her short. "Just like you, Mama! It is about time that we, too, did something, and all you can say is: I'm afraid."

I didn't worry overmuch about my mother's fear. It was a vague fear, and I knew that she would tend the wounded man well and carefully. As far as my sister was concerned, she was enflamed with youthful and limitless enthusiasm to do all that she could for the revolution. I thought to myself that the house might be burned down and that my mother or sister, or even both, might be taken to some camp. But as for the boy, my brother, I did not foresee any danger for him, for till then neither the occupying forces nor our domestic enemies had ever harmed children. I encouraged my mother, so that she seemed to forget her fears and the danger, but she burst into tears at our parting.

I kissed my sister and moved off toward the river with the patrol.

Though today my parting from Bojana certainly seems more moving than in fact it was, she was quite overcome by emotion. On the riverbank, from which little ripples were just visible in the darkness, quivering in expectation of the dawn, she threw her arms about my neck, moistening my face with her tears, and sobbed: "Perhaps I shall never see you again, Stanko, my brother, light of my eyes."

She had not even let me carry the little bag of food collected in haste. It fell from her hands, scraping on the pebbles, and I felt ashamed before my comrades at the tears that ran down my face. But because it was still dark I knew that they would be hidden, and I steadied my voice and began to speak about the wounded man, telling her to take good care of him. And she answered: "I will, light of my eyes, I will look after him, Stanko, brother mine. What will happen to us? Where are you going? Our sun is darkened."

So it was—I speaking of one thing, and she of another—that we parted. It checked my tears, though it filled me with an icy foreboding that our life was being destroyed, both what was and what was to be.

I had already taken off my shoes and was standing up to kiss my sister for the last time when I felt warm, bony little hands around my neck. I knew at once that they were my brother Mile's. He burst out in broken, passionate words. "Brother, take me with you, take me, too! Where you go I will go. I will be able to endure everything."

I began to console and dissuade him. Useless! He began to weep, complaining that he was not so little and that I had never wanted to do as he wished. For a moment I wavered; and then I thought: Even as it is there are too many useless mouths among the fighters, and I must not add to them without urgent need.

My comrades had already begun to ford the river, and I had to hurry. I kissed the two of them and went. Bojana and Mile followed me, hugging me, but the water was too deep, and I could hear their sobs mingled with the noise I myself was making and could distinguish the words "Why don't you take me with you?"

It was thus that I left home.

We could withdraw along the cliffs by the river or along the road through the village and thence into the mountains. I decided that we should not go through the village, because the river crossing, though exhausting, was safe and so that we would not awaken suspicion among the peasants that we had been at my house.

It was already beginning to grow light along the mountain slopes, and the river was like a shining yellowish metal strip. We had gone only a few hundred yards along the stony path through that cold dawn light when we came upon the porter of my school, Živko, who was known in the village as Žućo (Towhead) because of the straw color of his hair and mustaches. I was last in the file and, hearing behind me a crunching on the stones, I looked around and recognized him in the semidarkness. "I am going," he explained, though I had not asked him, "to have a look at my night lines."

So, I thought to myself, I am destroying everything by which I have lived, and still live, while he, even in days like this, does not forget to look after his lines.

We were now out of danger, and I slackened the pace to question Žućo about conditions in the village. I waited there with him till the darkness paled in the ravine.

Žućo was not a quick-witted man, but he was adaptable and talkative. Smooth and rational words flowed warmly and abundantly from between his short, jagged teeth under his sparse fair mustaches, like flour from a pierced sack, as someone in the village had once said. He was not a liar, though in his diffuse and pleasant chatter truth always turned out differently, softened, without rough edges, dimin-

ished and refined. Like his storytelling, he, too, was compliant
and obliging. His family life differed from that of the other
peasants; he never accused his wife of unfaithfulness, though
that was so evident that even he must have been aware of
it, and he never beat his children, but gave them advice in
a smooth even voice and with an inexhaustible lament for
his unhappy fate. He was one of those peasants who pass
their lives unnoticed, content to be a hindrance to no one,
but who knew how to console and appease.

I had inherited him as school porter, and we had got along
together well enough. During his military service Žućo had
been an orderly, and even when at work he had always been
hanging around the office or the cookhouse. Unsuited for and
incapable of heavy work, he was cut out to be a servant, and
no one in the village fitted the job so well. He guessed my
wishes and intentions in advance, as well as all the needs of
the school, though it was difficult to get on intimate terms
with him because of his reserve, which his chatter successfully, and I might even say skillfully, concealed. But I was
not on intimate terms with any of the other peasants either,
except for a few youths on whom I had political influence.

He told me freely enough that the peasants were alarmed,
using, to my astonishment, the political jargon of the insurrection. "Shame on them for a bunch of turncoats," he said.
"They are only waiting to serve the occupiers and become
traitors to our people."

He mentioned several peasants by name, mostly among
the well to do, who were only waiting for our withdrawal
and, chatterbox that he was, he wondered how I had got
there when only last night the enemy had occupied the
bridge. He even brought himself to ask: "Surely you must
have been at your mother's?" and looked at the brightly
colored peasant bag, tied with a cloth. He ended almost tear-

fully: "Poor Marija, what will happen to her? Without a husband, you on the run, and those two children, still quite small."

I changed the subject. We had just reached the pool where he had put his night lines. He quickly and calmly cast his eye on the pool and, though I had noticed nothing, remarked: "There's a fine trout, at least a couple of pounds. It would come in handy to fry for your comrades somewhere along the way."

He made me a present of the fish and wished me a good journey. That was my farewell to the village, for at the far end of the pool the gorge began, with the imprisoned river roaring in the morning mists.

# 3.

FROM COURIERS and from fighters who had passed through my district I came to know, some months later, that the counterrevolutionaries, soon after our withdrawal, had killed my family and burned them in the house, and that a few days later they had caught and shot the commissar, who had crawled out of the cave, probably to try to find shelter with someone.

But just two years after the withdrawal, in the summer of 1944, my duties, as I have already said, as well as my desires, took me back to my village. I had been transferred to the military security organization in that district. Its first task was to settle accounts with the bands of counterrevolutionaries that had retreated into the forests and were hampering the movements and the work of the authorities. So it hap-

pened that, in the way of duty, I had to investigate the case
of my own family.

It is very hard to put into words the feeling that overcame
me when I was told again of the disaster that had befallen
me; it was done, with every consideration and gentleness,
by the commissar of the division. As always in such cases, I
recalled clearly the most stirring and dangerous moments
and incidents—the moving farewell to my brother and sister,
the murder of the blameless child, and the recollection that
now revealed to me the tender and honorable disposition of
my mother. And as with everyone who has lost someone near
and dear to him, I felt as if something had been irreparably
torn from my own body. I who remained was not and would
never again be able to be what I had once been.

Because my comrades were present at the time the commissar told me of the incident, and perhaps, too, to defend
myself against this stroke, I reacted with the phrases: "That's
the sort of war we have been waging; no sacrifice can be too
great for freedom and for a life in which man will cease to
be a wolf to man."

I knew that my comrades realized—they could not fail to
do so—that my calm phrases were only superficial. But they,
with or without reason, saw in them a confirmation of my
spiritual force and, above all, of my loyalty to the revolution.
It is true that I did not shed a tear, but that was because of
the renewed shock and the greatness of my grief.

Later—I remember it was about twilight—I withdrew from
my comrades and went up to the crest of the hill alone, rejoicing in the rage and power of the wind, which wrestled
with the centuries-old beech trunks around me. I spoke to
that wind, perhaps even aloud, and not merely to myself.
"Howl, strike everything that stands in your way, and scatter
my sorrow to the four winds!"

Only when I came to my own house, right to its ashes, did I feel the irremediable depth of my sorrow and how insincere had been my public reaction to it. It was there that the feeling of burned-out memory, that consciousness of a murdered past now vanished forever, took form and made my life, and therefore my future, too, mere existence only, and awakened at every moment a feeling of incurable mutilation.

It was summer, as at the time of our withdrawal, and everything was as it had been then, and perhaps would be forever: the gray roof shingles on the houses on the far side of the river from my former home, the hills pregnant with blue around the unseen village, the green-and-white cliffs behind me reaching up to the heart of the blue sky, and immediately in front of me the green meadow and beyond it the river, whispering in shining ripples through the gray-green willows.

Yet everything was different, and it was just that lack of identity that weighed heavily upon me.

Surely those roofs had been less spitefully pointed when men had lived under them? Why was the river so loud that it filled the whole valley with a sullen ominous roar which perhaps did not come from it alone but from everything, from the whole expanse before me? The ravines were still precipitous, but not so sheer and proud.

Was I really in my own home, on the soil where I had first seen the light, or was all this, even all that had been this, only a beautiful torturing dream?

I walked through the house, of which only some unfamiliar walls, smoke-blackened and stripped to the stone, remained. Some sort of long thick grass had grown in the corners of what had once been the rooms, and behind the hearth an elder grew, gay and carefree, with creamy flowering clusters. Nowhere was there a trace of human life. A

lizard watchfully sunned itself where the glass windowpane
had once been in the room in which I had worked and day-
dreamed and had become a man. No household utensils or
bits of furniture were left. Certainly the peasants, after the
fire, had looked for anything that might be of use to them;
even the stoves and the stovepipes had been taken away. But
in the middle of the big living room, in which the *slava* had
been held and guests received, was a huge brown enameled
dish, broken and blackened and half buried in plaster and
dust.

I thought of looking for some bones, though the peasants
had told me that they had found nothing that could be
buried.

But that thought, too, confirmed my remoteness from all
about me. If anything had remained, it would certainly have
disappeared in the piles of dust and plaster caused by the
bad weather and by the legs and arms that had ransacked
and delved to steal a trivet or an unbroken coffee cup.

What had brought me here? And what had driven me to
investigate how it had all happened, though I could have
dodged it and entrusted it to someone else?

Who could tell?

Was I not yearning to find even a crumb of my childhood
and youth, of those moments of peaceful, joyful everyday
life?

Was I not delving into the past, unresigned to its extinction, to the impossibility of re-creating it in everyday life, of
bringing it into the future?

Was I not finding enjoyment in my torment and suffering, driven by the hope that they had perhaps not been so
terrible as I had imagined them?

Was I not driven to that search for human evil to determine my own fate?

# 4.

THE SAME MORNING that I had withdrawn downriver with my patrol, counterrevolutionary units entered the village—the occupying forces did not stray so far afield.

Captain Manojlo became commander of the local battalion, and Žućo his orderly.

The Captain at once began an investigation into the actions of my family—that is to say, a search for the commissar. For that he had, however, good reason.

When my comrades and I had brought the wounded commissar down the ravine, some shepherds had spotted us. The next morning the commissar was not with us, and, as I have already said, we had met Žućo in a place we could only have reached, since the enemy already held the bridge, by going down the ravine and passing my house. Putting these facts together, Captain Manojlo, and, even more, the experienced policemen who had at once taken up quarters in the police station, easily came to the conclusion that we had left the commissar with my mother. Furthermore, as was later proved at the enquiry, Žućo had lurked behind my house and seen that my mother and sister, and sometimes both together, went out somewhere as soon as it was dark. In the darkness he was not able to see where they went. He waited for them to come back, but could not determine from the length of their absence where they had been, for it was much longer than would have been necessary to get to the commissar's hiding place and back; the wounded man had evidently felt the need for company as well as for food. Žućo confirmed their nightly absences; and that was enough, even had there been no other suspicions.

When I think back over this today, I am again and again forced to conclude that nothing could have led me to believe Žućo capable of such an action. The most remarkable thing is that even today I am convinced that he was not dissembling when he said good-by to me in an almost friendly manner that morning and gave me the fish.

I have already spoken of his reserve, though what man is entirely frank? But that he, at no one's instigation, entirely on his own account, should have gone and pried around my house all night long—no, that I could not imagine, and I still wonder at it. It is true that his character was servile and toadying, and it was not at all surprising that he should have become Captain Manojlo's orderly. But that he went so far beyond guessing the wishes and needs of his master and did so without considering the disaster he would bring upon others—no, that I cannot get into my head. I do not think that he did it from servility—that servility was merely incidental—but simply that there awoke in him, usually so calm, reserved, and unmalicious that he did not even hate his wife's lovers though they were, so to speak, thrust under his nose, some unknown and unfettered nature of which till then he himself had not even been aware. Furthermore, he was a poor man, and it might have been expected that he would favor the insurgents and the revolution—and up to the time of our withdrawal he had done so, although irresolutely, halfheartedly.

In searching for an explanation I hit upon the most absurd and yet perhaps the most correct; that unknown and secret Žućo, which he bore within himself, was simply awaiting a favorable moment to break loose and give vent to his wrath and fury. Because among the insurgents such conditions did not exist, he looked forward to the return of Captain Manojlo, not only as would the good servant of a real

master, but also as some sort of regeneration—the final realization of his true and secret personality.

About ten days after our withdrawal the Captain, with a
group of police chosen from other districts, surrounded my
house just before dawn. The peasants from my village were
compelled to search the cliffs and mount guard. They did
not know what was happening in the house, not even when,
about ten o'clock, the police began to throw things out of
the house and smoke began to rise and flames, gleaming and
weak in the sunlit morning, began to gain a hold.

There were no eyewitnesses. Captain Manojlo was later
killed, and the police involved were either killed or disappeared.

According to the evidence of the peasants, it could be concluded that my people were killed before the house was set
on fire and that they were not shot. No shots had been
heard, and there were no screams from the burning house.

Only Žućo, who had been beside the Captain all the time
he had been in the house, could know what had happened
and how. He succeeded in hiding himself for a good year
after my return. But at last he, too, was caught. So everything became known—what had actually happened to my
family.

# 5.

DESPITE BEATINGS and the evidence against them, my mother
and sister did not show the slightest inclination to reveal
the commissar's hiding place. They justified their absences
at night by their need to visit the stock and to conceal things
taken from the house lest it, being an insurgent house, be

burned. But they were not able to show any of the things. The boy obviously knew nothing, though he might have suspected, and they did not put any special pressure on him.

Finally, after the usual threats and torture had proved useless, the Captain decided to force Marija to speak by threatening to cut the throats of her son and daughter before her eyes.

Žućo was unable to explain what it was that had led the Captain to think of such a thing, whether it had been some special detail or minor incident or whether he had already thought of it beforehand. But he did remember that the Captain had said: "We must make use of the fact that she is a mother. We must strike at her through her motherhood, and then she will start to sing."

The Captain was sitting in the big guest room, his shabby uniform jacket, with tarnished shoulder straps, unbuttoned, his cap pushed back, his legs, encased in down-at-heel military boots, crossed. He was dark and looked youthful, though he was already in his thirties, and, for a wonder, he did not have a beard like the majority of the counterrevolutionary leaders. He did not seem in the least excited, though he continually used the coarse words and oaths usual in the former royal army, in which he had served since early youth. He gave orders, which were carried out by Žućo and some unknown police sergeant, a tall wiry man with penciled fair mustaches, gray eyes, and a very sharp expression. This man bound both women and whipped them with a dried and twisted bull's pizzle, striking them at random. He also carefully thrust pins under their nails.

But it was at once evident that all that was useless. It was most of all evident to Žućo, who swore that he had begged the Captain not to torture them. "It's no good. You're wasting your time, Captain. I know what they're like. You could cut them into pieces and not a single piece would ever say a word."

According to the evidence, neither Žućo nor the others thought that the Captain was joking with his threat of throat-cutting. "But," said Žućo, "it never even entered my head that he would actually do it."

It was clear enough to my mother and sister, however. Yet they—and this was the strangest thing to everybody there, and was even a provocation—did not seem in the least frightened by the thought of their own death. Perhaps the tortures had made them indifferent. It sometimes happens that conditions may be created in which death seems the only way out.

My mother implored the Captain to kill her first, "so that I, their mother, do not see their torment."

The Captain only laughed. "That's the way we want it, and that's the way we will do it, just because you *are* their mother, so that your bitch's heart may be moved for your children at least and you will give up the bandit."

My sister, too, implored the Captain. "Do not touch my brother. He is blameless and knows nothing. If you really must cut my throat, then cut it if you want to."

The Captain said to my mother: "I will do this much for you. We will cut your daughter's throat first. She will be the lesser loss for you. To tell the truth, I do not like to cut children's throats, and I hope you will think it over before we put the knife to your son's."

It did not astonish me that my sister, who was already a member of the revolutionary youth movement and had even understood something of the new ideas, should resist all the tortures and be ready to sacrifice her life for a wounded fighter. She was like her father in everything; she was pale and slender, and very strong-willed and consistent whenever she accepted any idea.

Nor was I astonished that my mother should sacrifice her own life. But the lives of her children!

She was an ordinary peasant woman, illiterate and very pious, fat and slow-moving, a housewife so frugal that she could not even lend a faggot for a neighbor's fire. She had linked her fate with the insurrection and the revolutionary movement only because of me, and was always bewailing (I used to use that word when I reproached her) that it would be the end of me, since I had got caught up in that devil's dance.

It was true that from the time of the occupation she, like many other mothers, had begun to sympathize with the insurrection, though she knew that the insurgents did not believe in God or in nationality. In her view they were only continuing the earlier days of constant war. But that was not enough to explain her loyalty to the atheist commissar.

She could have known, and certainly she did know, that even if things were no longer what they had once been, no one could reproach her for betraying an unknown man to save the lives of her own children.

No, her attitude is beyond my comprehension.

This conclusion, too, though, is not accurate. I did not know all the details, the feeling within the house and what who spoke or felt; and Žućo's evidence was far from reliable. He had forgotten much and certainly was concealing much.

But when I combine all that I learned about what happened there with my memories of my mother, I sometimes see with a terrible clarity that she behaved thus just because she was ordinary, uneducated, and God-fearing. She had, it seems, something within herself greater and stronger than

her motherhood—some knowledge, some truth, some conviction, which took possession of her in those moments, which
convinced her that the betrayal of the commissar would be
an evil and a shame even greater than the death of her own
children.

As I have said, the Captain paid no heed to my mother's
appeal to take her life first. What is more, he did not even
bother to go on entreating her to think things over. It was
as if he wanted to find out whether a mother could be so
great a "no-mother"—he used that expression—as to sacrifice
her children for the sake of an outlaw and an atheist. From
Žućo's account it seemed that the Captain, who kept tapping
his boots with his riding crop, wanted to harden himself by
just such an act, by the slaughter of children before the eyes
of their mother, and finally destroy in himself every trace of
wavering. "May God be my witness," affirmed Žućo, "he
seemed to be forcing himself to laugh and even joke about it.
It was not so much that he was evil as that evil had carried
him away and intoxicated him."

Žućo certainly tried to conceal the further course of events
and to put the blame for the actual throat-cutting on the
police sergeant. But since I myself had heard from peasant
witnesses that Captain Manojlo had once let slip in his cups
that it had in fact been Žućo who had done it, it was not
difficult by cross-examination to force him to confess.

The Captain ordered Žućo to cut Bojana's throat first.

At the enquiry Žućo made excuses for his action; he had
excuses for everything. "I had to do it. The Captain would
have shot me had I refused."

And it was very likely that the Captain would have done
so.

Žućo continued to plead the commonest justification of all
executioners. "If I hadn't done it, then the police sergeant

would have. He was just waiting for the chance, and I would have lost my life for nothing."

In fact, the sergeant began to grin, and even asked the Captain: "What about the men having a bit of fun with this little bitch before we kill her?"

The Captain cut him short. "In my army I will shoot anyone who tries. We do not violate women, but exterminate enemies."

Dissatisfied and ashamed, the sergeant sat on Bojana's legs —her hands were already tied—and Žućo cut her throat. My sister did not try to defend herself. When her body twitched, it was reaction to the initial pain and the recoil of a living being from death.

"But I did not, like some others," said Žućo, "let her be tortured. My knife was sharp as a razor, and I cut through her windpipe at a single stroke."

I parried that with the question: "You say that the Captain forced you to do it and yet you had sharpened your knife beforehand!"

And he, like a shot from a gun, said: "I was expecting us to attack the Moslems, as in fact we did soon afterward, and I would not torture even them, though they are of an alien faith, and how much less a brother Serb and a Christian soul. It was wartime—and in war everyone who is ordered to kill must kill."

My mother did not shed a single tear for Bojana. She was in a sort of insensible, numbed state, as if she did not believe that what she had expected only a few moments before was now actually taking place. She no longer replied to the Captain's questions and threats. She only prayed to God, but even that she did mechanically, warning the men that God would punish them.

The boy, who alone had perhaps believed that the Captain's threat would not be carried out, knelt before the Captain when he saw his slaughtered sister and began crying and imploring him. "I am not to blame. I know nothing. Mama knows that I know nothing."

His mother made no response to his wails, but went on with her prayers and her muttered curses.

It seemed to Žućo that the Captain wavered for a moment. He did not kick the boy away with his boot. But the sergeant pulled the boy away, quickly threw him down, sat on his legs, and held his hands tightly behind his back with his sinewy fingers. Žućo stepped across the youngster, who no longer tried to resist, pulled his head back, and cut his throat, too.

Žućo remembered all these things, down to the minutest detail: how the boy suddenly ceased imploring, stopped sobbing, and rubbed his eyes, shuddering as if expecting a blow; he only cried out with the gush of blood. His mother gazed starkly at the slaughtered child. She whimpered incomprehensibly and then obediently lay down under the knife. No one sat on her legs, though she struggled violently when the sergeant thrust his knife into her throat, turning it in the wound, and cut through the windpipe and artery.

"That's how it is," explained Žućo. "He had tortured and killed so many people, he was afraid of no one, yet he did not know how to cut a throat. I did not cut Marija's throat. I begged the Captain: 'It is not right for me; we looked after the stock together as children.'"

When everything was over, the Captain ordered them to throw out all the food, utensils, and bedding. Then Žućo set fire to the house. They loaded the things on pack horses and drove away the stock. The cows lowed on leaving their stalls.

# 6.

THOUGH ŽUĆO WAS NO HERO, I was convinced that he had not done all that just because he was afraid of the Captain, but had used that fear as a justification to us and perhaps even to himself. Something beyond his control, something stronger than life or death, had sharpened his knife and guided his hand.

For example, Žućo was quite unable to explain why they had not shot them instead of cutting their throats. To me, such a method of killing seems more frightful and brings the executioner into direct sensual contact with his victim; the victim must be held still and the blood spatters the hands and sometimes even the face. Žućo was not only quite unable to see this difference, but he even regarded throat-cutting as natural, seeing in it something similar to a ritual sacrifice—the slaughtering of a sheep or a cock on a feast day. Such a victim seemed to him impersonal, a being different from a man, and hallowed even the executioner, freeing him from the bonds of sin. In truth, killing by the knife, which had, so to speak, become a part of the ideology of the counterrevolutionaries, was inherited from the ancient blood feuds of this land, probably from times when firearms did not exist. To cut the throat of someone of another faith meant not only the annihilation of an opponent, but also, by that direct bond with the victim, bathed by his blood, the killer was enabled to break free from any inherent regard for him. In some districts everyone in the community dipped a sop of bread in the blood of a slaughtered prisoner and made that act a kind of communion.

All that I knew well, but I could not understand.

I certainly did not carry out the investigation from any sort of curiosity, but mainly to make clear to myself and my comrades, and perhaps even to Žućo himself, the full horror of his behavior. He defended himself and explained: "You do not understand; you are of the new times and of different faith. You kill differently."

He showed how every man must be transfigured at the moment when he first takes part in the killing of men, no matter whom he kills or in what way. "It is not that a man loses his head," went on Žućo. "He even becomes more aware of himself. It is as if he becomes someone else, as if he himself were not doing it. When a man sheds human blood for the first time he is sad and troubled, but afterward it is nothing, it is even sweet, as if he could kill and slaughter everything living."

One thing, however, was sure. Žućo had no feeling of guilt, even though he pretended he had. What is more, it was as if he had been driven by something outside himself. If, for example, some pious man had reminded him of the sin, it would at once have unlocked something within him, and justifications and solutions would have poured out. Though he regarded lying, theft, rape, to say nothing of murder, in times of peace not only as a sin but also as something shameful and unworthy of a man, he considered the slaughter of my family—later he killed many Moslems also—as pardonable, even though sinful and inhuman, since he had done it of necessity and by the order of something stronger and, as it were, independent of himself. Not only I myself, as a fighter, and all grown male Moslems, but also all my family, were for him a hindrance and a mortal danger to some holy, unformed belief in some perfect life. Naturally, he did not believe that they were a menace to him personally—he would never have committed any crime for himself alone—but to his faith, the world to which he belonged, or considered that he belonged. He even justified this and explained it. "Is it any different from killing a neighbor for trespass? Faiths and peoples always fight among themselves. Either I kill them or they kill me."

Loot was not important and was not a factor in his crimes. He had not stolen a single thing from my house. True, he had plundered Moslems, but only incidentally, when killing and burning, seizing his opportunity just as previously they had done to his and similar communities. The desire for Moslem property was certainly very strong in him, but it was almost impersonal, an urge to extend his faith and his race into fresh areas. Even without this, he would have killed and exterminated Moslems. He did not try to hide it.

He was aware that he would be shot, not because his deeds merited it, but because the new authorities punished many less serious actions in this way. On the other hand, had I said to him "We will let you go and forgive you!" he would have regarded it as something quite natural and comprehensible. All through the enquiry he continued to address me as "Mister Teacher," as if he had always been my servant and nothing had ever happened between us. He seemed to feel no sort of hatred for me, though he would have cut my throat without a quiver of his hand, as though he were conferring the greatest honor and happiness on me.

I have no intention of trying to explain crime and its reasons, nor am I in a position to do so, especially this crime of Žučo's. In his case also, I only did my duty. I punished what was regarded as crime and I have told this as part of my own story.

When we took Žučo to the place of execution it was clear that he did not so much regret his own life as he did the world he bore within himself and of which he dreamed.

We placed him against the wall of my house, as a symbolic confirmation that justice had caught up with him, but before the order to fire was given, he drew himself up, small, weak, withdrawn, and obsequious, raised his head, and, looking far beyond us at the jagged mountain peaks and the sky blanched and quivering in the heat, hissed: "It's your turn. I would have done the same to you."

Only then did I realize that there would never again be any comfort for me and that my past was lost forever.

# Different Worlds

IT WAS IMPOSSIBLE to know exactly what had happened and how, because the sisters, Elizabeth and Katerina, or, as they called each other, Elza and Katy, had lived for a whole thirty years cut off from the other inhabitants of the town and from almost every living being.

They were the daughters of a large landowner, and before World War I, in Austro-Hungarian times, nobles and officers milled around them, though they were less noted for their beauty than for their breeding and wealth. It was said that they had been, so to speak, betrothed, but both their fiancés were killed at the very beginning of the war, at one of the fronts the old monarchy in its death throes had had to open on so many frontiers. So they lived through the war in a sort of widowed grief, loyal and withdrawn, in accordance with the class to which they belonged, with their standing in society, and with the education they had received. Even at that time the townspeople regarded them as inseparable, as if they were really only one person—"The Two Sisters," "Those Two," "The two Beljanskis"—though they were not even twins, Elizabeth being a year or two older than Katerina. In all their activities, the town regarded them as one; they went to church together, went to dances together, and made music together, the elder on the violin and the younger at the piano. Music was, and remained, their only joy and their only relaxation. But their complete identification began only after the war, or after the death of their fiancés.

The manner of their life after the war did not lessen, but, rather, increased, this impression among the neighbors, and their unity and identity became even stronger. Their mother had died earlier, and their father at the end of the war, so the two sisters were alone, exposed to the covetousness of aunts and uncles and to the blows of the agrarian reform, which overnight transformed them from the richest heiresses in the Danube region into landowners still rich but compelled to take account of every penny—for which they had neither experience nor ability. In the new state and changed social conditions not only their wealth but also the milieu in which they moved entirely disappeared. The people whom they knew and loved, all the landed and titled aristocracy of Austrian and Hungarian origin, emigrated to their own countries, while the Serbian aristocracy, insofar as it existed, either devoted themselves to banking and speculation or squandered their estates on cards, women, and drink. The Beljanskis did not have anywhere to go or anyone to go with. They were neither adventurers nor cocottes, so they withdrew to the ground floor of their not overlarge house on the outskirts of the little town, surrounded by a dense garden and protected by a red-brick wall.

There they lived right up to World War II and through it, going out more and more rarely and always together, and ever more infrequently receiving visits from fewer and fewer acquaintances and relatives. Thus they passed the age of marriage. And nothing would have been known about their life had not servant girls gossiped about this and that, or had not the sound of their music stolen through the house and over the wall.

The bailiffs of their remaining properties cheated them; that they certainly knew, but they were unable to do anything about it, for if they got new ones, they, too, would do the same in an even more cunning manner. Such conditions led almost imperceptibly to their becoming only nominal landlords. The bailiffs knew their actual income, collected it and doled it out, giving the sisters just enough to live on respectably. For although the bailiffs considered that nothing was owing to the two as "do-nothings," nonetheless they gave them something—they had to be careful not to provoke the sisters into making use of their rights and replacing them by others. The bailiffs feared the sensitiveness of the former large landowners; they knew their characters and habits very well. Properties and castles fell into disrepair and were sold for a song. But the sisters were dependent on them, since they knew nothing about agriculture and still less about financial affairs. They grew old and became impatient and peevish with the servants, but they managed to maintain their standards and their reputation. Perhaps they might have gone on managing to the end of their days had not events and changes, heedless of their habits or their wishes, overwhelmed them.

For twenty-five years all kinds of music could be heard from the house behind the red-brick wall. Musicians were rare in the little town, and therefore the sisters usually played duets together. In the town there was scarcely anyone who understood music, except for popular folk tunes. But in time the neighbors could interpret from the music the mood of the sisters, the extent of their income, when their birthdays were, and who their visitors were. Certainly these were only fragments of their music, which was varied and untiring, but they were the only indications of their lives available and comprehensible to the outside world.

World War II plunged the Beljanski sisters into still-greater loneliness and indigence. The bailiffs gave as excuses for their depredations the requisitions of the occupying forces, the plunderings of the peasants, and the seizures by the insurgents. Money had become worthless, and the sisters had to fall back on the raw fruits of the earth and on one old woman, who had also served their parents. They were never seen anywhere, and it was a rare thing for any acquaintance to visit them in those years. Even the occupying forces left them in peace, for there was no garrison in the little town to requisition rooms for its officers. Their music remained the only source of information about them, and it was said that even that became more hushed and melancholy in those years.

When the war was over and the new revolutionary government was set up, even less was known about the sisters, since no one took any further interest in them. The townsfolk were too concerned with their own misfortunes or enthusiasms.

The new agrarian reform, which left only about seven and

a half acres to those who did not work the land themselves, overnight deprived the Beljanskis of their remaining properties and all their income. But no one touched the house in which they had always lived until the housing shortage forced the authorities to commandeer their surplus living space. It was in this way that their ultimate fate was revealed.

The neighbors had noticed that their only visitor was a certain peasant, the one who had leased the few acres of land the agrarian reform had left to the Beljanskis. He usually came in a trap, sometimes in a cart, opened the yard gate, and let the horses loose in the garden. He did not stay long, and it was noticed that when he left there was always something on the cart covered by a tarpaulin. Sometimes it happened that one or two other peasants came with him, and then the corner of some piece of furniture could be seen from under the tarpaulin, and, finally, the legs of the piano.

In bad times they had always found a savior—some peasant or other. So had they with this buyer, the only one who still remained for the Beljanskis. He was their provider and their sole link with the outside world. It was through him that the authorities came to know the details of the end of the Beljanskis; for there had been no one who had taken any interest in them other than for official purposes.

The peasant had told the sisters in his own way about the changes that were taking place around them. He had brought them food, and they had paid him by giving him clothes and household goods. They now knew even less than before about prices, the state of the market, and what was happening in the world. Their ideas had become entirely confused. The old servant woman had died, and the peasant had taken her body to the graveyard and paid for the funeral.

In a few months the peasant had taken away furniture,

household goods, chandeliers, books; he had taken them all to the little town and sold them for a song, but had nonetheless made a good profit for himself. Finally he bought even the remaining acres of land; he had brought a lawyer and witnesses and done everything legally.

"They regarded me," the peasant said, "as their savior. And I was their savior. They used to call me 'our savior.' I never took anything from them that they did not give me themselves. And today there are no fair prices for anything; food is human life, and that alone has any value. I fed them and told them about everything, for they, poor things, feared to put their noses outside, as if the street were going to bite them. They could hear the youth-movement processions marching and singing and could make out the words of the songs. They began to weep and rush around the house wailing: 'The world is upside down! The world is upside down!' I said to them: 'My dear ladies, the world has not turned upside down, but you never go out, you see no one, and you live as your father and mother lived.' And they answered: 'No, no, the world is upside down, is upside down!' "

The peasant had arranged to pay for the seven and a half acres by installments. The installments, however, were not enough for the bare necessities of life. The peasant swore that he had not charged more than black-market prices for their provisions. But foodstuffs were expensive, even unattainable, for those who had no guaranteed source of supply. The sisters were forced to go on selling.

"Mad women," the peasant went on. "Good people, but mad, really mad. They did not weep about anything; only when they sold the piano and the violin did they weep. I, too, felt sad when I knew that their music would no longer be heard. But what could I do? I have a wife and children, times are hard, and I am poor. I could not give them things for nothing. I had plenty of trouble with the piano, too. The youth organization began to be suspicious of me. 'What are you doing with a piano, peasant? You must have stolen it from some bourgeois or other, from the national property.' I had to tell them straight out: 'They entrusted it to me; you can ask them yourselves.' They bought the piano and drove a hard bargain; they got it from me for almost nothing. As for the violin, I sold it to a gypsy; gypsies love that sort of thing. And later, later I don't know what happened to the sisters. They had nothing left to sell, and I was afraid that the authorities would suspect me of something, for they are even worse than the bourgeois. So I didn't go there again."

Though the housing authorities got no answer, they did not have to break into the house. There were no windows and no doors, and even the parquet had been torn up and the coat racks torn out of the walls. The house was empty and deserted, and the bodies of the two sisters were already decomposing. They had died of hunger, having sold the shifts from their backs and the beds from under them, but they had not gone out of the house into a world that they could not understand and that could not understand them.

# The Song
# of Vuk Lopušina

THOUGH I HAVE KNOWN the song of Vuk Lopušina from childhood, even now I cannot say that I have understood it in all
its aspects. I might almost say: That song is my life. Even as
my life has always been changing, and these changes I have
only noticed over long periods, so, too, it was with this song;
I have found new beauties and meanings after those I had
found in it before had proved to be less beautiful and significant.

Everything that a man writes with artistic pretensions he
writes also about himself. Nonetheless I know it is unbecom-
ing for a man to talk too much about himself. But how can

I keep that song separate from myself when its every sense expresses some period of my life?

Life is a point of no return despite our continual search for a resurrection and it does not outlive, nor is it able to outlive, song or picture, melody or sculpture; and it has seemed to me only too often in my solitary prison hours that the song of Vuk Lopušina still lives and will continue to live despite everything.

It is not something that was, or is, or is to be. It cannot be said that the song is an expression of reality in that it was created by some poet after the events described in it had taken place, so that the only reality in it is its creation and its form. The song is a work of art, a world unto itself, a world created anew, no less real for human beings than any other. Such worlds are necessary to man, for man lives as much by song and by ideas as by daily bread.

Influenced by this song at various times and in various ways, I have always sought in it the inspiration of poetic creation, the secret of its survival.

It is, however, one of the many, and at the same time one of the best, Serbian national ballads, a magnificent ode to the heroic death of a Montenegrin hero toward the end of the eighteenth century, and one that has sometimes seemed to me to be a reflection of my own existence.

Now the song has become more real to me than my own existence. Living here in prison, impotent and reduced to mere existence, I feel this the more because, even if I am not already in the decline of life, I am deprived of the illusion of resurrection and revival. Perhaps it is for that reason that I am at last able to speak of the song of Vuk Lopušina. By the very fact that my own life is fading away and has already to a great extent ceased to exist, the song of Vuk Lopušina seems to be more comprehensible in its beauty and significance, though my narration of it may even now be colored by personal factors. In any case, it cannot be otherwise; I am not to blame for having lived, for having relived in myself the song of Vuk Lopušina—that is to say, the life of Vuk Lopušina himself.

# 2.

AS FAR AS I CAN RECALL, the song of the death of Vuk Lopu-šina is not to be found in the earlier collections of ballads, certainly not the version I am discussing here. It was published for the first time by the Kavaja brothers of Nikšić about 1926. That version, however, when I compare it in memory with those sung by some *guslars,* has many omissions and lacks many remarkable details. But as far as I know, it is the only printed form of the song that gives any indication of its poetical and moral content. I knew of differing oral versions, and while spending the summer of 1946 at the house of Raško Jauković I took down with his help a variant sung by a *guslar* from Drobnjak for whom I had sent just because of that song. In that version, which must be among my papers, there are important details that are not to be found in the others, but not even that one may be considered complete.

The song of Vuk Lopušina does not, in fact, exist in its most beautiful version. In my youth there were countless versions, of which each had some special quality, but none of these was written down, nor did any skilled transcriber make from them a better and more complete example. So it may be that some of its details have disappeared forever, together with those who recited them and who certainly invented many of them.

For an even more important reason the song of Vuk Lopušina suffered a different fate from that of the other national ballads sung by the *guslars*. Of the songs of the *guslars* that have been created among us from the mid-nineteenth century onward—that is, from the time of the publication of the collections made by Vuk Stefan Karadžić and others—not one has any sort of value; they are banal in expression, without imagination, and false, in the deepest sense destructive to art. They show contemporary events in terms of the distant past, referring to them as if they had already been transformed and rarefied into myth. When a present-day *guslar* sings the printed version of a song, he keeps strictly to the printed text; this shows, incidentally, that the creation of the *guslars'* songs, the really artistic creation, belongs to the distant past. But that has not been the case with the song of Vuk Lopušina; the *guslars* went on adding to it, and not one of them, and I have heard many, kept to the printed text. The song was still being created and therefore could not have any final and polished text; the myth of the incomparable hero was still burgeoning and taking shape.

From that song, from that tale, flows an intoxicating sense of unfathomable reality, more real than anything known to our senses.

Though we are aware and know very well that Vuk Lopušina has without question been killed, he nonetheless goes on living in our thoughts and desires, so that not for a single moment is our hope extinguished that perhaps he has not been killed after all, but that the *guslars* have introduced his death to add to the beauty of the song.

# 3.

ALL THIS SEEMS the more real and moving, so vivid that one catches one's breath and one's mind is pleasurably darkened, because Vuk Lopušina has nothing superhuman and scarcely anything unusual about him. Even in our own times he seems possible and even probable, and tomorrow even inevitable, just as the Pleiades will move tomorrow in the clear skies of dawn, and the dogwood will not forget to burst into golden and tawny glory in the coming spring.

Our knowledge and records of Vuk Lopušina are, however, very slight. They are most complete in the song about him and about his death.

We are told, and it is confirmed by the sparse written evidence, that Vuk was born at Trebjesa, a village in the hill country near Nikšić. Somewhere I have noted down his father's name, which was also his until he won the sobriquet of Lopušina. That nickname became his surname and the family name of the tiny clan descended from him.

The story tells how he got that nickname, or surname, if you like. It was in this way:

As a youth Vuk was noted for his exceptional strength, and someone bet him that he could not slice through the neck of the best bull in the herd with a single sweep of his sword. When in fact Vuk did so, someone said: "He sliced it off like a *lopuh* (colt's foot)."

In the center of the field, amid the circle of astounded herdsmen, among whom the tribal chiefs were easily recognizable by their dress, their engraved weapons, and the severity of their glances, stood the gigantic youth, with his bloodstained sword in his knotted hand, smiling good-humoredly and just as astonished as the rest at the severed neck from which gushed great jets of warm blood. So that was the bull at whose bellow the whole mountain trembled and before which every living thing cowered, and this was the youth who had not even himself believed in his own tremendous strength! That was the beginning of the myth about Vuk, of the song about Vuk. Vuk had made a name for himself in the world in which he lived, and from that time forward all that he did would be remembered.

Truly it is so; we are remembered to the extent that we have succeeded in doing what no one before us has been able to do. That may be good or it may be evil. The good lives on, is quoted as an example and an ideal, and the evil is cited as a curse and a malediction. Of Vuk only the good has been reported.

He killed many men of another faith. But what else could he have done if he wanted his clan and faith to survive? Those men of another faith, who were called Turks but in fact were Islamized children of the same race and tongue as Vuk himself, had become so parasitical a ruling class that they placed their way of life, their faith, and themselves above and before everyone and everything, thereby entailing the enslavement or extinction of those who until yesterday had been their fellow clansmen. I say: They did it! And I think: It came to that because of the inevitable clash between human groups: one must die that the other may live.

It amounts to this: Vuk only did good, because absolute good and absolute evil do not exist, only good or evil actions whereby a man may extend or enlarge the narrow conditions of life by actions, whatever they may be, that ensure the continued existence of his fellows.

Vuk was already known as Lopušina when, despite his

father's wishes, he killed the Nikšić begs who came secretly to insult his patron saint and violate his womenfolk. He then fled to Rovac, to a clan in the pathless and precipitous gorge, whose pride it was, or so it is said, that it had never paid tribute to the Turks and which for two, if not three, centuries had been a haven of refuge for *hajduks,* or outlaws, and refugees from Turkish oppression.

From that cradle of heroism and evil, of violence and freedom, precipitous and inaccessible to outsiders, Vuk led a band of raiders, and continued to lead one until the day of his death. But not one single exploit of his was remembered or sung of till the raid that led to his death. It is not known if he was married there, though it was from Rovac that the line of Lopušina has sprung.

It is known that the Trebjesa leader at that time was the Serdar Mališa, who tramped as far as Russia, to the Orthodox Tsar, to ask for help for the scattered and defeated people of Trebjesa. Cetinje and Bishop Peter had little power, and Serbia was on the eve of the great Karageorge insurrection, both too far off and too oppressed to help.

Vuk was neither a headman nor of a family of headmen; only after his death were headmen chosen from among his descendants, because of his fame and reputation. In addition, the headmen could not abide him, probably owing to envy lest he cast a shadow over their leadership, and the Serdar Mališa himself, the leader of Vuk's refugee clan, was to forsake him at the moment of choice between life and death.

Vuk did not want to, or did not know how to, in my opinion could not, choose between life and death. He had already chosen the life of his clan, his faith, and the Serbian ideal. From the very start he lived for something that might have seemed to him eternity but which, at that particular moment, was merely spiritual and biological survival. In fact, Vuk lived and went on living to the time of his death with consistency and unselfishness, without choosing between life and death.

I have told of his life as it was recounted to me in the tales. How scant and obscure are the records of so massive and vivid a personality!

# 4.

LIKE THE MAJORITY, if not all, of the Montenegrin *guslars'* songs, the song of Vuk Lopušina is based on a foray to steal Turkish sheep. All the songs of such forays avoid the word "plunder," for it was not regarded as plunder, seeing that they were taken from an enemy.

That, too, is comprehensible. The poverty-stricken Montenegrins were at war with their Moslem overlords in order to be able to go on living, so they sang about that warfare and of that survival. Their songs do not tell us of the beauty, but of the raw, naked incidents of human existence. They give more facts and statements than poetry—if one may speak of facts and statements—and it seems to me that the songs were, therefore, clean, logical, poetical in the wider, the unconventional, sense.

Whether taken this way or that, the song of Vuk Lopušina indubitably raises this not especially exalted theme of the plundering of Turkish sheep to the level of sublime poetry and pure ideal. The reason for that is certainly not in the incident itself, nor even in Vuk himself—he was neither the only nor even the greatest Montenegrin hero—but in much else besides. To draw nearer to an appreciation of that beauty I must relate the incident—that is to say, the myth—

in the manner of both the song and the folk tale. They do not differ in essentials.

As do so many other songs, this one, too, begins with three good heroes—the Serdar Mališa, the monk Šundić, and the *iguman* of the monastery—drinking wine in Donji Morača and discussing where they can find the greatest booty. After sharp and dramatic altercations, they decide it would be best to strike on Krvo Mountain or at Petrovudna when the sheep from Nikšić are pastured on the hillsides and the Nikšić Turks are making merry in the town. By agreement the host of clansmen is at once summoned—from Pipera, Rovača, and Morača. When the men gather at the time fixed, the headmen order Vuk Lopušina to reconnoiter the sheepfolds and make sure that the Moslems have really left the mountain villages and gone to make merry in Nikšić. All day and all night Vuk reconnoiters "seventy-seven sheepfolds." This is the most beautiful and dramatic part of the song, and it makes it clear that the Turks are expecting a Montenegrin foray and are keeping their horses ready for battle. The song mentions that someone from Rovača gives them warning of the intended foray of the Brdjani and Montenegrins, and, in truth, it would not be in accord with tradition had there not been treason among the Serbs in every great undertaking, and every great and true tradition must have somewhere the theme of treasonable incitement. Vuk returns from his reconnaissance and in the morning is overcome by drowsiness and the host finds him asleep. The Piperi leader, Paun Šušović, rebukes him, saying that he was not told to sleep in the hay but to reconnoiter the Turks and Krnovo. Enraged, Vuk tells him of the Turkish preparedness at Krnovo and calls on the leaders and men to kill his sheep if they want meat, but that it would be foolhardy to attack Krnovo and the people of Nikšić. But that,

too, earns him a rebuke from Šušović; if he is afraid, he
should not scare his band as well. Overcome by anger, Vuk
seizes his dagger, but the men beg him, cap in hand, not to
waste time in quarreling. Then the men split up and begin
discussing where and when they should fall upon the Turks.
When they set out, Vuk calls upon the headmen, naming
Paun Šušović and the Serdar Mališa, not to betray him, and
then each goes his own way. Listening in vain when, according to their agreement, Šušović and the others should have
started the fight, Vuk realizes that they, having met with
opposition, have fled and left him unsupported. Despite
that, he decides to attack the Turks with his men alone. At
first they meet with success, and even take prisoner the girl
Zika Kajović, whom he had noticed while he was reconnoitering the sheepfolds. But soon the Turks surround him
and drive his men back. Vuk's men waver, want to leave the
sheep and flee, but Vuk rallies them and in the most decisive
moment of the battle checks the rout by his personal heroism
and example and repels the townsmen of Nikšić who have
been encouraged by the flight of the Brdjani and Montenegrins. The song says that during the flight he cuts off
Zika's head, so that the Turks cannot take her from him;
some versions say that he wanted her for himself, even
though he was already married. At the end, when he thinks
that he has escaped, he is confronted by the Turkish hero
Avdi Ljuca on horseback. The tale insists on describing Vuk
as being "chafed"—saddlesore because of the long time it
had taken to round up and drive away the beasts—but the
song only mentions that luck was not on Vuk's side. In the
first clash Avdi Ljuca—according to the tale, a small and
wiry man—cuts off Vuk's arm, but Vuk throws him to the
ground with his sound arm. Just then a pair of Montenegrins, who probably because of some blood feud had earlier

taken service with the Turks and fought alongside them, leap into the fray and kill Vuk as he bends over Ljuca. The spoils of battle remain with Ljuca, and he cuts off Vuk's head. The song ends by saying that the leaderless host was annihilated and that the Turks took seventy-seven Monte-negrin heads.

As can be seen, I have tried to give the content of the poem as simply as possible, and even as dryly as possible, because it would be impossible to recount the whole poem, and even more because of my intention to speak later on of its beauty, its drama, and its ethos. It is clear to me that to separate the plot from the aesthetic and ethical factors of any work would be unnatural and forced. Least of all would I want to do so in this case. But so that the reader may know what it is about and may follow what I am saying, I must do this. Such procedure is especially justified when one takes into consideration that this is not so much a study of the song of Vuk Lopušina as my personal experience of it and of its hero. It is as much my life as my literary reaction to it, which would remain obscure if the reader did not know the action and the more important incidents of the song itself.

# 5.

THE SHORTNESS of this song never ceased to astonish me, until I remembered that it is, in fact, one of the longest in Serbian folk poetry. While one listened to it or recited it, time passed irrevocably. I would have liked to make time stand still, or to prove that it is not possible to revive events long buried in the past.

As a boy, and also as a youth, I found that through this song, through my reliving its every detail, time passed slowly and agonizingly. The inevitable transience of life was evident in the song, or, to be more exact, in the surge of its verses, the shifting of its images and messages. It was not merely an order of events and the experiences of its hero, but it had its own independent and specific existence, like the isolated beech tree near our house, the river Tara, intractable among the mountains, or I myself in a world different from that within me.

For me, at all events, the shortness, the evanescence, of the song took the form of grief for the unhappy end of its hero. My grief went deep. I went on living, eating, sleeping, contending with everyday things and events, and the song ended. It did not go on, and after Vuk's death I could not even imagine what its continuation could be. Its noncontinuance, the impossibility of its continuance, aroused in me a strange feeling of remoteness from everyday life, if not of some personal evanescence.

Perhaps for that reason I was always sorry to leave the inn and the storytelling of the innkeeper, Pavle Danilović, from whom I, while still a schoolboy, first heard the song or the tale of Vuk Lopušina.

My father, too, used to recite to me the song of Vuk Lopušina, but a different version from Pavle's. My father added and rationalized, so that personages and events appeared more probable, more comprehensible, and in accord with the life I already knew. In its own way it was a very fine tale, convincing, polemical, instructive, and abounding in detail.

But to me Pavle's telling was more entertaining and more likely. He did not tell it as to a child, and perhaps not as to a human listener; he simply told it in order to tell a story. There was never a suspicion in his voice or words that everything had not taken place just as he had said. No more than my father, did he believe in poetic exaggeration or in the fantastic, and he, too, did not embroider or enlarge upon heroes and their exploits. But this song he accepted and recited as if it were just so, something needless to prove, since it was true in a different way from everyday truth and from the ideas and the life familiar to us. It was for him a world as true as the world of everyday, though unattainable through the senses, and his low and husky voice, rumbling as from some great distance, conjured up both the inexplicability and the inevitability of poetic reality. For that reason Pavle, in contrast to my father, who even while he was reciting remained the man he was, was transfigured into quite a different man, remote from this everyday world. That transfiguration was so complete and clearly drawn that he vanished with all his ugliness and illness, and it seemed to me that he was no longer a man, or at least not as other men, but a character from the fable he was relating. He became all goodness and beauty, such as one can only imagine.

Sometimes it seems to me that I remember the innkeeper Pavle and his inn only because of the true and incredible tale of Lopušina, though Pavle, more than anyone, was not in the least like that song and its hero.

Pavle was small, with a mottled, rather puffy face. He was wasting away from some unknown disease. In addition, he was goitrous, and every few moments used to cough to get his breath back. Though he was not without reputation and integrity, no one ever said of him that he was a hero, from which I concluded that he was not one. Sparse, very black and grizzled mustaches hung down on each side of his mouth, and his lips were thick, the upper one cleft, pursed in an ugly way around the amber mouthpiece of a silver cigarette holder which he always used as an outward sign of an imagined aristocracy.

But no one was able to tell tales as he could. Indeed, telling tales was his greatest talent and his main occupation.

For what was his inn? A little house by the road, with a single small room and a pantry behind it and a hut nearby in which his wife, Savica, cooked and where she sometimes spent the night. Only coffee and plum brandy were served in the inn, and one could also get fodder for horses. There was nowhere to spend the night unless the one and only bed was handed over to the diffident guest, that of Pavle's neat and orderly wife, who, though it did not seem so, had the last word and would not allow dirty or lousy guests to spoil her freshly scrubbed yellow planking, bleached sheets, and probably her only blanket, which, always white and smooth, fell from the bed to the floor under a colored bedspread.

Pavle's reputation, therefore, was derived from his skill in telling tales. He knew how to tell them in a thousand different ways; they were full of jokes, which he always inserted at just the right moment, pausing to give them significance, but rarely and scarcely perceptibly laughing at them himself. With the headmen, with my father, he spoke seriously, weighing every word, considering himself their equal, but never failing by an apt word or gesture to show his respect. Toward his fellow villagers, as poor as he was himself but dirty and bowed by work and every kind of lack, he did not noticeably stress the advantage of being a man who did not need to work like a horse and was even invited to sit among the headmen "as a man among men." On the other hand, he did not become too familiar with them; his manner with them was curt, as if he were hastening to some important task, though he never hurried, nor was he able to hurry. He dressed accordingly: in serge, such as only the well to do

wore, though somewhat threadbare. His shabbiness was not
noticeable because of his cleanliness, such as was rarely to be
seen. Pavle always wore a clean white shirt. His body, too,
was strikingly clean, and his well-kept hands, rather puffy
at the wrists, had soft, pinkish, uncalloused palms and fingers.
Pavle's stick, too, was not quite like a peasant's; as with the
cigarette holder, he was never parted from it. It was heavy
and knotted, like those some peasants know how to make
from blackthorn, but so well turned and smooth that one
could see at once that it was factory-made.

It was obvious that he pretended that his way of life was
better, more distinguished, and wealthier than in fact it was.
But perhaps, the devil knows how, that sense of personal
betterment, that participation in a better but nonexistent
way of life, was his real, his deepest and most cherished conviction. Though others, grown men, knew him better than I
did, and though they grumbled about his airs and graces,
they did not see anything unnatural in them. It could even
be said that it was not wholly imaginary, as if he had been
born, or had, in any event, learned, to live without laboring
like a peasant, though he lived on little and from little.

Not only did he never do anything on his tiny holding—he
always stressed that he was a sick man—but even in the inn
itself he never raised a finger to do more than was demanded
of a good host, to converse well and pour out a glass of plum
brandy. He never brewed the coffee, because he regarded
that, as well as all cleaning and mending, as woman's work.
His meadow and pasture he let out on half-shares, or paid
day laborers to work on them; everything else was done by
Savica.

Even Pavle's disinclination to work was not obvious to the
eye; he was born to chatter, to greet men with fair words and
a welcome glass. Nor was any preoccupation with work evi-

dent even in Savica, despite her diligence. She was quietly capable and, unlike her husband, very taciturn. Though she knew how to rest and sit down and welcome people cordially, one got the impression that even in those moments she was thinking out or completing some task or other in her mind. She was never late in anything she did, though she, too, never showed any noticeable haste. There was never the slightest mark on her cooking utensils or rubbish in her yard, and the firewood in front of the hut was always stacked according to size: logs, faggots, chopped wood, and sticks. Pavle was known to snap and swear, especially at the peasants or lodgers. But no one had ever seen Savica angry. She used to caress the neighbors' children and give them dried pears and plums, which she always had in the storage cupboards hidden in the dark corners of the hut and pantry which were crammed with who knows what treasures of her work and her frugality.

In contrast to her husband, Savica was a healthy, upstanding, and singularly beautiful woman.

I mention Savica's background, and Pavle's, too, because that was the cause of the discord between Pavle's public bearing and his private life, which perhaps did not really exist, but was only created by my imagination, seeing that I believed—and suffered whenever I found that belief unfounded—that a man should behave according to what he thinks and feels.

They said, and it was true, that Savica had conceived while still unmarried, which was regarded as one of the greatest disgraces, and that after her marriage to Pavle she still carried on secret love affairs, and certainly not with the village youths but with the headmen and other respectable men. The peasants, who jested coarsely whenever love matters were in question, said that it was no wonder that she was unfaithful, since she had an old and sick husband, and they explained her lapses in youth as the reason why she had married Pavle.

There were even mischief-makers who asserted that he knew all about his wife's behavior but that he, sickly and embittered, could not make up his mind to revolt and throw her out of the house, as he ought to have done and as any real husband would have done if he did not want it to be said that he was worse than any woman. But no one was ever able to prove anything. No one ever mentioned Savica's lovers by name. It was all rumor and gossip; in a village they always know everything, even if it is not seen and not heard.

I, too, believed it to be true. Even now I believe that Pavle knew or at least suspected the truth. But for him it was important, above all, in fact decisive, that no one could prove that Savica was unfaithful and that she afforded no occasion for open reproach. She carefully concealed her unfaithfulness and did not even have to deny it, because for him it did not exist.

From the facts that came to my childish knowledge I did not draw the same conclusions as the mischief-makers, that is to say, that Pavle was dependent on his wife for his living and overlooked everything, and that Savica only needed a husband to cover up her affairs.

That was how it appeared from without, and was indeed so. But beneath that, beneath reality and despite the facts, everything was different and much more complex. What could I know of the complex relations between woman and man in my eighth or ninth year? And what could I know of Savica's loves when not even her nearest neighbor knew anything reliable about them? But nonetheless I knew everything, or almost everything.

In the village they usually spoke coarsely about love and relations between man and wife. Even when they took place shamefacedly and secretly, everyone understood and guessed. Only I was unable to understand why men must enter into such relations with such vehemence; children could surely be born without such bitterness and passion. And because the property of my eldest uncle marched with Pavle's and on his death passed to my family, I could, herding cattle on it and naturally inquisitive, go to the inn every few minutes, and was thus able to notice things others did not. It may have been because of these visits that Pavle's liking for me grew somewhat stronger than for the other children, whom he and Savica, childless, greatly loved.

Savica behaved toward the more worthy and respectable men differently from those women who were not gossiped about, and who, strangely enough, were not, for the most part, beautiful. Her behavior was especially noticeable when neither Pavle nor any other adult was present. In time I got used to noticing traces of that unusual behavior even when she was not alone.

Who knows? Perhaps even I would never have noticed had not one of the men to whom she behaved thus, in her own special manner, been my father. Oh, I could not help noticing when a strange woman won the good will of my father, an affection to which she had no right, and how my father not merely did not resist her attentions, but even willingly accepted them.

On such men—and on my father—Savica used to smile in a special way; her smile played about the corners of her trembling, dark-red, slightly open lips, and at the same time she looked boldly at them with her round and shining black eyes under thick black eyebrows curved into a bow and almost touching. When doing this she wasted words even less than usual, and her pale face became even paler, drained of color and rigid. At such moments she would carefully, as if carrying a waterpot on her head, with her long, delicately cushioned fingers toss aside her plaits, heavy, shining, and black as tar, and her firm rounded breasts would swell provocatively. The conversation between them, between her and my father, even in front of children, would at once be cut short, and she would use her eyes and lips, and her whole body would grow tense, as if in the grip of some stiffness or spasm. She was big-boned, like many Montenegrin women, but, differing from them, she was of softer shape and fuller in the hips; and at such moments those hips by their swaying movement, now left, now right, seemed to be taking part in some magical and to me quite incomprehensible dance. Oh no, they never suspected that she might be a witch, but they said that she could tempt an eagle from the skies! Savica served such men with special care, and, though she was always well and cleanly dressed, whenever one of them put in an appearance she would change her shawl for a veil and her simple blouse for a velvet jacket that both framed and displayed all the warm and swelling breadth of her breasts and the delicacy of her tall and rounded shape. Only such a man would she accompany to the yard when he left. The yard stretched for nearly forty feet in front of the inn, and she would keep her eyes fixed on him as she leaned on the pear tree, yearning for him, and willing him to turn back.

Nonetheless, she was no whore, and not even the most malicious held that she was. It was clear that she made a shrewd choice of men, and whatever she did secretly with them she managed to conceal so skillfully and unobtrusively that it offended no one's moral feelings. Since in her loves she looked for no profit and since she had an old and sick husband, all, though slandering her, silently conceded that she had a certain right to such a life. She was beautiful and healthy and kindhearted.

Though she was mistress in all household affairs, she was frank with her husband, and, judging from all accounts, she was also humble and obedient. They never quarreled, which was quite exceptional in conditions in which a woman was regarded as almost a slave. That certainly strengthened the opinions about Pavle's dependence on her, but it also revealed that their relations were firm and serious, founded on something that others did not know and were not able to understand.

In fact, these two were considerate, even tender, to one another in the smallest details. They had based their life together on some silent, unspoken agreement by which each of them remained what they were both in public and in their intimate life. It could not be doubted that Pavle would have driven his wife out if he had caught her in unfaithfulness, which he secretly certainly suspected, and that she would have left him at once if he had reproached her for anything of the sort without proof or if he had ever lifted a hand against her. Though weak and pusillanimous, he so held to his reputation that he would not have thought twice about throwing her out, and she was so independent, even stubborn, and able to look after herself that she had nothing to be afraid of if she should leave him. But nothing of the sort ever happened or entered the head of either of them. They had built up their own special life together, in which each was free and satisfied, despite the fact that it was not in harmony with the lives of those around them or with established viewpoints and customs.

So I, too, though like others I could not reconcile such relations between Pavle and Savica with my moral ideas, not only reconciled myself with things as they were, but also went more and more frequently to their nest, not overwarm and welcoming, but clean and well-ordered and tolerant in every way.

For a long time I was unable to understand fully how such a woman—and I mean such a woman!—could at the same time be so good, so serious-minded, so tolerant and kindly, even as to this day I have been unable to reconcile myself to the idea that so weak-willed and ugly a man as Pavle knew how to tell such mighty, irresistible, exalted, and true tales.

Must there be so many and such great contradictions between the song and its creator, between life and the way it is lived?

I loved both of them, life and song, Pavle and Savica, and their relationship, though I was always powerless to reconcile myself to it, divided as I was between the joyous immediacy of meeting them and the inescapable moral laws that make man great and invincible. That was my first and unavoidable experience of the clash between the beauty and truth of this fable and the cowardice and deceitfulness of everyday life. I could not manage to reconcile these things or to equate them. When Pavle died, Savica was left alone, sorrowful and suddenly grown old.

But the song of Lopušina remained and went on growing in all its beauty and significance, as I, too, lived and grew and matured.

# 6.

I HEARD THE SONG again later from many *guslars*. But not one of them have I remembered. There was no need, for among them there was one, my elder brother, who made a place for himself and for that song in my youth, and made me forget all the others.

Not even in childhood could that song completely express everything in life and in the outside world. Still less could that be in youth, when all the limits of knowledge and experience are tremendously extended, and the world, having lost its frontiers, becomes attainable and comprehensible.

But the song continued, in a different way, to live within me like a recurrent motif, one of the aspects of my existence.

First of all, there were Vuk and my brother, blended, despite their differences, as if one were not from the song and the other from everyday life.

As a child it had seemed to me that I, too, would be Vuk Lopušina. I even thought of myself as the Vuk of the song. I, too, would in the end die, but in such a way that I could still rejoice in the world and men and myself. Between Vuk and me there was no age difference, at least nothing insurmountable in the future, even though he had lived in the distant past. Though stronger and better than others, he was possible and attainable even in my own person, although there were no longer any Turks or any plundering of their herds. I cut off their heads and rounded up their flocks on the mountains and took Zika Kajović to wife, but since I was not quite clear as to what that might mean, I arranged for her to be a shepherdess who knit me stockings of the whitest and softest wool in the world.

As a youth I soon came to grips with every sort of day-to-day reality and with the idea that past times would never return. It was not without sorrow that I realized that I had longed in vain to be Vuk Lopušina. I had thought too much about the moment of death and had so adapted everything that the Turks did not kill me and were themselves routed. I already knew that there is no return from death and that even if the soul continues to live after death it has no part in this world; a world that in any case was such that one could not leave it merely to identify oneself with a hero who had once existed and of a type who would never be again.

But it seemed to me that my brother, even if he could not be Vuk Lopušina, could be someone rather like him. It was not by chance that he preferred to sing that song and enjoyed singing it, adding an additional line here and there and raising and intensifying his tone, especially when he sang of Vuk's recklessness in the moments when the choice between honor and selfishness, heroism and faintheartedness, between life and death, was put before him.

My brother certainly did not realize my hidden longing, my unattainable ambition, to be Vuk Lopušina. But he was right when he felt that I rejoiced in the beauty of the song, and he would sing it for me to the gusle whenever I asked him. There was not a single verse I did not know by heart, not a stave my brother might sing, or a tone by which he would stress some word, that was not familiar to me. Nonetheless, every time he sang it I enjoyed it anew. The passion of love and the other joys of life cannot be renewed, but this was a pure enjoyment of something that was always the same, unchanging.

What was it that drove me to listen a hundred times to the same song from the lips of the same singer? Not once did I find it boring, not once did I not experience that sweet shudder, as sweet as love, as inevitable as death.

Certainly the fact that I was living in the last days of the dying epic and mythical Montenegro contributed to this. It was a song of the youth of my country and my people, a song of the times when they arose from foreign enslavement, clan rivalry, and the anonymity of serfdom to grow proud in pure ideals and moral sacrifice, which became inherent in the land and the continuance of the race. Vuk Lopušina apparently acted like other Montenegrin heroes; he plundered sheep and cut off Turkish heads. But the plundering was for him only a pretext, a way of settling accounts with the Turks in the name of a moral ideal which grew within him as a part of his life and his blood and his every thought. Vuk did not care about sheep, but about Turks, and took no heed for his own head, but only for his honor, for a continuance more lasting, more unselfish, and therefore more personal.

Furthermore, the song abounds in magnificent and living images, so real and dramatic that they impress even the foreign and the prosaic reader. How much more, then, was a listener impressed who was still living in the surroundings whence the song arose and devotedly attached to the skill and experience of a real and sincere *guslar*?

But there was also something else in my enjoyment of it.

That song, transfigured, remained throughout my youth as a vision of an unattainable but personal world. As such— unattainable, inimitable, even imagined and taking place in a world of fantasy—it became reality for me because I enjoyed it in a different, but no less intense, manner than my first loves and my first victories over the adversaries every man encounters by the very fact that he is alive. For that reason I enjoyed the song in a special way and more than any of the others, and it became inseparable from my way of life and thought. A fiction became for me a reality—a reality more beautiful than everyday life, but no less essential and inevitable.

Even now I cannot explain why it should be just this song of Vuk Lopušina and not some other work of art. But it seemed to me that, should I ever understand it fully, it would at least reveal for a moment why I was alive, why I thought and behaved in a manner predestined. I remember that I had no feeling of unreality and emptiness because the song told of an unreal, nonexistent, and implacable world, nor was there anything humiliating in my powerlessness to correlate Vuk's personality and actions with my own.

Everyday life became more and more interwoven with the life depicted by the song, which I so much desired. It was as if I had the foreboding that the beauties and the events of the song could never happen again; but I could create fresh beauties and in fresh unforeseen events still be great in the inimitable manner of Lopušina.

Nowhere, in no aspect of everyday life or in my fantasy, was there anything that could convince me that it was possible to encounter such beauty as in the song. Its beauty drew me, disturbed me, and excited me, even when I had not been thinking directly about it, like a dream of the unattainable or the achievement of the possible and probable. It was like a continual and fateful adventure. I lived in its beauties and in the sacrifices of its hero. I strained, as what human being does not, to create my own reality, to create new worlds.

Already existing literary forms, especially those from the beginning of the twentieth century—those of Dučić, Šantić—were for the most part molds for these spontaneous yearnings. But not having found their proper form, these yearnings remained unsatisfied, unexpressed, stifled. Certainly I was not conscious that by those strivings I was trying to create new realities; they fulfilled an inner need to "describe," to "picture," to "imagine."

But the song about Lopušina was something more, deeper and more significant, an example and an inspiration. It seemed that direct and immediate reality were inherent in it, transformed into a work of art.

I knew that my brother in no way resembled Vuk Lopuš-

ina, despite his daring, and, I would again say it today,
after his heroic death, his willingness to die for some supernatural and unattainable goal. These characteristics of his,
common to all the heroes who were so wrapped up in their
exploits that they never thought of what might befall, often
made me think that there are men who are created for wars
and insurrections, for during them they fulfill all their destructive creative force and are inevitably killed, as if to confirm their predestination, proving thereby their own and
man's power of final and incomparable sacrifice for abstract
and impersonal reality—for an ideal. While he was singing
about Vuk, raising or lowering his voice to accord with the
sense and form of the song, restraining and intensifying the
fire of his dark eyes, half hidden under thick eyebrows, I
felt not only that the song lived in that reality—for him and
for me—but also that we were living in it and that, even
though I should wish, I would not be able to free myself
from the past inspired and resuscitated by the song.

The past lived in that song, was transformed into its espe-
cial but nonetheless direct reality.

I loved my brother with an unconditional love and at the
same time saw in him Lopušina, identifying one with the
other despite their lack of kinship. Was I not longing to link
past and present, to wipe away time by the feeling that I,
too, should create such a work, such a world of beauty and
vision, as that song?

My brother sang of Lopušina, and there was no one but
me to listen to him in our lonely house amid the forested
peaks, in the summer twilight which soon swallowed everything but the words and the sense, so that they became purer
and more immediate. The dusk swallowed my brother, too.
There remained only Vuk Lopušina, and perhaps I myself
and my power of conjuring up Lopušina. When Mother

brought out the lamp, reproaching us for wasting time singing, the petty unlovely world of everyday things would return. My brother would sing another two or three verses
and then hang up the gusle, and I would not urge him to
continue, though he had broken off at the most dramatic
passage, the reconnoitering of the sheepfolds. The real world
and the world of art, each real in its own way and linked together, cannot be merged and reconciled.

The song was never so lovely, or my brother so dear and
unfathomable. Life had so many possibilities.

# 7.

TO EXPERIENCE the world through others and to be forced
to play our part alongside them is one of the aspects of
human destiny. I felt my first love throes through my brother,
and Zika Kajović, the heroine of the song, was our common
love.

We loved Zika, each in our own way, and held similar
views about Vuk's behavior to her—that is, we agreed that
Vuk cut off her head so that the Turks could not take her
from him.

Certainly one cannot speak of love in its usual form, for
how could a man be in love with a character from a song,
even had she ever existed? But even so, it was love, filled
with a passionate yearning. Still less could there be any dis-
pute about Vuk's behavior, for neither of us could even think
of using violence against women or the helpless. Nonetheless we agreed with Vuk, with his finality in everything, even
when he killed the woman he loved—in our fantasy he already loved Zika, since we, too, loved her—rather than allow

the Turks to take her from him and ravish her young beauty.

Adjusting the events, especially those of the songs and myths, according to his views and moods, often momentary and therefore capricious, my father was never able to understand how so great a hero as Vuk Lopušina could cut off a woman's head. Such an act is unknown in Montenegrin tradition, both because it is inhuman and because woman is considered to be of a lower order, with whose blood it would be improper for a hero to stain his arms. Furthermore, my father insisted on referring to the tradition that, though no more reliable than the song, did not stress that Vuk had killed Zika. Father even grew angry when my brother would not skip that passage. But my brother, as if to spite him, insisted that that was what the song said and that he must be true to it, and he sang the passage with defiance and tragic intensity. I longed for him not to omit it, though I grieved at Zika's death every time he sang of it. It was wonderful that Vuk had cut off Zika's head, and yet it would have been wonderful if she had not been killed.

The great drama of Vuk and Zika—and why not also mine and everyone else's?—was foreshadowed when Vuk went to reconnoiter the mountain pastures and the Krnovo sheepfolds.

Omer Kajović, Zika's eldest brother, calls on his mother to prepare clean clothes for him, since he has a foreboding that the next day he will be killed when settling accounts with Vuk Lopušina, for, being a hero and a real man, it is not right for him to die improperly and unprepared; he must fight for life to his last breath and look death confidently in the face. Vuk "both saw and heard" all this, and at last approaches the Kajović cabin. When he gets there, there is something for him to see; nine Kajović brothers have their horses ready saddled. The horses are snorting and tugging at their reins, and the brothers are arguing with the Montenegrin renegades about who will be first to take a Montenegrin head when on the morrow they attack Vuk Lopušina at Krnovo. The Turks do not even mention the other heroes and leaders, as if there were no one else in all Montenegro. Zika urges her brothers, above all, the eldest, Omer, to take her in good time to Nikšić, so that on the morrow she should not become a *hajduk's* slave, that she, loved by so many brothers and brought up to wealth and all good things, should not have to break wood and stones barefooted, slaving for and serving those who have till recently been her serfs. Vuk thinks her "very pleasant." Omer consoles her, saying that she need fear no one while he has a head on his shoulders and while any of her brothers are alive. Death is easier than the shame of his only sister being seized from him, even worse should she be seized by *hajduks* and serfs.

Because this song is not an account or a chronicle, but a drama, it does not dwell on the conflict between Lopušina and the Kajovićs, but it briefly takes note of the event and dwells on the clashes and the passionate exchanges between men of differing and hostile worlds. Vuk Lopušina announces his presence from the mountain slopes; he is not one to attack perfidiously and unseen. "Are you at home, Omer Kajović, and have you prepared a meal worthy of you and me?" Omer's mother, from whom her son had yesterday demanded new clothes, answers, summoning him to battle and to death: "Come on, mountain brigand, if it be so written that you should kill my Omer." Vuk massacres the Kajovićs. That wonderful Kajović mother is not even mentioned after she leads her children to the slaughter. The song speaks of the Turks with pride and respect, and the poet only says that Vuk took Zika prisoner, for the *hajduk* did not make his raid solely because of her, but to kill and enslave all that belonged to his enemies.

Vuk and Zika belong to different worlds, but until death, and even in death, they cannot be separated. When Vuk, abandoned, retreats with his men before the jubilant and triumphantly victorious Turkish pursuers, he could clearly have escaped had he been willing to leave to the Turks what he had taken from them and what he considered to be his by right of heroism. In those fateful moments Zika becomes Vuk's destiny and the conscience of the Turks; unreconciled for a single moment to the idea of being a slave or to love by force. Her struggles to get away betray the movements of the host. She defies Vuk and death and calls by name on her uncles and nephews, Turkish heroes and headmen, not to let her cross the Morača alive into Montenegrin slavery. The fighting rages around her; the Turks might even have withdrawn had it not been for the girl in whom burned all the hatred, all the implacability, of their struggle with the serfs and the insurgents. One after the other, at the shrieks of the girl, the foredoomed Turkish heroes charge and die. At one moment they even seize her—she was in the charge of a young man from the Morača, and the youth was frightened—but Vuk recaptures her and, when he realizes that his men are routed and that the Turks will at last succeed in taking her from him, he cuts off her head with his sword. This is no longer the warring of men—it has gone beyond every human, moral code—but a war between two faiths, which have come to grips for their honor, their place in the world, and their name.

It is obviously impossible morally to justify Vuk, even from the viewpoint of his own times, though the extermina-

tion of an alien faith was not at that time regarded as immoral or inhuman, as it is today, even when it was not a
question of the survival of an ideal or of a race.

I stifled my conscience not to have to judge Vuk's behavior
from a moral viewpoint. According to some sort of logic,
which has no link with my understanding and is in some way
independent of me, I felt that Vuk was right. But because
of the beauty of the song and the continuity of the theme—
hatred against everything Turkish—I felt, I knew, that I
would never have acted in that way, and would never have
been able to hold up my head again if I had. But Lopušina
was something else! And not because he was without conscience, honor, and unselfishness. Even when he kills Zika,
he gives his own life to save the son of Father Dragović, for
he would have been ashamed to admit that he had forsaken
the child. And not because the song was so beautiful—a work
of art cannot be immoral, even though it may be indifferent
to morality. It was and is a question of something different,
of something incomprehensible, or comprehensible only with
difficulty, some power Vuk possessed even without knowing
it, which made it possible for him to remain moral while
paying no heed to established moral codes and customs. It
was some sort of existence outside the usual, some ethic over
and above the day-to-day code. There is a feeling that Vuk
kills Zika, toward whom he felt some attraction and with
whom the struggle to the death finally united him, as a way
of settling accounts with something within himself, with
reconciliation and wavering toward the Turks, with his own
passions and desires.

Implacable worlds and two beings legendary in their death.
Everything should have been love, but was, but had to be,
hatred and death.

Every thicket along the Tara, stifled by the summer heat,

concealed Zika. The scent of Zika rose from all the mountain paths, and I held my breath in the hope that I should come upon her on the topmost peak of the Bjelasica. Unattainable by day in the open, she gently crept into my dreams and, unbidden, joyously held me in her warm arms.

I had to search for Zika, and I searched for her, even though I knew that my every longing for her was in vain.

I did not wish, I did not yearn, to fight. But what was I to do without love, without life? For Zika, for love, a man must struggle and go on struggling to the end. A man must prolong his existence, must seize love from reality and bring it into his world of beauty and renewal. A man must renew life and create beauty, or disappear.

To search for Zika.

# 8.

ONLY A THIRD of the way through the song is Vuk Lopušina first mentioned. But every verse anticipates and heralds his appearance and his character.

From the very first lines, unusual events are foreshadowed. The Moslems are glorified. If something noteworthy is to take place, there must be some personality capable of piercing the veil of convention, established viewpoints and relationships. The words, too, are unusual, chosen and placed in such a way that one perceives the play of events and at the same time anticipates a great action, a great idea. At the very beginning, the monk Šundić and the Serdar Mališa almost come to blows over the choice of a place for the raid. The monk taunts Mališa with avoiding great risks and jeers at him, saying that it would be better, since he is afraid of lead-

ing a raid, to return to Trebjesa and cultivate the Turkish
holdings and plow the Turkish lands for a third of their
produce, as his ancestors had taught him to do—the harshest
and most shameful taunt that could be made to a man who
has lost all that he had for the sake of hungry freedom in a
strange land. Relations between the headmen and those who
agree to follow them are tense, fraught with anger, with
harsh words and drawn swords. Had it not been for the
*iguman* of the monastery, who appeals to God for help
against this sin which would shame his old age, blood would
have been drawn and the headmen, who acknowledge no
authority above their power and their clans, would have
killed one another. Despite this, the picture of the monastery
is wonderful, deeply spiritual; the white *lavra* from the times
of the Nemanjas glitters among the mountains like the morning star among the stars. When at last the headmen agree to
attack Krnovo and begin to muster a host among the clans,
they do not forget to tell the leader of the Rovača clan to
bring Vuk Lopušina with him. Vuk has taken refuge with
the Rovača clan, as also has the Serdar Mališa, for Vuk is a
skilled raider and knows the Krnovo mountains well. Although they do not like him, Vuk is the only hero whom the
headmen call by name.

Vuk himself only appears when he is told to reconnoiter
the mountain pastures and folds. He is, in any case, purely
a man of action, who does not plan or consider. The poet
even then does not speak of Vuk directly, but only through
his weapons. He describes them and tells of the great Turkish
heroes who once owned them and whether Vuk seized them
from the living or the dead. But from that time onward, the
song is devoted to Vuk, his actions and his ideas.

The reconnaissance, the longest and most dramatic part of

the song, is devoted entirely to Vuk, as also is the end, which describes his death.

Vuk spends days and nights in the mountains. He reconnoiters the power and pride and determination of the Turkish heroes; in every mountain hamlet, at the cabin of some hero, as in life, as in a good song, as in Homer, he meets with fresh experiences, unforeseen events, and preparations for the fight. He comes across one Turk who is afraid and he taunts him openly on the mountainside to flee to Nikšić in time, but the famous Duro Bajrović curses his cowardice and says that he needs not fear the fight so long as his, Duro's, head is on his shoulders—only serfs are afraid and need someone to give them courage. This Duro Bajrović takes a horse with him wherever he goes and on the horse an ornate Damascus gun. Vuk outwits him, though he cannot kill him lest he reveal himself as a spy, and tries to steal the musket from the pack horse—such was Vuk's daring and cunning! But when he cannot do this, he breaks down the door of Duro's fold and kills his two sons; the song does not say if they were still children, and the poet quickly and shamefacedly passes over this inhuman exploit, even as later he does not dwell on the killing of Zika. But it must be known, without attempting to justify Vuk, that his greatness does not lie in the fact that he does not do evil, but in his heroic defiance and his unsurpassed self-sacrifice. He meets evil with evil. He is an exiled peasant whose folk have been killed and raped and his home burned, so he pays back in the same inhuman measure by destroying the seed of his oppressors. Tahir Ljuca is putting his horse through its paces for the morrow's battle, and another hero is digging a trench above his cabin. Hero after hero, picture after picture, incident after incident, the song tells of the preparations of the begs, convinced that they are born to power and lordship, and of the unbridled daring of the *hajduk* Vuk, whom the ruthlessness of the begs has convinced that there is nothing left for him but to exterminate his former masters until he, too, is killed.

Then, after the reconnaissance, the quarrel with the headmen, the battle and the death.

A hard death, a death the like of which is not to be found in all the Serbian poems, only too rich in deaths. It leaves behind it an unspoken summons, which could not be disregarded, to fresh struggles, to extermination. The poet says: Wolf to wolf, beast to beast, will not fight by night when neither can see nor recognize the other, but *hajduk* to *hajduk*, man to man, will fight by day or by night though they do not know or recognize each other. So, too, Avdi Ljuca against the possessed Vuk; the poet uses just that word, "possessed," by which he expresses both Vuk's strength and violence and his berserk heroism and implacability. As every death in life or in a good song is unique, so, too, is Vuk's: Ljuca cuts off his arm, and the half-dead Vuk with his other arm seizes Ljuca by the throat and hurls him to the ground. A treacherous bullet strikes Vuk from behind. The avenger places Vuk's head on the walls of Nikšić, above the serfs, above Montenegro, above the Turkish glory and lordship—above good and evil.

Vuk's father is at his grave in the mountains: the grave is longer and wider and the headstone on it higher than the other graves, than the graves of common men. The mountain grows to the stature of the dead hero, and his death is made known throughout all Montenegro.

Who knows, who now remembers, the name of that mountain?

But Vuk's grave is not forgotten, and his death has become a song to be remembered for all time.

While the Serbian tongue is spoken, Vuk Lopušina will be a seal upon Serbian life, a special conception of the world and of man's existence in the world.

For Vuk has conquered reality and taken from it the sense of the impossible. This the song about him has done. He had to die, for man is mortal, and it was not given to him to survive, to overcome the real and the impossible. The song has remained, to survive with him through its beauty, despite time and reality, whether Vuk's or ours. Vuk did not imagine the song. But it found him and immortalized him.

The song cannot die, nor need it fear oblivion.

# 9.

THERE STILL REMAINS my unaccomplished plan, to retell, re-create Vuk and Zika, to tell the song once and for all. It is well that it has happened so, for it would not be a re-creation, but only an imitation. It is something that can be created only once.

After so many years, when the song has already lost for me the living significance I once gave it, and when my life moves into its peaceful concluding phase, all that I am able to do, and all that I will do, is to tell of my intentions and what the song has meant to me.

Vuk Lopušina is an exceptional figure in the tragic and bloody destiny of Montenegro and the Serbian people, and the song about his death, unpolished and incomplete as it is, is one of the most harmonious and moving symphonies of the survival of a man and of a people.

Setting out from reality transformed into myth and at the same time myth transformed into reality, art maintains an unbroken sensual and visionary link between man and the past.

I would like to return to my youth and my homeland, to the song of Vuk Lopušina. I am withering away in my longing for them. But there is no way back. Today there are new realities everywhere, but the only thing real to me is this longing. My decline has begun, and I seem to see the day and hour of my death. Then shall I be free of everything, even the song that has ensorcelled and inspired me since I first came into this world.

If only such a song could be inspired by me . . .

# The Leper

*To Jovan Barović*

THE VILLAGES along the way already knew all about it, even if the headman, Todor, had not talked with everyone he met and had not let it be known in the inn. He had obviously spread the news intentionally. But not even his fellow villagers, those who knew him best, had at first been able to understand why, when telling of this evil and misfortune, he had stressed his own special role.

Very soon that, too, became clear. The town doctor, an officer of the Austrian occupation forces, had said that Lazar, a prominent and obviously fairly well-to-do peasant from their village, had been stricken by leprosy and that he must therefore be isolated from the rest of the world. The military authorities had entrusted Todor with the job of choosing some suitable house in the village in which to put the sick man, and had given him strict orders to see to it that no one should come into contact with Lazar.

The evil rumor spread ahead of Todor, and the householders gathered at his still-unfinished stone house, which, with its unweathered shingles, shone white on the great hillock in the center of the village.

The fine spring day was already drawing to its close when Todor arrived at the village, and though he could see the men crowding around his house from afar, he did not hurry. Instead, he lingered at every house along the way to tell the wives, or the children, if there were no elders present, the terrible news that everyone already knew and to inform all and sundry of the grave task that had been laid upon him. He knew that Lazar's illness was called "leprosy" in the doctor's language, and although that word sounded far less frightful than did the people's word for that same evil, it seemed to Todor that in this word, in its unfamiliarity, there lay some special significance. So he liked to keep repeating it, often adding: "The scall indeed. It's much worse, if there can be anything worse. It's leprosy, leprosy!"

Thus Todor appeared to the eagerly waiting peasants, who greeted him impatiently, clearing their throats as after some great effort. He took off his cap, wiped his high, bald, heavily wrinkled forehead, lowered himself into the heavy chair that his daughter-in-law skillfully pushed forward, and asked his wife for a glass of plum brandy—"To give me heart," he put it.

No one expected Todor to offer him plum brandy—it would be too much to ask of him to honor all of them, stingy as he was. Nor was there any reason to; everyone's thoughts were turned in quite another direction. And Todor did not think it necessary to wonder why he was drinking alone. Was he not tired out, bearing such evil news with him all day long?

"And so," said Todor, emptying his glass, "you have already heard what sort of evil has fallen upon Lazar—leprosy, or, in our language, the scall, if there is anything worse than that. But this evil has not struck him only, or his house only; it has also been laid upon all our village. Who among us will be able to take a wife? Who will let one of their girls come to us? Friend will be divided from friend and brother from brother. Even more, may God not grant it, should this sickness appear in any other among us—Sodom, no less!"

The peasants did not like Todor. Squat and heavily built, with sparse, fair, almost white mustaches, hollow cheeks, curly beard, and fleshy, slightly crooked nose, he gave an instant impression of a man cunning and even ruthless in pursuit of his own advantage.

In fact, that was just what he was. Not that the other peasants were in any way different; each one of them looked after himself and his own interests first. But there was something special about Todor. As some hunting dogs have an exceptional sense of smell, he had a special gift of sensing and smelling out anything that could bring him profit and strengthen his position in the village and the neighborhood. And, what was even more important, he chose unerringly the method that led to success.

He was scarcely fifty, but his authority, not only in the family but also in his numerous clan, had for long been unquestioned. In time it had spread over the whole village, too, at first under the national authorities and now under those of the occupation. Relying on his strong and united clan and still more on his own power and cunning, he had always been elected. The position of headman, moreover, brought no pay, and men assumed it unwillingly. But it brought its possessor into contact with the higher authorities, and that alone gave him precedence over others, especially if he knew how to profit by it. If, for example, it was necessary to muster a gang for compulsory labor, and during the occupation that happened more frequently than under the despotism of the former king, it was the headman who drew up the list of peasants, and he could, without infringing law and order, assign any person on days of his own choosing. Also, he could gain advantage when there was aid, such as flour and sugar, to be apportioned, even if he did not apportion a larger share for himself, which Todor did not blush to do. The peasants grumbled against him, especially after the arrival of the Austrians, when they began, rightly or wrongly, to regard him as a henchman of the foreigners. They no longer elected him; the occupation authorities appointed him. And even had there been anyone to take over the headman's duties—and especially under the occupation everyone avoided doing so—there was no one who knew as well as Todor how to adapt himself to conditions. He was born to rule, the peasants said. Had he been of better line or of greater wealth, they said, that man would have won a kingdom for himself.

So no one even tried to contest Todor's authority, though it more and more brazenly infringed the established rule and ever more shamelessly interfered in the everyday life of the peasants.

Lazar alone knew how to mock at the headman's dignity and at the same time to enforce justice even when it seemed that there was none. But he was in many ways a law unto himself, and, above all, he was under the spell of the gusle,

the one-stringed fiddle of the national bards, and the songs of
olden times. He even rhymed such songs himself. And what
seemed even stranger to the peasants was that he was devoted
to books, which he borrowed from the schoolteacher and
even from the town library. In the village, it is true, he was
loved, because he did not give himself airs and was ready to
give the shirt off his back. Even so, there were few among
the peasants who would associate with a man who believed
that the truth and the justice of the national tales and songs
really existed and were possible, and who preferred to turn
the pages of a book rather than harrow his meadow at the
right time and in the right way.

There was one other peasant, Jovan, who did not curry
favor with Todor. He was a *hajduk,* an outlaw, who had
been outlawed long before. The national authorities had
put a high price on his head, and the occupation authorities
had increased it even more. Who would have anything to
do with such a man? The only man in the village who dared
openly to say anything good about him was, to be sure, the
eccentric Lazar. The two were blood brothers, kin to one
another by that incomprehensible and eternal bond between
song and heroism, between the gusle-player and the *hajduk.*

Especially now, after the village had been stricken by evil,
it never entered anyone's head to contest Todor's authority
and powers. It was a question, one might say, of the existence of the village. Not only was it exposed to contagion,
but the occupation authorities threatened that they would
banish anyone who disobeyed the doctor's rules, and came
into contact with the sick man, to the lazaret on an island
in a distant sea.

The peasants knew that Todor had only been waiting for
some misfortune to strike down Lazar in order to free him-

self from this thorn in his flesh—the more unpleasant and unwanted just at this time, when the Austrian authorities, because of bad harvests and famine, were ready to offer work on the roads in exchange for food, thus giving the peasants a chance for profit. But no one could deny that what Todor undertook and wanted to undertake was of advantage to the village. They all knew that there is no human enterprise that some human being will not turn to his advantage, and they suspected that Todor would in one way or another turn Lazar's and the general misfortune to his own profit and would increase his power over the village by the strict measures against contagion, whose execution would devolve on him as the sole authority in the village.

But who could say anything against that when the life and the reputation of the village were at stake?

The peasants submitted to Todor's orders and advice as never before.

When, as was the custom, they began to discuss which house or hut should be set aside for Lazar to live in, and how they should behave to him or see to his needs—and the peasants showed great compassion in this matter—Todor interrupted them. "Let it be Widow Mijoljka's house!" he said.

Mijoljka's stone cottage on the little knoll in the center of the village was in sight of all, sufficiently near the head-man's house for him to be able to watch the sick man and see that no one came into contact with him, and also sufficiently far off for the headman's children to avoid contagion.

The peasants began to cough nervously and look questioningly at one another. The house was ramshackle, and the roof let the rain in. But Todor cut them short. "Let it be as I have said. And anyone who does not want to obey, let him go where his eyes see and his legs carry him! While

I am what I am, I will not let the village suffer because of a bunch of blockheads."

So the meeting ended.

# 2.

THOUGH THE VILLAGE was only about an hour from the town, it took the Austrians a whole morning to bring Lazar back to it.

Guards were placed at all crossroads early in the morning, and when a squad of soldiers started out with Lazar, there were only deserted streets and windows along their route and, behind them, the flames of the hut in which the sick man had been housed. Ahead went a patrol of three Austrian cavalrymen and two civilians on foot, and about two hundred yards behind them Lazar, quite alone, disheveled, unshaven, and bareheaded; he must have lost his cap somewhere. About three hundred yards behind him came two bullock carts loaded with quicklime, which soldiers with shovels scattered wherever Lazar had walked; he had to keep to the right-hand edge of the road. The movement of the cortege was made even slower because the bearded doctor, who rode just behind the first cart, did not know Serbian, and his orders to Lazar on how to walk and when to stop had to be transmitted through a foxy sergeant major who, also on horseback, was on the doctor's left.

Had Lazar been shackled and had his guard been a little closer to him, it would have looked like the cortege of a man condemned to death. Even so, it looked like a procession to the place of execution. The slow convoy advanced, leaden and silent. Only the doctor's orders, which seemed even harsher because they were given in a foreign language, and the curt shouts of the sergeant major, known throughout the whole district for his severity, and for that reason probably chosen to command the squad, could be heard. Lazar himself moved like an automaton, a puppet on a thread jerked at the sergeant major's commands, with hands hanging wooden and lifeless.

No one wondered at his helplessness and docility; for a month past there had been gossip about his illness and the fate that awaited him. Though that winter he had noticed painless sores on his body, he had paid no attention to them until they had begun to spread. When they had broken out around his mouth, experienced older peasants had warned him that they might be something serious, even the scall. The very thought of this had caused him intense anxiety, not so much that he feared for his life—after all, he would have to die one day—but because it might infect his family and the village. So he had hastened to the foreign doctor, for there was no other to go to. The doctor had quickly realized the nature of his disease and placed him under strict guard in a hut until everything had been made ready for his total isolation. As soon as they had shut him in the hut, it had at once become clear to Lazar that some serious illness was in question, and the day before his departure for the village, the doctor told him the truth and explained how he must behave.

Lazar now knew that he was condemned not only to a slow and torturing death, but also to something still more terrible—to isolation from men. He used to say that when the doctor told him, his first thought was to take his own life. But man's nature is such that when he is at the end of his tether there are always so many tasks at home and

for friends, unfinished and unstarted, that it seems a shame
and a sin to die.

So, not even a full day after the terrible realization, everything was turned upside down—men toward him and he
toward them—and everything, the woods and the fields, the
houses and the river and the sun in heaven, looked different.

The peasants waited for him in sympathy at the crossroads, but the dull glances of the guards checked them. Not
even those whom he knew could bring themselves to greet
him, not so much that they feared the illness, for they must
have known that it could not be transmitted by words, as
from stupefaction at what had happened to him and also
from fear of the authorities, lest they or their henchmen
would take it amiss and regard it as a proof of past, and
therefore perhaps also of future, links with the sick man.
Only one old man, at the first crossroads, took off his cap,
as if before an icon. And, what was still stranger, two schoolboys, sons of one of the neighbors, did the same just as he
was coming into the village. Lazar himself avoided greeting
anyone, for that might seem that he was asking for help,
which, in any case, could not be given him and, which was
worse, the authorities might suspect that anyone whom he
greeted might have been in close touch with him and perhaps was also infected.

So he walked submissively and despondently, not because
he was afraid of the sergeant major, for that was all one to
him, but lest by some unthinking action he might harm
someone.

With every step a greater and more inescapable emptiness
opened before him. Not only men, but also things and the
whole countryside disappeared from his life, as if they, too,
were afraid he might infect them. On the bridge, just before
entering the village, he halted, perhaps remembering his

childhood and youth, which he had passed around and in the little river, and spoke aloud, though no one heard. "Farewell, water and meadow, earth and sky, and you, too, heroic people of Serbia!"

In his native village it was still more empty, still more frightening.

He had expected something of the sort, for within himself he, too, shared the ancient belief that leprosy was not only a mortal illness but also a punishment by higher powers for terrible sin. No one could remember any of his clan who had been afflicted by the disease. Nor had he ever seen anyone who suffered from it, but with childish horror he had listened to tales in which there had been rare sufferers who had isolated themselves in some hovel or cave in a lonely spot. For many years men had pointed out their kin and had been unwilling to join in marriage with them. One such clan had been known to Lazar; men had said of it, although no one remembered when it had been: "Lepers lie among them!" Such a fate now awaited him and his descendants— who knew to what generation?—perhaps as long as any trace of them should exist. It would not help him in the least that he, as a peasant who had read and who had understood, knew that illness is not the consequence of sin, but of contagion. What was important was how men behaved in the face of illness: awe and emptiness had met him at the threshold of the hut and had accompanied him step by step, as if some merciless and omnipotent higher power had vented its wrath upon him.

Nonetheless, when even his own village greeted him in this way, he was crushed and appalled.

When the convoy entered the village, at the point where the bridge over the little river marked the border of the village common land, Todor and two of his relatives were

waiting. The headman first of all took off his cap and greeted
the doctor and the sergeant major. Then he greeted Lazar,
but naturally without taking off his cap. He reported that
everything had been made ready for the accommodation of
the sick man, and then, at the sergeant major's order, took
his place in the procession behind the doctor. His two relatives, giving Lazar a wide berth, joined a pair of soldiers
who till then had been mounting guard at the crossroads,
and went hurriedly along the path that branched off from
the main road to the village, which sprawled over hum-
mocks overlooking the fields.

The path led upward, and as soon as the head of the
column crossed the bridge the whole escort moved on. But
the deeper the column penetrated into the village, the more
deserted it was. By order and from fear, not a living soul was
outside the houses. Not even the cattle or poultry were there,
only the chained dogs, which barked furiously. Not even his
own kin awaited Lazar; not his wife, his daughter, or his
son. Not even his mother. They, too, had been forbidden.

At the top of the rise he looked toward his own house—
an old stone building at the farther end of the village. He
halted, half joyfully, half sorrowfully, when he noticed his
family gathered on the stone balcony. He could even see a
movement among them—they had seen and recognized him.
Memories and pictures of still-living, unextinguished life
crowded into his mind. Tears ran down his face. Staggering
and bent, and wiping the tears from his face with his hands,
he obeyed his orders.

When the procession arrived in front of the headman's
new house, Todor shouted to Lazar to turn to the right, to
the widow's cottage. But he, unthinkingly, probably because
he had grown accustomed to taking orders from the sergeant
major, once more halted. At that moment Todor's wife, a

plump, still-good-looking, dark woman, came out of the house and greeted Lazar. "May God be good to you, Lazar!"

Todor flew at her, leaping out of the convoy and threatening her with his stick. "Into the house, hag. May the dogs chew your carrion!"

The woman fled, but the sergeant major shouted angrily at Todor: "Who gives orders here? I or you?" Then, even more sharply, he shouted to Lazar: "Forward! Forward and turn right!"

As soon as he turned into the narrow walled alley, the widow's cottage could be clearly seen on the crest of the hillock. The leaders had already stopped in front of it, and the procession resumed its slow even course.

It had been clear to Lazar as soon as they had turned near the headman's house where they intended to put him, and he went readily into the cottage, as if it were his own. He at once recognized in it things taken from his own house—the black cauldron, already filled with water, a recently planed wooden platter, a shallow copper pan, and in it a small cut loaf and a hunk of cheese, and his wooden spoon with the carved handle; in the corner were a striped pillow and a thick white blanket. There, too, were his gusles, hung by their plaited leather thongs on a wooden peg in the place of honor.

His tears flowed again, but he did not even notice them this time. After he had glanced around, he went outside to thank the doctor for saving the people from the evil that had fallen upon him. But there was no opportunity, for the doctor and the sergeant major, some way in front of the cottage, were giving their final instructions to Todor, who noted them carefully, cap in hand—though it was not clear whether he had taken it off as a mark of respect or because his head was sweating.

When they had finished and gone away, Todor took from a nearby wall a longish stone like a boundary mark and set it in the path in front of Lazar, about ten yards from the door of the cottage. When he had finished, he noticed Lazar's tears and, thinking, wrongly, that he had begun to weep on seeing a boundary beyond which he dare not go, said: "Don't think hardly of me, Lazar. May God be my witness that I do no more than that which our ancestors laid down and is to the advantage of the village. And this, too, you must know: farther than this mark you must not move, but behind it you are protected by God and the law, and not a hair of your head may be touched."

Then Todor took another stone like the first, counted out ten long paces from the first and stuck that, too, in the earth. Then he once more turned to Lazar. "You may go as far as this one, and whoever wishes may go to that one—ten yards, as the doctor instructed us."

The soldiers scattered quicklime up to the mark Todor had first set up, then threw a few shovelfuls about and went back to the carts. The procession set off on its way back. The doctor and the sergeant major now rode ahead. They halted in front of Todor's house, and Todor yelled at his wife to bring snacks and plum brandy.

Lazar sat on the stone doorstep and buried his head in his hands.

Thus began his new life—and his death.

# 3.

DAY IN, day out, having nothing else to do, Lazar watched from his hillock and knew who moved in the village and who did what. He became so skillful at this that he could tell, even at night, by the barking of the dogs, by the lanterns and the still-unextinguished fires, or by some distant call or whistle or the creaking of a door, who visited whom and when he returned home. From what he heard, and even more from what he saw, he drew his own conclusions about conditions and relationships in the village. And besides, at first the peasants did not shun him overmuch and placed a semicircle of stones around the farther boundary mark on which they sat and talked with him. Lazar found in the yard behind the house another stone and put it up at his own boundary mark in order to be a little nearer and not to have to shout to make his visitors hear, as he had to do from the doorstep.

Thus, even against his will, although his isolation strengthened his desire to take part in the life of the village, Lazar became a sort of center for all the complaints and misfortunes of the village.

He would watch the clouds, the winds, and the sunsets. He had known something of them earlier, and now drew conclusions about the weather. The peasants came to him, too, as to a wise and upright man, and complained to him about everything that worried them and asked his advice. They came when they wanted to know whose beasts had been straying, and also from sheer inquisitiveness, to ask who had gone where or who had been visiting whom.

On feast days, as evening fell, a few of them would gather and ask him to play for them on his gusle. His singing and the words of the song now seemed clearer and full of meaning. The songs would attract others also, even the children, who listened from a little farther off, just as inquisitive, but a little afraid as they looked at the bearded human apparition.

Not that Lazar had changed greatly; it even seemed as if his health were improving. In fact, either because he had no chance to shave or because he wanted to hide his emaciation and his sores, his black, slightly silvered curly beard had covered his face, and his neck was also covered with thick hair. His skin looked as if it were sooty, probably because of his constant sitting in the rain and sun, but a sort of waxy bluishness showed through its wrinkled blackness. His clothing was old and ragged. But he was himself largely responsible for that; he wore rags because he would not let his family bring him anything of greater value; it was a shame, he said, for him to wear it when it could be of more use to the younger and healthier. He ate very frugally, arguing with his mother and his wife, who took turns bringing him food and water, about every rich dish, saying that they should have given it to the children or eaten it themselves. "Whenever you bring me something tastier or richer, I keep thinking of your need and your lack—I eat it and it eats me!"

It seemed to Lazar, and even more to his family, that, although outcast, he would live out the remainder of his life in touch with his family and with the village—in fact, with the world of men. Even his death, despite its obvious inevitability, did not seem so terrible. "It is different," he said, "when one dies among one's own people."

Sometimes it even seemed to his family and to many in the village that he was not ill. Though he could not help with his hands, he nonetheless took part in everything by word and thought.

So it went on until midsummer. But on the eve of Ilindan —the feast of St. Elias—there was a change.

The year before, the occupying authorities had tried to hold the customary *sabor*, a mountain gathering, on that feast day, but the villagers, some spontaneously and some by persuasion, had refused to meet. The occupiers, certainly instigated by those who supported them, wanted to restore as many of the normal customs as they could, the more so because it was now the second year of the occupation and it seemed to them that there was more reason and justice for this. In truth, there was little chance that the people would go to the *sabor,* for there were few who could take part—the stock had been almost wiped out by requisitions. But the occupying authorities issued an order that this year the *sabor* would be held on the land of a neighboring village, which was close to the road and the hamlets.

To go or not to go to the occupiers' *sabor* was the subject of discussion in the village. Lazar, too, was involved by the very fact that he was a fellow peasant and still took part in village life.

It was then that he first noticed Todor's disapproval of the visits paid him by the peasants. It was shown in two ways.

Todor and his relatives did all they could to dissuade the peasants from visiting Lazar and exposing themselves to danger and suspicion. This was not without effect; many who were Lazar's relatives or were friends who had shared every good and evil with him for years ceased to visit him, though they were secretly sorry for him and in sympathy with him.

Futhermore, Lazar noticed—and there were some who confirmed it—that Todor or one of his men was always watching carefully from the balcony of his new house to see who went to visit the leper, and when the visitor came back, Todor would stop him and obviously ask him what they had been talking about.

This unceasing interference with his visitors and the supervision and the questioning worsened relations between Todor and Lazar more quickly and more deeply than either would have liked. The intentional and provocative supervision especially irritated Lazar in his suffering, as though he himself were not taking the greatest care to prevent his terrible illness being passed on to others; and Todor could not bear that this outcast of God should, so to speak, divert men from him and from his plans.

Lazar had no desire, or even will, to quarrel with Todor, and still less to rake up old feuds. It was obvious to him that, even if he had not been an outcast, he had no hope of succeeding in his opposition to Todor, who was cunning, farseeing, and in league with the authorities, as well as supported by a stronger and more united clan. Lazar knew that Todor would make good use of his illness as a pretext to unite the village against him and to crush his influence among the peasants.

But just the same, even as before his illness, Lazar was unable to remain silent and not say what he thought about village affairs. He felt this to be his inalienable right, whether he were healthy or ill. He said: "The village is as much mine as anyone else's. I was born and brought up in it, and I have made sacrifices for it and even risked my life in quarrels and fights with other villages about forest and pasture rights. My home and my family are here, and while I have breath in my body I must take an interest in it!"

His son, Stojan, had already reached manhood, and his daughter, Ruža, was ready for marriage. Though leprous, he had not ceased to be a father, and he felt that his life would be continued in that of his children. A similar feeling and a similar justice were shown in his relations with his

wife, Milica, and his mother, Ikonija; he loved them tenderly and devotedly, the more so because he was now re-
signed to the fact that he could be of no more service to
them than to give them a kind word now and then.

Most important of all, the country was disunited and
under the heel of the foreigner. Many thought that it would
be best for them to bow their heads until a stronger power
smashed the Austrians, while others rebelled and called for
resistance in the name of honor and glory. There was no
one who could stand aside, even had he wished, for it was
his life that was in question. Not even Lazar was able to
remain indifferent to the misfortunes of his country. "This
is my language and my country," he declared. "Man lives
by this as much as by bread and water. Montenegro is as
much mine as anyone else's. No woman has brought it with
her as her dowry."

Thus circumstances involved Lazar in village affairs, since
he was still a man among men, and therefore also brought
him into conflict with Todor.

The quarrel became especially sharp after Zarija visited
Lazar about twilight one evening. Zarija was Lazar's *kum*,
and so had with him that very close relationship that Montenegrins have with a godfather and with the best man at
their wedding.

"What sort of celebrations and *sabors* are these under the
rule of the foreigner?" exclaimed his *kum*, flushed and foam-
ing with anger. "The land groans, and the very stones cry
out under the foreigner's jackboot, and they say that Serbs
should make merry! Let Todor and his henchmen work for
that. By God, we have had enough of him and his . . . He,
too, has become almost a foreigner. This is no longer a
village, but Todor's estate, as if his grandfather had left it
to him! But you, dear kinsman, lift up your voice; God gives

you the right and you can dare to do so. You are a leper, and no man can harm you any more."

"Just because I am a leper, kinsman," broke in Lazar, "Todor and his gang will profit from it. You will be the first, *Kum* Zarija, who, if troubled times come, will not make a stand against Todor's might. To be fair, that is nothing to wonder at. Terrible is the sword in Todor's hands; he will accuse you of being infected and will scatter you to the winds."

Zarija swore that he would stand fast, and went on exhorting Lazar. "Never, kinsman! Rather would I change my faith than call myself henchman to Todor. Everyone has his eyes fixed on you and places his hope in you, for you can, you dare, say what others do not even dare to think, for there is no greater evil that can happen to you. Even though you are afflicted—and that affliction is from God and may happen to anyone—you are still our fellow man and a human being. You are our hope and our inspiration."

So Lazar, who was already in conflict with Todor, took it on himself openly to inflame the villagers against the *sabor,* against hollow rejoicing and slavery.

He noticed how Todor stopped his kinsman Zarija in front of his house. He could not hear what they were saying, and it was getting too dark to see clearly. But he was able to see how Todor paced up and down angrily and yet, nonetheless, offered a glass to Zarija. Even after it had grown dark, they brought an ember from Todor's house two or three times to light Zarija's pipe.

Next day, in the evening, his wife told Lazar that Todor was furious with him and threatened to stop all conversation with him. Todor had also said that Lazar was taking advantage of the fact that he was a leper and was harping on everything that came into his head and sticking his nose into village affairs. "That leper wants to play the headman in the village," Todor had said, "but only over my dead body!" Lazar had never wanted to be headman. It was not in accord with his contemplative and poetical nature. Especially now that he was a leper, no such thought ever entered his mind. But his wife's account embittered him; though he was devoted to death, he was still alive and a son of his village, of his clan and of his country. Leper as he was, he had no way of defending himself from Todor; that he knew very well, but he did not recognize Todor's right to silence him, to bury him alive. Quietly, so as not to cause his wife sorrow, he withdrew into his cottage and his solitary meditations.

What could he do? How could he defend himself? How could he warn the peasants that it was not so important to Todor to preserve the village from contagion, seeing that the sick man was already isolated, as to strengthen his hold over it and to force it, willy-nilly, to turn the national misfortune into dance and merrymaking.

During the night an idea sprang into the leper's mind—the gusle, the peasant fiddle of the Montenegrins, the one weapon left to him. He wondered, so he said later, why this idea had not come to him earlier, but it had come only when his anger had subsided and various phrases and thoughts against Todor had begun to form in his mind. He got up from his bed, took the gusle in his hands, and sat on the doorstep. The night was warm and clear, and he felt joy, even power, looking at the limitless and familiar expanse. The gusle responded eagerly to the bow and the twang of his fingers, and he began to sing, not one of the old songs, but a new one, against a fresh evil and a new injustice, but one whose meaning every child in the village could understand.

Thus, almost without design, began the senseless and unequal struggle between the leper and the village headman.

# 4.

THE FOLLOWING EVENING he sang to his visitors the song that had come to him during the night, and it spread through the village, and the people began to gather around him.

On the day before Ilindan, with the first rays of the sun, Todor came to the boundary mark in person and began to read Lazar a lesson.

"What do you think you are doing, wretch! When God struck you down, did he also afflict you with madness? Has it ever been and is it ever likely to be that a leper, an outcast of God, shall be a leader of the people? Instead of gaining some sense from the curse of God that has fallen on you for all your life, you insist on railing against God.

"Let me tell you, if you go on doing whatever comes into your stubborn head, it is my duty to save the village and the people from you. The people lap up your sweet words like cattle at a salt lick, but they do not know what they want, nor do they see from what side danger threatens. I know that, and, by force or by kindness, I will bring them salvation. I will show them the way.

"Now they have begun to gather around you as if you smell of myrrh and are not falling to pieces in your rottenness! What sin will you lay on your soul if one day, now or later, your illness passes to others? Who will halt the infection? And whoever has not been poisoned by you, the evil one will snatch away without trace.

"Even if you do not like Austria and the Austrians—nor do I like them, but I suffer them because I must—why should you turn the people from the authorities and lead them into misery? Men must live, even if you have no care for your own life, and they must buy and sell and make merry at the *sabor*.

"I am no friend of the Austrians, nor are any of my kin, I swear by God. But for the village, for the people, I will, if need be, rely upon the Austrians and call on them for help. I will surely never allow a madman and a leper to deceive the village by tales and songs, so that not only its body but also its soul goes rotten!

"It is the leprosy in you that talks and sings. God still keeps you alive as a punishment and a curse upon the people! What have you to do with the village, leper and outcast! I am the village; it is I who keeps ward over its life and its existence. I work my fingers to the bone and place my head in jeopardy for it.

"So I tell you for the last time; stop meddling and keep a rein on your tongue and root out these fancies. Thank God and me that you still get a crust of bread and a drop of water and that I have not yet sung you a song still unsung."

Lazar listened to him calmly, or, at least, so it seemed. He spoke almost as if he were not replying to the headman but continuing his lonely meditations.

"God has punished me with leprosy and you with an evil heart and a selfish soul. Though my body is leprous, my words come from a pure heart, and I cannot, I cannot unsay them, for I would be sinning before God and before my own conscience.

"Though the contagion has fastened on me, I am still a

living creature. That may happen to anyone. What I have said, I have said also when I was not infected, and I will go on saying it to the hour of my death. It may well be that the illness fell upon me to try my soul. My words are true and I am willing to suffer for what I have said.

"You know well, Todor, that I have always sought after justice, and that we have both taken oath on it. You will say there is no scale on which to measure justice! Nor is there! But men always know what is just and what is not, as they know how to tell night from day. There are men, and you are one of them, to whom justice is what they lust after in their heart and who would consent to kiss the devil himself and to live in hell's flames to have their opinions asked and to lord it over others.

"I can see very well the misfortune that I am bringing upon myself, my family, and my clan, but I cannot do otherwise. I dream that we two work in harmony and that you see justice as I do and approve all that I say, but when I awake everything is different; the widows weep and the poor and the weak bend to your will. Now you are trampling Serbdom under your feet just because of a miserable profit at the *sabor.*

"At first I thought it over, but now, after I have considered it well and my eyes have been opened, I could not stop even if I wanted to. There is a force that drives me on, even greater than my love for my clan and for my kin.

"Even cattle need more than their trough, and how much more does man, who was made in the image of God.

"It may well be that it is the leprosy that speaks and sings in me. It has forced me to see even that which I did not see before. There is no happiness in power and in wealth—we shall all of us die just the same—but only in good will toward

all men. The human race would be destroyed if it paid no
heed to its soul. Men must strive to do what I speak of, even
if they never succeed.

"I am an outcast and powerless. I know that the hornless
cannot compete with the horned. Exercise your power over
me. If my time has not come today, then it will come tomorrow, and men will not look at leprosy as they have done
from time immemorial, but as at any other disease. Even
were this not so, I want only to die in peace and leave an
honest memory behind me.

"Do, Todor, whatever you have a mind to. I cannot do
otherwise than as I must."

Todor made no attempt to interrupt Lazar, though he
was filled with impatience, as if this man were telling him
things long known and his words were needless and meaningless. When he began to speak again, Todor refrained
from harsh words and threats. What is more, he tried to
persuade Lazar, either to win him over or because he really
did not wish him ill. It was not clear which.

"Lazar, my poor fellow," he said, "don't talk like that. If
you come to evil, think of your wife and children and of
your old mother! Think to what misfortune you are con-
demning those who are blameless. You may well go on living
for another ten or twenty years. We will bring you all you
ask, will cherish you and visit you.

"All that I want, may God be my witness, is to be able to
treat you as a man among men. But do not meddle with
village affairs. The village is mine. When you meddle with
the village, it is as if you placed a firebrand on my roof. If
you meddle with the village, you will be dancing a round
dance, with the devil. Do not stick your nose into the
authority I have won with such great toil. You will be
thrusting a stake into my heart. If you feel like singing, then

sing the songs you have sung until now. Song is yours; authority mine. Otherwise, I will cut you off from every living being. Get it well into your mind, you poor devil, that there is no greater defilement than that you suffer from; even should you be cleansed of your leprosy, you are still instigating the people to evil and misfortune! It is as if you had become possessed and no longer listen to anyone but yourself and understand no one's words but your own!"

Lazar was unable or did not want to answer. (Those who knew him well held that at that moment he rejected life and his future and let them bring whatever they should bring, for he composed a new song.) He disregarded everything they had been saying and began to ask Todor about his family and his stock and his harvest. And though the headman was a greater landowner than any in the village, he replied against his will. Todor thought—so he said later—that the contagion had turned Lazar's mind. And though he had earlier made up his mind not to give way, he decided to argue with the leper no longer. "I told him what he must do. He must come to his senses, or his family must convince him to do so. If nothing comes of it, then I will strike at him as if he were my bitterest enemy."

So their conversation died out in the sultry heat of the morning. Todor went back whence he came, and Lazar remained on his stone doorstep alone.

# 5.

IT LOOKED AS IF the conflict between Lazar and Todor would die out.

Todor went on keeping watch on Lazar and dissuading

the peasants from going to see him, but he did not touch him or his.

Nor was Lazar eager to begin a fresh strife with Todor. In any case, nothing came of the *sabor,* and Lazar's first song, in which he had not mentioned Todor by name, was soon forgotten, and if anyone quoted anything from it, it was in passing, in order to remember that there was still in the village one man—a leper, it is true—who had openly stood up against injustice, even though no one had had any benefit from it.

Peace reigned in the village, but outwardly only. The tension was evident and grew of itself, through malevolent comments and mocking couplets, which, in distorted form, reached Lazar from Todor or Todor from Lazar. There was tension even when they looked at one another from a distance, a tension so stubborn that each of them would sit for hours unmoving lest the other think that he had moved from weakness. More fatefully, the conflict was intensified by the life of the village, which went on its way, and was bound to go on its way, without taking heed of what was thought of whom or of who spoke of whom while at the same time forcing everyone to take sides with one or the other.

The Austrians made a record of how much building timber the village had to cut and bring into the town before the winter—by St. Demetrius' Day. There was no way of avoiding this and, since there were no state forests to cut, it would have to come from the village property.

Todor decided that the richer peasants could be relieved of this task by making payment to the poorer. This would have been accepted without grumbling if the question of pasture rights from the cleared forest had not arisen, and had not Todor, on the pretext of the hunger and shortages in the country, put these lands up for public sale, so that the richer peasants staked their claims even before the forests had been cut down. Naturally, he and his relatives were among the richer peasants.

The majority in the village, though secretly grumbling, approved Todor's action at the village meetings, in order not to find fault with him and because they themselves did not know of any more just solution.

In the already tense and divided village, question after question arose, and Todor solved them all without hesitation. There was no one else able to do so, or else they did not want to or did not dare suggest anything better. Lazar, infected and isolated, was least of all able to do anything. But there was one thing he could do, and, spurred on by one of the malcontents, he did it; he sang a song against the injustice that many suffered.

This time he named Todor openly. It would be neither right nor heroic, thought Lazar, to avoid mentioning him, since everyone knew to whom the song referred. However, he did not curse or abuse him, but beseeched and begged him to take heed of the poor, and recalled that Todor himself had often spoken of justice and uprightness.

Although Lazar hoped that his songs would influence Todor and arouse his conscience, perhaps even lead him to discuss things and come to an agreement about the village and its needs, he expected, knowing Todor, that the reply would be a sudden and ferocious attack. It was clearer to Lazar than to anyone else that Todor was unmatched in cunning and more capable than anyone else of dealing with all life's difficulties, and that he did not wait for deliberations and decisions but did only what he himself considered to be equitable.

But the gusle cannot remain silent or speak lies.

Lazar did not have to wait long for Todor's answer.

On the eve of Mala Gospodja, the Birthday of the Virgin, September 8, Todor summoned the peasants early in the morning and forced them to wall up Lazar.

It may be that the doctor had ordered Todor to do this, or perhaps he had made the decision himself to enclose Lazar behind a double wall. First the peasants scattered quicklime everywhere around the house, and then they got on with the building. The walls were built foursquare and separated from one another by about the same distance as the boundary marks.

The work progressed very rapidly, as if the workers were taking part in a race. Some brought stones, of which there were plenty in the vicinity, and piled them up at the angles of the future walls, while others—those most skilled in building, among whom Lazar's *kum,* Zarija, was the most zealous —laid the foundations with the biggest of them and rough-hewed the stones.

Todor supervised the work, shouting now to one group and now to another what had to be done. He paced out the distances between the walls and drew on the ground with the sharp end of his stick where they should go. He paid no attention to Lazar, who was sitting silently on his doorstep, as if the whole business were no affair of his. The more the work progressed, the more the headman displayed a sort of cheerful and carefree gaiety. "Ha, my falcons," he encouraged the workers, "soon we shall have meat roasting on the spit and can turn down our glasses!"

Lazar meanwhile looked toward his own house and saw his family standing on the balcony, as if turned to stone. They, too, were filled with wonder, not so much at what was being done as at those who were taking part and how eagerly they were doing it.

Lazar's fellow villagers worked with unnatural haste, as if they wished to make an end of something shameful as quickly as possible, but at the same time they were glad that the work advanced so easily. There was no house that had not sent a worker. Lazar counted them over and over again, recalling the friendships or trials he had shared with each one of them, and noting those who had visited him and had urged him to sing his songs, reproving him for not being harsh and open enough. These were now among the most zealous, both in work and in rejoicing.

Zarija, tall and bony, toadied to Todor, though Todor had not asked anything special of him, and bullied the stone-carriers for not working fast enough. And when Todor's son, who was constantly serving the workers with plum brandy, offered him his flask, Zarija, smoothing his thick brown mustaches, said: "May you have every fortune with this work, Todor, as with every other."

What had happened to Zarija? Had Todor managed to win him over that very evening when he had returned from his visit to Lazar? Had Todor made him change his mind? Lazar could not understand what had happened to him and all the others that they had turned so against him. He could come to no clear conclusion. They watched him morosely, with glances filled with hatred, the fiercer because they could not find any justification for their actions. He thought it over, and said to himself: "All very fine. I am a leper, and they must wall me up so that the illness will not spread to children or stock or any other living thing. But why do they do it so silently, with no sort of explanation, and with so much joy and hate?"

He was so astounded at this change in the men that he asked questions of no one, not even of his *kum,* who represented a Christian kinship from time immemorial that is not a thing to joke about, and whose life had once been saved by Lazar, who had taken him in when wounded. But Zarija gave an explanation, not to Lazar, but to Todor, when Todor reminded him to leave an opening in the wall through which Lazar could get his food. "I wouldn't," he said. "I'd build that up, too. It is true that we two have a sacred relationship, but it is just as you said well and wisely: The village is even above that! The village must be preserved, and nothing else matters!"

But Todor would not agree that no opening be left. "Let him still be able," he said, "to see his wife and children. We will close that later if he does not behave himself as he should."

It was very bitter to Lazar to see how his *kum,* whom he had known better than himself and who had shown himself a hero in war, relied on Todor, asking him even the smallest detail; shall we do this this way, or how would it be that way, while Todor pretended not to notice and would approve and then say, in a superior, condescending sort of way: "Good. Just as you say. But no, no . . . it would be better this way."

It was especially strange to Lazar that neither in the last few days nor on the evening before had he noticed the peasants gathering for a discussion at Todor's house. That meant that Todor had ordered them to come to work without first asking them. That was an infringement of established custom, by which the headman, even for some unimportant task, would call a general meeting to obtain the approval of the majority, if the whole village were involved. This time Todor had not done this, relying perhaps on the doctor and on the incontestability of Lazar's illness and the danger that threatened the whole village. But despite that evident infringement of ancient custom, the peasants had obeyed him as never before, and diligently walled up Lazar.

Even bitterer for Lazar to muse over was that the foundations of the walls, especially the inner walls, had been made so wide. At first he thought that they would be ordinary dry-stone walls, roughly knee high, such as are built around a meadow to prevent stock from straying. But the foundations showed that the walls would be much higher.

"Why do you do that?" exclaimed Lazar. "I should be out of my senses if I tried to leave here."

But no one looked in his direction; only Todor, morosely and ill-humoredly, replied: "It is not you that we are walling up; it is your disease."

And Zarija supported him. "The filthy leper! Leprosy can attack anyone, but I could never have believed that Lazar would become an outcast from the village!"

Thus, while it remained inexplicable why the peasants had so easily accepted Todor's lack of respect for the village meeting, the width of the foundations was explained about noon. The walls rose above a man's height, so that Lazar could not be seen by anyone except by one or two through the narrow entrance.

Then, at Todor's call, the workers stopped and gathered around a roasted ram and some barrels of plum brandy. The roast was Lazar's bellwether—he recognized it by its twisted horns—and the casks of plum brandy were from his cellar—one of them had a new pinewood tap, which Lazar had only recently driven, after the first tasting of the cask he had kept for his *slava,* the feast day of his patron saint. Lazar had paid for his own walling-up out of his own poverty. But no one even noticed this; they drank the plum brandy and cut slices off the roast with the enjoyment of those who are

hungry and thirsty. Lazar made no mention of this, probably from pride and also in order not to show that he set
any value on his property. But he could not resist from
shouting: "It is you who have walled yourselves up, not me.
And you, *Kum* Zarija, you have made yourself nothing, a
thing for Todor's servants to mock and push around."

After that there was no more talk between Lazar and his
fellow villagers. Early in the afternoon the walls were finished, and briars were piled on top of them. The outer
entrance was made waist-high, so that his food might be left
on it.

The workers began to disperse. Lazar guessed that from
the cessation of the clatter and the hum of conversation.
Through the narrow opening in the outer wall he could
just see Todor, who was sitting on a pile of stones and puff-
ing out great clouds of white smoke from his pipe, and, a
little lower down, Zarija, with his hands crossed in his lap.
There were some others, too, heads of families, sitting
around Todor. He could not hear what they were saying,
but from the nodding of their heads he could gauge that
it was something important and confidential.

The shadow of the wall fell across the courtyard. That at
once seemed a hardship to Lazar, though he had never taken
advantage of the wider space. He withdrew into the cottage,
poked the fire, and held out his hands to the warmth. Then
Todor called for him. He walked slowly back across the
courtyard and stuck his face, lit by a meaningless smile,
through the entrance.

"So," began Todor, "we have agreed to tell you that we
will pull down these walls if you end your singing and stop
gathering the people about you."

"*Kum* Lazar," broke in the harsh voice of Zarija, "your
torments are no easier for me to bear than if they had fallen

upon myself, but I would regret you no more than a dog
if you do not stop your songs. I, too, was led away by them."

Lazar's face darkened and hardened into a bitter grimace.
"Leprosy is, I know, an incurable disease, but I do not lie
to you when I say that this other illness is no easier for me.
I cannot stop singing, so do what you will."

With angry curses and threats, the heads of Todor and
Zarija withdrew.

Lazar remained alone. Twilight fell, still warm and sum-
mery. He picked up the gusle and began to sing, more and
more ecstatically as the darkness deepened. He knew that
even if someone heard him, no one could understand him.

He sang to himself and the stars.

# 6.

BUT HE DID NOT remain entirely cut off from the village.

True, no one except the members of his family any longer
came near him. Through them he got to know what was
going on in the village, and although he did not sing to
them or tell them of his songs, something of what he would
have said about conditions in the village filtered through
and was noised abroad.

Therefore, Todor called Lazar's wife and son to him and
threatened them. But they could not think how he could
make things any worse for them. They had not stepped over
the wall, so he could not take advantage of that to say that
they could spread the disease, nor could he prevent the sick
man being visited by his family because of the scandal. And
mere talking did not carry leprosy.

The peasants, even Lazar's closest relatives, had changed

sides, and now fawned on Todor. They brought him gifts and did services for him free, and no one ever went to see Lazar's wife and children. Lazar was able to see something of this, for the walls were not so high as to conceal either his own or Todor's house, both of which were on rising hillocks. So the relationship between Lazar and Todor continued to worsen despite the fact that Lazar was walled up and, even more, that no one any longer showed any sympathy for him. His wife told Lazar that his words and songs were quoted in the village, although no one could actually either hear or understand them. She said that they embittered Todor and his men and awakened fresh hopes in the village.

But if Lazar and his family could not imagine what Todor could still do against them, Todor found pretexts in the very fact that they were alive, and, one way or another, they still had to live.

Even before his illness, Lazar had guessed that his daughter, Ruža, had had her eye on a young man of Todor's clan, but of so distant a relationship that the headman could not have any special influence on his marriage. Slow and careful observation quickly confirmed Lazar's presentiments and fears.

He had never once seen Ruža and the young man together. But he had seen her in a white kerchief going up the hill for wood or to the meadow by the brook. Soon the young man would go after her, usually by some other path which joined hers. Her little swathed head flickered amid the greenery like a flower until it was lost behind a turning or in the undergrowth, and the young man, in green military trousers, could scarcely be seen except for the fact that he usually carried his dark jacket hanging over his right shoulder and his shirt showed white. He swung his free arm

and looked like a butterfly walking on the field or on the
hill. The girl and the young man did not stay long together;
he would leave first, very slowly, loitering on his way, while
Ruža moved with the same flickering motion as when she
had come.

Lazar's watching had begun before the walling-up, and
now he continued it through the tiny attic window. How
and when they met and separated told Lazar how their love
developed and in what way. Recently, on the eve of the
walling-up, he had sensed a change; their meetings were no
longer every day, and the young man returned from them
hurriedly, as though running away, while Ruža walked halt-
ingly, and, once, it seemed to him, though he could not be
sure because of the distance, that she was wiping away tears
with the edge of her kerchief.

His ancestors and brothers had married girls without even
asking them, though the girl's willingness was usually known
beforehand. Earlier, Lazar had been expecting the young
man's relatives to come and ask for his daughter's hand. But
when he had found out that Ruža was meeting the young
man secretly, he began to fear for her reputation. He had
never spoken of it either to her or to his wife, but he followed wakefully the course of her love. This change made
him uneasy. He adored his only daughter and was sorry
that she was suffering. The young man was modest and in
dustrious, and Lazar was aware that any hindrance to their
love could arise because of his illness only, through the fear
of the young man's family of being allied to a leper. His
daughter's misfortunes affected him heavily.

He had decided to discuss all this with his wife, though it
would be hard for them to come to an agreement at so great
a distance, because they would have to avoid speaking
loudly in case an outsider overhear them. But his wife herself

broached the subject. It was about noon on the fifteenth day after his walling-up.

First of all she looked carefully around, and by that alone Lazar knew that she wanted to tell him something important. Someone must have been passing nearby, for she remained waiting, following with her eyes someone whom Lazar could not see. At last, with a wave, as if saying good-by to the unseen one, she made a trumpet of her bony hands and shouted as softly as she could: "Ruža wants to be betrothed."

It was at once quite clear to Lazar, even had Milica not made a motion with her hand toward Todor's house, that they had been putting pressure on the young man to jilt his only daughter. The headman had certainly been frightening him and threatening to drive them both out, for he would not allow lepers to be born in the village, and it might well be that he had mentioned that distant Austrian island, too. Now it was clear to Lazar why his Ruža in the last few days had gone only twice to the fields, and the young man's path had not crossed hers, nor had the butterfly hovered around the flower. The young man, evidently, had already been subject to pressure and no longer went to the tryst. Lazar recalled that he had seen this the day before from his hiding place. From the plum storage behind the cottage he had watched her movements for a long time, till she had hurriedly occupied herself with some task in front of the house.

Lazar could not find a word of encouragement or consolation. Nor had Milica one. "They speak shame of her," she called out. This meant that Lazar's enemies had already bruited Ruža's love abroad and, in telling and retelling it, they had, as usual, added embellishments of their own.

For the first time since he had fallen ill and had quarreled with Todor, Lazar was at a loss for words. Milica noticed this and tried to comfort him. "We will suffer and endure everything, as we have done up till now."

But he could not find peace. He told his wife to ask Todor to come for a talk with him.

His wife did not know what was in Lazar's mind when he asked for Todor. Perhaps he intended to promise not to sing any more if his family were left in peace. That seemed the most probable and understandable, since now there was no one who could hear his songs. Perhaps he wanted to plead with Todor, or to bribe him. Certainly he had some idea in his mind, but he was searching for a way out which did not exist.

Todor did not appear for three days. And on the third day he recommended: "He should have come to his senses in time. Now it has gone so far that it can no longer be stopped."

There was no way back—either for Todor or for Lazar.

But Todor now had other ideas; he could link his relative with some more powerful family and thereby strengthen his own position and reputation. Any concession to Lazar and his family would mean giving fresh fuel to the gossips and the malcontents in the village. Lazar's leprosy was now welcome to Todor.

All that was now evident to Lazar, even had he not observed new movements and new friendships in the village. From what he had shouted to his wife, it could be seen that it was now clear to him that his powers were less and that his descendants would be snuffed out. "Who would marry a leper or give their daughters in marriage to one?" he exclaimed to himself and to the world which could not hear him.

This, then, was real, total death, for which he felt himself the more guilty in that it did not threaten himself only, but also the blameless young being in whom his life should have been prolonged. After thinking it over, he came to the conclusion that everything would have happened just the same even if he had not sung his songs and even if he had not been stricken with leprosy, because Todor would still have gone on in his way and he in his own. Yet it was harder for him because he could do nothing about it, though he still had his strength. Had not Todor acted similarly before? Had he not forced himself on the village as headman? Had he not seized the village common land, even without Lazar's leprosy? Now Lazar was a powerless outcast, condemned even in his children. He could not, dared not, go outside those walls, nor would anyone come near him, even had it not been for Todor's threats. And, like every hermit and mortal, fain to violent and extreme conclusions, he called to his wife when she informed him of Todor's refusal: "It is Todor's soul that is leprous. He, not I, is the real leper!"

His words gradually came to be known, and his family was cut off as if it, too, were leprous. He knew that. Therefore he implored his wife to wash her hands of him and that no one should come to see him, so that the reproach should be lifted from them and men again begin to associate with them. But they remained loyal to him. Nothing that was his could be taken from them, and they went on living isolated, concerned only with themselves, in a more and more tender mutual love.

They loved him, too, and became the more attentive to him as it seemed less and less probable that his life and the breaking down of the walls about him would come to an end. His son and daughter came to see him even more often than before.

When, one day in early autumn, the wedding guests were

making ready the young man whom Ruža had loved, she came to her father to seek consolation from him. It was about noon, the time the members of his family usually came. A golden haze shone around the white-skinned, black-eyed girl in the stone passage. Owing to the war there was not a real wedding feast, but shouts and the hum of conversation could be heard from the young man's home. Ruža only asked her father: "How did you sleep? Can you eat anything, Father? Do your sores hurt? Is the loneliness hard for you?"

Lazar began to weep. It was so long since he had last wept that his tears gave him a sort of relief, as if they revealed some hidden power within him. "Forgive me, Daughter!" he sobbed, and came toward her, but, conscious of his illness, he stayed about halfway between the two walls.

Then, in the noontime brilliance, she saw as he stood erect how weak he had become and that fresh sores had broken out on his hands and face. But she did not weep. Divining his thought, she cut him short, almost brusquely. "Don't be sorry for me, Father. If that is what he is like, then he is not for me!"

Lazar knew his little girl well. He recognized himself in her. He knew her through and through, even bodily; she had a mole like his, but on her left cheek. He made a step toward her, embracing empty space and watering it with his tears.

# 7.

ABOUT THAT TIME Lazar had a pleasant and unexpected visit. It was at dawn, when, as was his custom, he came to the doorstep to enjoy the freshness of the air, take joy in the day, and to see what the weather was going to be like. He expected a fine day, for the mists were rising from the valley. There on the doorstep was his dog, Garov, lying with his head on his paws, waiting for him.

At first Lazar was so astonished at the proximity of a living thing that he did not call Garov. The dog rose slowly on his forelegs, but went on looking at the man, quivering and obviously hesitating, uncertain whether he would find a friend or an enemy. He had clearly broken loose from his tether. Part of it was still hanging around his neck. Wandering about the village, he had come upon the tracks of the members of Lazar's family, and these had led him to Lazar's cottage, where, picking up the scent of his dear master, he had leaped over the entrance barrier and into the courtyard.

Lazar, thinking it over, was filled with joy at the meeting. But what was he to do with the dog? If he were to keep Garov until his family came—he would really like to play with him—then someone might notice them taking the dog away and denounce him as a carrier of the disease. But how was he to drive Garov away? If he shouted, the dog would recognize him, be filled with joy, and rouse the neighborhood. Then he would no longer be able to drive him away from the cottage. Lazar thought that he ought to go inside. But what would guarantee that the dog would not go on staying there in the courtyard waiting for his master, seeing that he had already scented him?

Garov, also, thinking it over, was of two minds about what to do. Slowly, stretching out his smooth rounded head, he came toward the man, who could not make up his mind whether to call him or drive him away. At first from some distance off and then nearer and nearer and from one side, Garov began to sniff at him. His sniffs became quicker and quicker. He was trembling more and more, as if on the track of something very dear and precious to him. Till then he had not looked at Lazar, as if his appearance in no way interested him. At last he jumped up and quickly nuzzled Lazar's legs. He sniffed quickly at his hands, one after the other, and then once again at his legs. Then he moved back, looked into Lazar's face, and at last, finding something that till then had been lacking, he threw himself with a mad leap of joy on his master's breast.

Forgetting everything, Lazar squatted down so that the dog could embrace him and he could stroke the dog.

Standing on his hind legs, Garov snuggled his head into his master's breast and in his lap. He touched his face with his damp muzzle and licked the wounded palms with quick motions of his red tongue. The two rolled over on the grass and, Lazar unused to movement and the dog exhausted by his sudden outburst of joy, sat down beside one another. Garov went on whimpering and licking his master's hands, and Lazar, to comfort him, began to tickle his ribs and behind his ears. That was what gave Garov the greatest pleasure, softly and slowly as only his master knew how. He stretched out lazily and good-humoredly at his master's feet, baring his teeth in a grin and sticking out his tongue.

Garov was no ordinary dog, either in appearance or in nature. Lazar had got him when he was still a puppy from a shepherd, a relative of his wife, who had bred him by crossing his Shar Mountain bitch with a smooth-haired and very powerful dog of some foreign breed which he had looted from a dead Turkish officer at the time of the war with Turkey. The powerful dog had taken the shepherd's fancy, and, since the bitch was in heat, he thought that the pairing would result in a powerful dog, a match for wolves and with long hair to resist the mountain cold. His expectations were not entirely fulfilled. The result was a very power-ful but smooth-haired litter, sensitive to cold but very tough and brave. In time these dogs became well known through-out the whole district for their ferocity and loyalty. Nor was Garov any exception; no one, even among the family, dared go near him except Milica, who fed him, and Lazar, who had played with him ever since he was a puppy. Though Lazar's long absences during the war had estranged the dog from his master, Garov had not forgotten him, and last winter, which Lazar had spent with the stock in the moun-tains, an understanding had been born between them, such as can only develop between man and dog in common struggle and isolation.

Garov did not hesitate now. He was overjoyed that he had found his master. But Lazar was filled with doubts and un-certainties. The dog was necessary to his house, though they had little stock left. He could mount guard against wolves and robbers, who had increased in numbers because of the misfortunes of war. But how could he send back to his family a dog he had stroked and which had licked his open sores? A dog certainly cannot be infected with leprosy; Lazar had never heard of such a thing. But perhaps it could carry the disease? And even if it could not, Todor might think that it could and, since a dog cannot be kept shut up like a man, for it is not worthwhile to feed an unprofitable animal, he would certainly kill Garov.

So Lazar decided to keep the dog until he could talk it over with his wife. He climbed to the top of the wall, pulled down a couple of briars, and put them across the entrance in the outer wall in case Garov should take it into his head to run away.

So began an exceptionally happy morning for Lazar. He was no longer alone, and he could even talk to Garov, who

had earlier been accustomed to listen to him in the mountain
shelter, in truth yawning a little when the story was too
long. He took the dog with him to visit every corner of the
yard, waiting patiently till he had sniffed at all the corners
of the house and lifted his leg at the stake to which his prede-
cessor had been tied. Then they went around the space between the two walls, but since there was nothing of interest
there, Lazar took his guest to visit the cottage. Garov was
not a house dog but there, too, he quickly sniffed at everything and then went to the spot that seemed to him the most
likely place for his future duties—the entrance to the inner
wall.

"Just look at him!" joked Lazar. "He knows what his job
is! But you've nothing to guard here. No wolf or *hajduk*
will ever come here. But guard it, guard it, brother, since
God made you for that. As for me, I will go and get break-
fast. There's little enough. I was not expecting guests, but
I will find something for you, even if I have to go hungry
myself!"

Just as Lazar began to blow up the fire on the hearth, he
heard Garov's sudden loud bark outside.

Lazar had not yet reached the doorstep when a shot rang
out, followed by the sharp yelp of a dog. He ran out. Near
the outer entrance Garov lay with his head between his fore-
paws. He was motionless, and blood was flowing from his
shattered skull. Before the entrance, on the far side of the
wall, stood Todor. Smoke was still coming from the barrel
of his shotgun, and from Todor himself came seemingly un-
malevolent words. "Anything you have touched, no other
living being must dare to touch!"

For the first time Lazar broke out in curses and hatred
against the headman. Then he knelt down by the dog. The
body was still warm, but nothing of Garov moved. Lazar

caressed him, his hands covered with blood, and wailed softly: "My dear one, my sorrow! You came to bring me joy, and you have found death! How are you to blame for man's evil? My Garov, my brother!"

Then Todor brought workers, and they walled up the outer entrance. In the future Lazar's food would be left on the top of the wall, so that there would be no way to get to the leper.

Lazar deeply mourned Garov. He dug him a grave in front of the cottage, a full-length grave, and laid him with his head to the east, like a man. Then he covered him with stones, as when they bury a man, so that the earth would not fall upon his face. Then he filled in the grave and set a stone there, as they do with a man. Garov was now where he could see him, so that he should not be forgotten.

There was nothing now that could divide dog and man.

# 8.

LAZAR WAS NOW RECONCILED to the fact that he would never again speak with a living thing; how much less likely that anyone should ever come to seek him out.

Yet one dark, wet autumn night a dull knock at his door awakened him. He did not reply at once, for he was unable to believe that his door would ever again resound to a knock.

"Brother, blood brother, it is I, Jovan!" A well-known but long-forgotten voice came through the ramshackle planks of the door, accompanied by a frenzied barking of dogs in the village.

The sound immediately restored Lazar to the life from which he had been expelled an interminable age ago. He leaped to the door, but, while still fumbling with the bar, he remembered. "Jovan, in God's name, brother, you can't come in—you will take the illness!"

But Jovan overwhelmed him with words, and even knocked once more. "Open! I must talk with you!"

They could not talk through the door, lest anyone overhear them. But Lazar could not get it out of his mind that Jovan might catch the contagion. The fear of infecting someone else had grown even stronger in him with time. He offered to talk with Jovan through the door. Jovan refused.

"I am a *hajduk*. It's all one to me. No evil will touch a *hajduk*. And I want to see your sores, blood brother mine!"

Lazar gave way.

Refusing to yield to oppression, Jovan had taken to the mountains even before the occupation. When, in 1915, the foreigners occupied Montenegro, he did not even wait for the first green leaf before he took to the forests. His reason was an insult by some sergeant major to the Montenegrin coat of arms. Jovan had trampled on the sergeant major's cap, with its imperial crest, and then escaped, thanks to his speed and the darkness. The Austrians had at once interned his family somewhere in the vast and godforsaken expanse of their wide empire, and Jovan had continued to live as a *hajduk*, prowling about the town and his village. This in itself would have given the authorities a headache even if he had not waylaid and plundered their road patrols and beaten up their sympathizers. Usually he worked alone or with two or three companions and attacked when and where no one expected. There was a heavy price on his head and, because he was the only outlaw from a village in the vicinity of the town, they made special efforts to lay hands on him.

Until he had been taken ill, Lazar had kept in touch with him, brought him food, and given him information.

But their blood brotherhood dated from even earlier. Jovan was ten years the younger. When their friendship began he was just a youth, whereas Lazar was already married and a grown man. The difference in years confirmed their friendship, and in its cordiality there had been something of the devotion and respect between father and son. Jovan's marriage had brought them still closer together. Lazar had helped him to get into touch with one of his relatives from a more distant village, and he had married her. Lazar's wife, Milica, had become like an elder sister to Jovan's bride, had introduced her to married life and told her the customs of the village. The two families had become, so to speak, merged into one, and the wars, with their bloodshed and sufferings, had made their comradeship firmer, sharing all their hopes and trials. The only reason Lazar had not joined Jovan in the forests had been an agreement between them that Lazar should remain for some time longer in the village in order to help the outlaws.

"You see, brother," Lazar began, squatting by the hearth, "I cannot even shake hands with you. And I am ashamed that you should see me so disfigured. I do not see myself, but I touch myself and sometimes see my reflection in water. I am much disfigured, brother."

Jovan could not comfort him, and answered simply: "It is from God. We cannot escape, nor should we run away from it. I would have come to visit you before, but sometimes I could not and sometimes the Austrians and their henchmen prevented me—so nothing came of it."

The fire began to burn up, and the blood brothers, sitting on tree stumps, smiled joyfully at one another.

But Jovan soon said in words what Lazar had read in his face.

"You are indeed disfigured, but you are still what you always were, except that you have become terribly thin."

"It eats me from within. It does not hurt, but I feel how it is eating me. It is like this; I wake in the night and it does not alarm me, but I can see that I am falling to pieces and drying up. It is a filthy illness. You must not risk catching it, blood brother."

Jovan laughed. "And why not? What can harm a *hajduk?* Once you put your head in the noose, then nothing seems hard or terrible."

"That is so," Lazar agreed, "but a man should not take risks without reason. That is his first duty, more important than all else, save honor."

"True, but friendship is as great as honor."

The walls of the cottage were lit up by the flames on the hearth, and the things in it were shown in all their roughness and poverty.

"Where and what sort of men are they who walled you up alone, Lazar?" breathed Jovan. "I had plenty of trouble before I cleared the briars and clambered over the wall—and not one wall only, but two. Where can I catch them?"

"What will you, brother?" Lazar answered mildly. "They have walled me up alive. It could not be otherwise, if you look at it fairly; not only was I contagious, but I was a hindrance to Todor."

Jovan clenched his teeth so hard that the shadows leaped on his firm cheekbones. "I had thought to kill this Todor, and, to tell the truth, that was mainly why I came."

Jovan's green eyes stood out under his thick eyebrows. Lazar knew that with his blood brother this meant a cold anger and a resolve to stop at nothing, so he began to calm him. "Don't even think of it, in God's name! His clan is a strong one; it will see both you and me buried. He does not do this for the Austrians, but for fear of contagion and of our local quarrels. It is reasonable enough if you consider it —every man must preserve what is his, even Todor. For love of me, brother, don't. I want to die in peace, free of sin except for the leprosy that has stricken me."

They remained silent, not understanding one another. Jovan unbuckled his cartridge belt and hung it on the ramrod of his rifle, which was leaning against the wall. Then he took off his cloak and hung that up also. He was a small man, though strong and wiry.

"I have never asked you if you weary of life in the mountains, brother," Lazar said.

"How shall I put it to you? Yes and no. It troubles me to think that there are fewer real men. The Montenegrins, brother mine, sell their souls for a coin or a trifle, as if they had never known honor and heroism! Save for that, nothing troubles me; a live man can endure anything. But, brother, now I am with you, I have something else to ask you. While you were well, I did not remember to ask you where you hid those rifles and munitions we did not hand over at the capitulation. I hope to have more company in the spring, and though Austria is indeed a great power, a suffering people is fiercer still."

Then Lazar began to doubt his blood brother. Had it not been for the arms, would it ever have occurred to Jovan to come and visit him? Was it misfortune that had driven him? For without arms and without a larger band he had no life. He had come in late autumn, when the snow could make everything white! An unarmed band and a great need had driven him, and not the bonds of blood brotherhood.

Lazar told him at once where the arms were; he could hardly take the secret to the grave. But his suspicions of his blood brother remained, and he could not help wondering. "Good, brother," he began, without looking at Jovan, "tell me honestly, as you have always spoken the truth about everything, would you have come to see me if it had not been for the arms?"

Even before he finished speaking, he felt that he had not been right to put his friend in such a dilemma. Jovan was looking fixedly into the fire, unraveling his own indecision in the play of the flames.

The silence lasted, more and more painful and oppressive, and the village dogs, which Jovan's passage had disturbed, were once more silent. At last Jovan turned his head, overgrown with grizzled hair and beard and bright in the firelight. He looked calmly and openly at his blood brother and spoke equally calmly. "To tell you the truth, brother, had I not been an outlaw I would have come to the boundary mark to see you, like the dearest ones of your family. But now, over the walls and when it is time for me to go to my winter hiding place, I would not have come to you if my companions had not sent me, since they had need of arms as of heads on their shoulders, and that is both arms and head to me. For I am responsible not only to you and to myself but to all Serbdom and to my band. Believe me, brother, when I tell you: I am sorry that I cannot regret it, but, since I had to come to you, I decided to come to you as we two have always and everywhere come to one another, and would not shun you or talk to you through gates and walls. For since I had to come to you, I wanted to come and be with you as a man and as a blood brother, such as I have always been and will continue to be while I have a head on my shoulders. We are one, we have been one, and we will remain one. Both of us are outcasts, each in his own way."

His blood brother's frank speech brought so much consolation and joy to Lazar that the tears ran down his face. "May God forgive me, brother mine, since you will never come to me again. And you, too, forgive me that I doubted your true heart!"

Jovan went on warming himself at the fire, and they continued chatting about whatever came into their minds, of Jovan's trials in the mountains and of Lazar's in his illness, till Jovan rose to leave. But as though he did not think that this would be his last meeting with a living being and still less with a man dear to him, Lazar advised his blood brother: "Take care, Jovan. Look after yourself, lest some enemy delight in betraying you, for you have worse enemies among the Montenegrins than among the Austrians. Now, when you jump over, go around Todor's house and make for the gully, to reach the mountains as quickly as you can. Be on your guard against dog and man, against wolf and *hajduk*, against fire and water. While you are alive, it is as if I, too, were of your band and fighting the enemy to the death."

He accompanied Jovan to the wall, and they embraced, with words of love and loyalty. The *hajduk* vanished over the wall in the moist darkness, and Lazar went back and sat on his rain-soaked doorstep.

The dogs barked even more furiously than when Jovan came, but Lazar did not hear them. He did not feel the dank chill beneath him; it was as if it were not he who was alone in the blackness of the night.

# 9.

NOT TWO DAYS PASSED before Todor ordered a fresh and final walling-up of Lazar.

Everything was merged in gray, the mist on the peaks and the fine incessant rain, and Lazar would likely not have known that the work had begun about noon had not Milica appeared shortly afterward with his food.

First they had to tear down a piece of the outer wall and spread quicklime between the two walls. Then they began to build up the inner wall. Through the passage Lazar saw Milica, at the point where the outer wall had been torn down, standing with hands outstretched as though they had been cut off. She stood seemingly turned to stone herself, waiting for that stone which would cut off her husband forever from her and from the world outside.

Lazar realized why they were doing this, and Todor did not hide it. "The outlaw came to you," he shouted. "Shall outlaws and outcasts meet one another? The Austrians will raze the whole village to the ground because of you!"

This time Todor seemed much bigger to Lazar. He was dressed in a goatskin coat and hood. Looking at him beside his wife, so small and wizened, he could not resist shouting: "No power lasts forever!" Those were his last words and his final farewell.

For the entrance, so narrow that a man could scarcely get through it, was walled up in a trice, and in the space between the two walls they put two dogs. Their barking could soon be heard. Then they went on to build up the outer wall again. When everything was ready that evening a keening broke the unaccustomed silence. It was Lazar's mother mourning, as had never before been heard within man's memory, for her living son. But no one could know if Lazar heard it—he would certainly not be able to understand the words, and he gave no sign. The mourning went on until nightfall, and then the moist black silence lay over the village and on Lazar's walls.

But during the next few days, usually in the evening, an attentive ear could hear the wailing of the gusle from Lazar's cottage.

Then, as if by agreement, the whole village would fall silent, even Lazar's dogs; and even in Todor's house no noise or shouting could be heard. During the day Lazar could still be seen from the outskirts of the village, but it was not possible to judge what he looked like, and he was not able to report anything to anyone. The peasants brought him his food in turn, on a long shovel from one wall to the other. His family were forbidden to go to him except when their turn came. But because the peasants brought food whenever it happened to occur to them, Lazar was unable to guess the order and so could not wait to see any one of the peasants or one of his own family at the farther wall.

It seemed that he was not especially keen to see men, or else that he was self-controlled enough to suppress that longing. He was content that every day, about noon, he could see his family on the balcony of his house—three women in black kerchiefs and his son, who welcomed him, as he them, as soon as he came out on his doorstep, by waving white cloths.

But Lazar did not outlive the winter. One day when the snow had already begun to disappear and the brownish earth on the sun slopes began to be tinged with green, no smoke came from Lazar's cottage, nor did he come out to the doorstep about noon. His food was taken back untouched, and the dogs between the walls, already run wild in their stony isolation, howled in mad grieving. In the evening, Lazar's gusle was no longer heard.

So it was for two days. On the third day in the morning they broke down the walls. The dead Lazar did not answer from his bed, and no one dared to go inside. They set fire to the cottage, and the flames lit up the village until far into the night.

The walls fell apart and became overgrown, and with them every remembrance.

From them, from the ashes of forgetfulness, exactly thirty-eight years later, arose this fable from the walls of the prison at Mitrovica.